"I'm not excusing my behavior—"

"Good."

Sam stiffened imperceptibly. Rose doubted he'd been treated with anything less than deference in ages. Where she got the brass to be cheeky she didn't know, but remembering he had the power to alter her life for the worse, she thought better of acting outright insolent.

His lips tightened, but he soldiered on. "I had hoped you might consider forgiving me on account of our past...association. We were good friends once, or don't you remember?"

Her fingers tightened into the arms of the padded leather armrest. As far as she was concerned, the word *friend* was an insult to what they'd shared. He'd been her reason to wake up each morning and her last thought each night. Even now, there were nights when he filled her dreams. Without him, she'd been wretched. The world had been fierce and frigid. If not for the Lord and His guiding hand, she didn't know where she'd be.

"How could I forget?" she whispered.

Books by Carla Capshaw

Love Inspired Historical

The Gladiator
The Duke's Redemption
The Protector
The Champion
Second Chance Cinderella

CARLA CAPSHAW

Florida native Carla Capshaw is a preacher's kid who grew up grateful for her Christian home and loving family. Always dreaming of being a writer and world traveler, she followed her wanderlust around the globe, including a year spent in the People's Republic of China, before beginning work on her first novel.

A two-time RWA Golden Heart Award winner and double RITA® Award finalist, Carla loves passionate stories with compelling, nearly impossible conflicts. She's found that inspirational historical romance is the perfect vehicle to combine lush settings, vivid characters and a Christian worldview. Currently at work on her next manuscript for Love Inspired Historical, she still lives in Florida, but is always planning her next trip…and plotting her next story.

Carla loves to hear from readers. To contact her, visit www.carlacapshaw.com or write to Carla@carlacapshaw.com.

Second Chance Cinderella

CARLA CAPSHAW

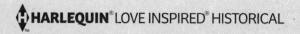
HARLEQUIN® LOVE INSPIRED® HISTORICAL

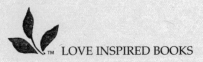

LOVE INSPIRED BOOKS

ISBN-13: 978-0-373-28272-2

SECOND CHANCE CINDERELLA

www.Harlequin.com

Printed in U.S.A.

Thy word is a lamp unto my feet,
and a light unto my path.
—*Psalms* 119:105

To Dottie, her favorite Andrew
and our second chance at friendship.

Prologue

Devonshire, England
November, 1833

"Please don't cry, Rosie." Sam Blackstone gazed into the glistening blue eyes of the only girl he'd ever loved.

A few feet away, Ezra Stark's magnificent coach stood ready to convey him to London and a new life filled with possibilities—a far cry from sleepy Ashby Croft, with its cob-n-thatch cottages and meandering muddy lanes that led to nowhere.

Rose's slender fingers curled around the frayed edges of his open coat front. "I'm afraid you won't come back to me," she whispered. "I don't know what I'd do without you."

"Don't be a daft little goose." He tried to cajole a smile from her, but the effort was a lost cause.

Painfully aware she'd been abandoned by everyone else who should have cared for her, he pulled her close and breathed in the light scent of rosewater she'd favored ever since he'd bought a bottle for her birthday last spring.

Her sadness tore at his heart. She'd endured more disappointment and hardship in her sixteen years than a soul should have to bear in a lifetime. All he wanted was to make her happy.

He kissed the top of her head, savoring the feel of her in his arms. He dreaded leaving her, but he had to go. Mr. Stark had made it clear he wanted to be away before the village fully awakened.

"Listen to me, luv." Sam dabbed Rosie's tear-streaked face with the embroidered handkerchief she'd fashioned for him last Christmas. "This is our chance. Mr. Stark thinks I have a real gift for numbers. The clerk's position he's offered me is a stunner of a job. At sixty quid a year there'll be no need for more gambling or thieving to earn our daily crust."

He motioned to the ramshackle inn across the rutted street where she slaved as a maid for a pittance. The stagecoach waited out front and several travelers were already milling about in preparation to leave. "I want more for you than working your fingers to the bone day in and day out. Maybe someday we can even buy a cottage by the sea like we always dreamed of."

"But…" She glanced nervously toward the gleaming lacquered coach and matched team of four gray horses nickering impatiently. "What if Mr. Stark isn't who he claims ta be? What if—"

"He is, Rosie, no doubt. I told you before, if you'd seen how high-an-mighty Sir Percival was bowing and scraping around him you'd know you needn't fret." He tucked the handkerchief in his coat pocket and cupped her shoulders. The threadbare gloves she'd darned for him too many times to count did little to protect his callused hands from the late-autumn chill.

A gust of wind tugged at the brim of Rose's worn brown cap, exposing her golden-blond hair. Having grown up as orphans, neither of them was used to the fineries of life, but if he had his way, it wouldn't be long before she was turned out in the softest linen and richest silks. She deserved jewels and servants to see to her every whim. He was bound and determined to give them to her.

"I'll be back from London within a month…afore the trees are bare. I'll save every ha'penny and the minute I come back we'll get married just as we always said we would."

A ray of sunlight pierced the gloomy morning. A tremulous smile turned her soft, pink lips. "I like the sound of that. It's about time I brought you up to scratch."

"And here I was thinking I'd finally be making an honest woman of you." He grinned. "Jus' proves how much we need each other."

Her faint smile faltered. "I can't help feeling something bad is bound to happen."

"Worrywart." He tweaked her chin and laughed, despite the tightness banding his chest. How he dreaded leaving her when she was so afraid. They'd never been parted more than a day or two, but there was no help for it if they were ever to be more than a pair of bootlickers. "I'm going to town, not to war, sweetheart. Besides, even if I turned up my toes—"

"Don't say that!" She leaned back in the circle of his arms, her stricken gaze pinned to his face. "I couldn't bear it if you were taken from me forever."

"You could never be rid of me for good. We're a

pair, you and me—the sand and surf, the moon and stars—"

"A goose and 'er gander?"

"Exactly." He chuckled, relieved to see her smile. His thumb brushed tenderly across her wind-reddened cheek. He pulled her back against his chest, pleased by her wish for him to stay. His mother, whoever she was, had discarded him on the steps of the orphans' asylum and no one else had ever cared a whit about him, except Rosie. "You have to know you're all that matters to me. All I'll ever care about."

She sniffed against the rough wool of his shirtfront. "You say that now, but you might meet someone, a pretty London miss who—"

"Silly girl." He squeezed her, snorting at such nonsense. She was as irreplaceable to him as his own heart. He'd been a lad of three the first time he saw her, a red-faced infant who'd been dumped on the orphanage doorstep. Even then he'd known she'd be important to him. In the sixteen years since, they'd become inseparable. She was everything to him, the reason he breathed and dreamed.

He nuzzled her ear. Squeezing his eyes shut, he missed her already. "I love you," he said gruffly.

Her arms tightened around his waist. "You know I love you, too. More than anything."

A few feet away, the coach's door swung open. The forbidding presence of Ezra Stark remained out of sight inside the magnificent conveyance, but there was no mistaking his tone. "It's time, Blackstone. Or have you reconsidered my offer?"

Sam stared at the tufted, burgundy velvet lining the door. The luxurious fabric probably cost more coin than he managed to scrape together in a year. How grand it would be to be like Ezra Stark who, according to the lads down at the pub, had more wealth than he could spend in ten lifetimes.

The shadowed figure moved within the coach. "The day is wasting, man. Make your choice."

Now that the moment of reckoning had arrived, Sam wondered if he was making the biggest mistake of his life to leave all that he knew and everything he held dear. His hand still clasped in Rose's tight grip, he took a step forward then stopped. His gaze darted back to Rose. Her chin quivered.

If she asks me to stay once more, I won't go. I won't rest till I find a position in service somewhere and—

"I sketched this for you." She reached into her dress pocket, extracted a small roll of paper and handed it to him. "Don't look at it until you're gone. Promise you'll come to fetch me as soon as you can, Sam. I know you want to find us a proper place to live, but I don't need anything grand. I only need you."

An ache swelling in his chest, he ignored Ezra Stark's silent demand for him to hasten and accepted the gift. He leaned forward and kissed Rose's cold lips, committing their softness and her warm response to memory. "You have my word as long as you promise you'll wait for me."

"Now who's being a silly gander?" She pasted on a brave smile. The rain began to fall, helping to disguise her tears, but he wasn't fooled. Pulling her crocheted shawl tighter around her shoulders, she hugged her small waist. Deep-blue eyes watched him with equal parts of uncertainty and trust. "Never doubt me, Sam. I'll wait for you forever if need be," she promised as he climbed into the coach.

Chapter One

London, England
September, 1842

It was the woman's hair that drew Sam Blackstone's full attention. The waterfall of gold tumbling down her narrow back from beneath a serviceable black bonnet reminded him of Rose Smith. As the blonde disappeared into the sea of pedestrians, his mood soured that same instant. The last thing he wanted or needed was a morning poisoned by memories of the past.

Relying on the years of strict mental discipline he'd employed to rise from being a village ne'er-do-well to one of London's most prominent stockbrokers, he forced memories of Rose's betrayal from his mind and descended the wide front steps of his elegant Mayfair townhouse.

In the past nine years, he'd played the game well and few challenges remained. He'd acquired more wealth than he'd ever dreamed as a young orphan in Ashby Croft. Far from going to bed with an empty stomach gnawing his ribs, sleeping in a drafty hovel and wearing itchy rags, he dined on delicacies, lived in a mansion and dressed in the finest Savile Row suits. Few rivaled his influence in financial circles. His advice on monetary matters was sought by everyone from potato farmers to Parliament members.

His driver opened the coach's door. Sam climbed in and sat heavily on the black, embossed leather seat, impatient to get underway.

As he waited, his gaze slid back to the Georgian edifice he'd acquired three years earlier. The echoing monstrosity boasted every luxury and admirably performed its duty to impress, but the residence was devoid of human warmth or cheer. He much preferred to spend his waking hours at the city offices of Stark, Winters and Blackstone or overseeing the firm's vigorous trade of commodities at the Exchange in Capel Court.

"Beggin' yer pardon for the delay, sir," his driver, Gibson, said over the din of the busy street. "Oxford's in a tangle. The fine weather's drawn everyone out. I 'spect there's nary a church mouse to be found indoors at present."

The coach finally pulled away from the curb. The pungent aroma of horseflesh and smoke carried on the air. Sam consulted his pocket watch before extracting several reports from the leather portfolio he'd brought with him. Not one to waste time when there was more wealth to be gleaned, he shuffled through the pages.

The list of figures blurred and the brisk activity all around him faded as his mind wandered to the taunting vision of the woman with blond hair. Something about the stranger beckoned him to find her, but he remained in his seat, determined to shut her out with a stubbornness that bordered on vice. She was nothing and no one to him. True, she'd been of similar height and build as Rose. And that golden hair—such a unique color. What if, by some twist of fate, Rose had come up to London and—

He scrubbed his hand over his eyes, dispelling the wild notion before his imagination grew to unrealistic proportions. Nine years had come and gone since he'd left tiny Ashby Croft. He was never going to see Rose again, and frankly, good riddance. Far from waiting for him as she'd promised, she'd married another bloke within months of his leaving. If a heart could break into a thousand jagged pieces, his had the day he'd returned to Devonshire to collect her and learned she'd thrown him over for someone else.

As much as he'd tried to forget her, the foul taste of her faithlessness had tainted every day for him since.

Despising the black mood overtaking him, he stuffed the reports back into the portfolio and closed the latch. The flow of vehicles congesting the street had slowed to a standstill. "How much longer, Gibson?" he demanded. "The 'Change opens in an hour."

"Yes, sir, but—"

"Bother this." Sam thrust the door open and climbed down from the vehicle. "I'm certain I'll find the pace more brisk if I walk. Pick me up at half past six as usual…if you manage to be free by then."

"Forgive me, sir, but shall I make that half past five? I overheard Cook say you was dinin' with guests tonight."

Sam frowned. He'd forgotten all about his dinner companions, including Lord Sanbourne and his beguiling daughter, Amelia, who was to serve as his hostess for the evening. "Right you are, Gibson. Half past five."

The driver tipped his cap with a quick, "Aye, sir," before pulling along the curb and setting the brake. The matched pair of gray geldings hitched to the conveyance whinnied and shook their heads as though disappointed by the loss of their morning exercise.

Portfolio in hand, Sam started off, shouldering his way through the occasional gaps that opened between his fellow pedestrians. He pressed his top hat tighter to his head to keep it from being dislodged by one of the frequent gusts of wind. At Oxford Street a seemingly endless row of traffic forced him to wait on the crowded corner.

"My, what a glorious day," a lady in front of him cooed, nearly poking him in the eye with her ruffled parasol.

"Indeed, 'tis marvelous," her elegant companion agreed.

Sam supposed it was true. The sun shone with undaunted enthusiasm, and rather than fog or London's usual gray haze of coal smoke, the air seemed clear for once. Pots of flowers graced the steps and entryways of the grand terraces on both sides of the busy thoroughfare. Their late-summer blooms shone in shades of bright pink, fiery-red and, to Sam's everlasting irritation, a golden-yellow that once again reminded him of Rose's burnished hair.

Gritting his teeth, he headed toward Regent Street.

He wasn't one for mysteries. He understood himself well enough to know that if he didn't at least try to ascertain the truth of the blonde's identity his imagination would pester him forever.

Aware of the unlikelihood of finding the stranger in the crush of people and that a solid quarter of an hour had passed since he'd first caught sight of her, he soldiered on as though some insistent, yet invisible force were pulling him forward.

Half a block later he began to wonder if he should retire to Bedlam. If there'd ever been a wild-goose chase, he was on it. Feeling foolish to his core, he scanned the hustle and bustle along the street and shook his head at his own stupidity. The woman, whoever she was, had disappeared like a vapor in the wind.

Annoyed by the bitter disappointment that assailed him, he wedged the portfolio under his arm, removed his top hat and combed a hand through his short, black hair. With a sinking heart, he wondered if he'd ever be truly free of Rose Smith.

His hat back in place, he was determined to forget the blonde and the lunacy that compelled him to chase after her. The pounding of workmen's hammers making repairs on the row of buildings behind him mixed with the call of newspaper boys and the clamor of horses and carriages. In the distance, the bass notes of a church bell announced the ninth hour.

A momentary break in the rank of pedestrians allowed him a glimpse of his quarry on the corner at the next block. His heart kicked against his ribs. He sprinted after her, her lovely hair drawing him like a lodestar as he pushed through the gaggle of people meandering along the footpath.

A gust of wind swished the lady's cape up and out behind her. She carried a battered valise he hadn't noticed before, and the black garb she wore appeared to be the typical frock of a servant.

A passing barouche and row of horse carts impeded his progress at the corner of Holles Street. For a few, tension-filled moments he feared he'd lost her again, but the way cleared in time for him to see her stop in front of a Palladian townhouse on the east side of Cavendish Square. Although she stood in profile, the details of her face were obscured by the bill of her bonnet. Her head nodded as she looked from the front of the building to a piece of paper she held.

The paper gave him pause. Rose didn't know how to read, or at least she hadn't when he'd known her. Perhaps she'd learned in the past nine years, the same as he had acquired new skills and bettered himself.

He picked up his pace. "Rose!" he shouted, drawing startled looks from the other walkers, but he paid them no mind. "Rose!" he called again, dodging several horses as he crossed to the square. No response. Either she didn't hear him over the activity in the street or he had the wrong woman altogether.

And yet she seemed so familiar. The fluid way she walked, the expressive tilt of her head… The cape she wore made it difficult to tell, but now that he'd had a better look, she seemed shapelier in the hips and bust than his Rose had been. But wasn't that to be expected? She was no longer a girl of sixteen, but a mature woman of twenty-five.

The mystery lady disappeared down the townhouse steps leading to the servants' entrance. Sam yanked off his hat and broke into a run. A door slammed just as he reached the front of the house. He moved to the narrow flight of steps he'd seen the woman take and stared at the scuffed black door that led to a basement and the source of the rich aromas filling the air.

Sam slapped his hat against his thigh in frustration. He considered inquiring after the woman but discarded the notion. Servants were often a prickly lot with an abhorrence for being intruded upon by outsiders.

Besides, what would he do if he found out his quarry did happen to be Rose? Strangling her wasn't an option and he doubted she'd come willingly to the door to hear his abysmal opinion of her.

He noted the address. The townhouse boasted mansion-size proportions, wide front steps, imposing columns and lead-glass windows. If he wasn't mistaken, the edifice belonged to Baron Malbury, a shifty fellow who'd risen to his current status through the untimely death of his predecessor in a boating accident the previous month.

Sam had been reluctant to take on the self-important, nearly impoverished peer as a client, but if Malbury employed Rose, he'd have to reevaluate the situation and determine the best way to use the connection to his advantage.

Sam returned to the corner across the street and called to a newspaper boy leaning on the gas lamp.

"Aye, govna?" the boy rang out as he bounded over to him. A child of no more than seven or eight, he was unkempt with dirt smudges on his cheeks, his muddy-brown hair uncombed. His ragged clothes were too big for his scrawny frame and the hungry look about him reminded Sam of his own miserable childhood. "You wan' ta buy a paypa?"

Sam shook his head. He'd already looked over *The Times* at breakfast. "What's your name, young man?"

"Georgie, sir."

"Well, Georgie, I have a proposition for you. How

would you like to earn a quid for say…ten minutes of your time?"

Georgie's brown eyes rounded with a hopeful eagerness he couldn't quite hide. "If it ain't on the up and up, me mum—"

"Oh, it's honest, all right. You needn't worry. I want you to go to the servants' entrance of that residence—" he pointed to the Malbury mansion "—and ask if there's a maid by the name of Rose employed there. If so, ask if her name was Rose Smith before she married. Do you think you could do that for me?"

"That's all I 'ave to do for a 'ole quid?"

Sam nodded. His gaze slid back to the mansion. His eyes narrowed on the glossy front door. Curiosity burned in his veins. "Yes, and if you hurry I'll give you two."

Georgie took off at a flat run.

Praying she'd come to the right place, Rose knocked on the kitchen door. Ever since she'd become a Christian eight years ago, she'd relied on the Lord to direct her path. Relying on His guidance eased her mind when the shifting letters and numbers others seemed to read with ease made little sense to her.

The scuffed black door swung open. "Ye're late," said a young, frowning kitchen maid.

She blinked, surprised to see a woman instead of a footman answer the door. "I know. I apologize. The coach from Paddington station suffered a broken wheel." Her heart racing from the mad pace she'd kept in her failed attempt to arrive on time, she switched her battered valise to her other hand and descended the final step into the basement. A blast of heat assaulted her along with the aroma of roasted fowl. "I had to walk the last few miles and I lost my way a bit. I came as quick as I could."

The door slammed shut behind her as the dour-faced Scot ushered her farther into the entryway. A stone arch separated the small space from the ovens and activity of the kitchen beyond. The harried staff reminded her of the frantic crowds in the maze of streets outside.

"Then yoo'd best get settled an' tae work straight awa'," said the maid. Dressed in a column of black wool and a sullied white apron, the young woman inspected her with a quick, unimpressed glance. "I don't ken how ye bumpkins in th' coontry work, but our cook, Mrs. Pickles, isna a body for tardiness or excuses of any kind."

Taking exception to being called a bumpkin, Rose bit back a tart reply as she followed the maid down a hallway that led to a spiral staircase. Before leaving Hopewell Manor, the Malbury family's country estate where she'd been in service for the past eight years, she'd been forewarned of the infamous Mrs. Pickles's reputation as a taskmaster. It was said the cook ran her kitchen like Wellington at Waterloo and with nearly as many casualties.

The mere thought of losing her job made Rose's stomach churn. It was imperative that she make a favorable impression on the irascible woman who held Rose's job in her hands. Rose was on excellent terms with the staff at Hopewell Manor and only in London for a fortnight to help with a shortage of trained servants in the townhouse kitchen, but that did not mean she couldn't be dismissed. The tragic death of the previous baron and his wife had put the livelihood of every Malbury employee in jeopardy.

Apparently, the new baron had inherited the title and lands with very little coin to sustain the expenses that accompanied the prize. His servants worried he planned to terminate long-term staff in favor of importing cheaper, Irish labor. Nothing could be taken for granted, nor a foot placed wrong. She could not afford to be sacked. Finding another position was nigh impossible for anyone and doubly so for a woman in her precarious situation.

"My name is Rose Smith, by the way," she said over the banging of pans and calls for more boiling water.

"Ah be Ina McDonald."

"Have you been in service here long?" Rose asked as they reached the third floor.

"Six months. Five and a half too many if ye ask me. Min', th' auld baron an' baroness were kind enough, but Mrs. Pickles makes every day a sour circumstance." Ina took a skeleton key from her skirt pocket and unlocked a door across the hall. "Ye'll be sharin' quarters wi' me whilst ye're here. Keep yer belongings tae yer own side of the room an' we'll get on jus' dandy."

Rose found the converted attic similar in size to the room she shared with Andrew at Hopewell Manor. Her former employers had always displayed a unique sense of Christian charity toward their servants' well-being and the snug space was pleasantly situated. Morning sunlight and a cool breeze streamed through two dormer windows dressed with faded blue curtains. Simple white moldings edged plastered walls painted in a cheerful shade of yellow.

Three single beds hugged the opposing sides of the room. Ina had claimed the one left of the door and arranged her few belongings with obvious care and neatness in mind.

"Hurry, if ye ken what's good fur ye." Ina headed back to work. In a rush to follow her, Rose moved to the bed nearest the windows and set her valise on the scuffed, but freshly swept wood floor. She would have to make up the bare mattress later.

She hung her cloak and bonnet on the wall hook at the end of the bed before opening her valise to fish for a fresh apron. The faint hint of talcum clung to the extra work frock, Sunday-best dress and other belongings that filled the case. With no more time to find the small mirror she'd brought, she did her best to repair her hair and repin the long blond tendrils that had bounced free when the coach suffered its broken wheel. She wished she could remove her shoes and rub her throbbing feet. They ached from miles of walking and she had a long day ahead of her.

As she stood to tie the apron around her waist, she glanced out the window and took in the bird's-eye view. Amid the colorful parasols and scurry of pedestrians, a tall man on the corner of the square across the street drew her attention. The refined dark business suit and top hat he wore vouched for his importance, but there was a solitary quality about him that she recognized in herself.

Despite the need to make haste, she remained nailed to the floor. The distance between her perch and the square kept her from seeing the gentleman's face. She willed him to move closer.

Instead, the newspaper boy he spoke with darted toward the Malbury townhouse whilst the man turned his back to her and made for one of the ornate, wrought-iron benches set along the gravel path. Tension wafted off him in waves.

A flock of pigeons scattered like feathers in the wind, jolting Rose from her musings. With no more time to spare, she dragged herself from the window and shut the door behind her as she left the room.

The stirring of curiosity toward the stranger surprised her. Not since Sam had she noticed a man with any personal interest on her part. After all they'd meant to each other, he'd simply forgotten her. He'd been gone for over a year before she'd given up all hope and admitted to herself that he'd cast her off the same as everyone else in her life had done. In turn, she'd banished him from her heart and mind—or at least tried to.

"How good of you to join us," a stern voice said the moment Rose reached the bottom of the stairs. It took a moment for her eyes to adjust well enough to see the gaunt, gray-haired woman in spectacles at the opposite end of the hot, dimly lit corridor.

"I am the household's cook, Mrs. Pickles. You shall report to me or the housekeeper, Mrs. Biddle, while you are employed here. Ina informed me your less than punctual arrival this morning is due to the state of the roads and an unreliable vehicle. I shall let the incident pass this once, but do not test me on future occasions. I do not abide tardiness in my kitchen. Since we're short staffed, you will work as a between maid whilst you're here. However, since the lion's share of your time will be spent in the kitchen and scullery, rather than the rest of the house, you shall look to me should you have any questions. You are expected to be ready for work promptly at half past five each morning. To my way of thinking Mrs. Michaels allows you far too many liberties at Hopewell Manor. Be mindful that those privileges won't be extended here."

A ring of keys she extracted from her pocket jangled as she unlocked and opened a dark-paneled door. "What are you waiting for? Come into my office, and be brisk about it, if you please."

Rose's black skirts swished around her ankles as she rushed past the older woman whose rigid spine, stiff shoulders and prim collar made Rose wonder if she'd bathed in starch.

The spotless office smelled of pine oil and drying herbs. A battered bookcase bowed with old crockery and receipt books stood in one corner. Rose checked her posture and waited like the wayward servant Mrs. Pickles apparently believed she was. The cook folded into the chair behind the heavy oak desk with the ease of bending stone and removed her wire-rimmed spectacles.

Fifteen minutes later, Mrs. Pickles released Rose to work. Armed with the names of her superiors, the litany of her duties, a lecture on propriety and a key to her room, Rose aimed for the door.

"And one last thing," Mrs. Pickles said the moment Rose turned the smooth brass doorknob. "I trust you aren't in any trouble. Your personal difficulties won't be tolerated in this household."

Rose paused, unable to hazard a guess as to what the cook meant by that cryptic remark. Was she warning her against the prospect of bringing Andrew up to London? "I assure you I'm only here to do my duties to the best of my ability, ma'am. I'm grateful for my

place at Hopewell Manor and look forward to returning there once you no longer require my assistance.
If you're referring to my son, he's staying with a relative in the country. I assure you I have no intention of
bringing him here."

Mrs. Pickles returned her spectacles to the bridge of
her nose before folding her hands into a tight knot on
the desktop. "Ah, yes, the child." Her thin lips curled
distastefully. "Michaels mentioned him when she
wrote to me about you. It seems everyone at Hopewell
Manor, including the former master and his family, is
quite taken with the pair of you. However, you are no
pet here. I warn you that I'm wise to women of your
questionable character, who put on airs and mimic their
betters—"

"Pardon?" Rose grew hot in the face. She didn't
mimic anyone. Aware that most people considered her
far beneath their notice, she'd made a concerted effort
to capitalize on the education she'd received while living at the orphanage.

Although her inability to learn to read embarrassed
her, she'd striven in other ways to improve herself. She
had no wish to disgrace her son or give the other parents and children additional reasons to look down on
him because of her lowly background or poor speech.

"—and bear children out of wedlock, then take advantage of the charity of others. Be aware that this is
a respectable household. If you wish to sell your fa-
vors or dangle men on a string, then I suggest you go
elsewhere for I'll have none of your antics taking place
under this roof."

Offended to her core but forced to tread lightly lest
she lose her much-needed employment, Rose prayed

the Lord would guard her mouth. "Mrs. Pickles, I've made mistakes in the past to be sure, but I promise you I don't participate in the behavior you've described."

"Then be so good as to explain why, within minutes of your arrival, a boy came to inquire about you at the behest of a man waiting across the street."

"A boy?" She frowned.

"Yes, the paper hawker from the opposite corner. He asked if Rose Smith worked in service here. When Miss McDonald told him you did, he explained about the man who'd sent him, then promptly ran away."

The image of the well-dressed gentleman popped into her mind and an unexpected surge of excitement made her heart flutter. "Did the lad happen to mention the gentleman's name?"

Mrs. Pickles shook her head. "Am I to assume you may be familiar with the identity of your admirer?"

"No, ma'am." Rose's hand tightened on the door-knob. "I haven't the slightest idea why anyone would seek me out. This is my first venture to London and other than asking for directions from a rag woman a few streets over, I've spoken to no one."

Mrs. Pickles stood, her expression skeptical. "You may claim you're not looking for a man, but according to the boy, there is definitely one looking for you."

"I assure you, ma'am, I—"

"Yes, yes, you've no idea who he might be," the cook said. "We shall see. Off to work you go. We've got a busy day ahead."

Rose wasted no time leaving the office and making her way to the scullery. Smarting from the house-keeper's accusatory manner, she despised her lowly lot in life and her inability to defend herself. The foul

odors rising from the buckets lined against the stone
wall gagged her. Towers of breakfast dishes stood beside the sink filled with food-crusted pots and pans.
Dampness from shallow puddles on the floor pervaded
the small, windowless closet of a room.

Resentment rippled through her. Thanks to someone else's whim, she'd been sentenced to the kitchen's
dungeon once more. The years she'd spent toiling her
way up to kitchen maid, then cook's assistant might
as well have never been.

After fetching and heating the necessary buckets of
water, she filled the sink and rolled up her sleeves before placing a stack of plates in to soak. She reminded
herself to be grateful she had a job at all. The walk
through London's crowded, fetid streets this morning
had proven she could ill afford to be particular. At the
best of times, females had few, if any, real choices and
a woman like her—with a young child to care for and
no husband to rely on—had fewer options still.

Thankfully, she wasn't alone. She had the Lord to
depend on and He had yet to fail her. She never forgot
that before she loved Him, He had loved her. Even in
her darkest hours, when she'd been near starving, expecting a child and leeched of hope that Sam would
ever return, He had not forsaken her. Instead, He'd
brought Harry Keen into her life and then the Malburys, a loving and godly family who cared more for
people than convention. Without them and their will-
ingness to take her on despite her being an expectant
mother, she would never have been able to keep Andrew or supply a roof over their heads.

Picking up two of the buckets by their rope handles,
she headed outdoors. The thought of losing Andrew

chilled her to the marrow. He was a gift from the Lord and the center of her existence. She'd do anything to protect him, to ensure he remained with her and in the happiest home she could provide. If that meant scrubbing pots and pans until her fingers bled, then that's what she would do.

The first luncheon dishes arrived to be washed just as she finished drying the last pan from breakfast. By midafternoon, her hands were raw from the hot water and strong soap, and her feet ached from the hours she'd spent standing on the unyielding stone floor. It was a great relief when Ina fetched her to help the chambermaid make beds upstairs.

Early evening found Rose back in the scullery, another teetering mountain of pots and pans beside the sink to be washed. Hearing Mrs. Pickles's joyless voice in the corridor set her teeth on edge. She glanced around for a bucket to empty outside as an excuse to escape the stern woman.

"Smith, there you are." The cook stopped in the doorway. "I have revised instructions for you tonight."

Rose faced the older woman. "What am I to do, ma'am?"

Mrs. Pickles dried her hands on her long, white apron. "You're to go with Ina to a house on Hanover Square. There's a well-to-do gentleman, a Mr. Samuels, I believe, who is short staffed for a dinner party he's hosting this evening. Baron Malbury is keen to win his favor and has graciously offered to send the two of you to assist."

"When are we to leave?" She wrung out her dishrag and laid it over the edge of the sink to dry.

"Immediately. I've already given the address to Ina.

Be certain you change your apron before you depart. You look like day-old porridge," she tossed over her shoulder as she left.

Rose wiped a trickle of perspiration from her temple and pushed back the damp tendrils of hair falling around her face. As she climbed the stairs to her room, she removed the offending apron and wished she could crawl into bed. Exhaustion crippled her. Considering the day had started with a carriage accident before dawn and gone progressively downhill from there, she began to wonder what trials the night held in store.

A downpour accompanied Rose's unfamiliar trek through Mayfair's confusing maze of slippery cobblestones and fog-shrouded streets. Her shoes squeaked from more than one dunk in a mud puddle and her soggy bonnet had quit shielding her face from the rain two blocks earlier.

The short jaunt should have been uneventful, but due to a pugnacious individual who seemed to believe he owned the entire footpath, Ina had been pushed off the curb and sent reeling into an open sewer. Her twisted ankle and filthy skirts left her unfit for work. After calling a hack to convey the other girl home, Rose had pressed on alone.

Shivering and keenly aware that she was late for the second time in the same day, Rose made use of the knocker on the glossy, black kitchen door of the Samuels's townhouse. As she always did when visiting a new place, she worried she'd misread the address and come to the wrong establishment.

The door swung open. Heat from the stove and the delicious scents of savory dishes emanated from the large work area beyond. A uniformed footman stared down at her.

"Hello, I'm Rose—"

"My name is Robert. Weren't there to be two of you?"

"Yes." She explained about Ina's predicament. "She twisted her ankle and had to return home."

"I suppose that's why you're late?"

She nodded.

"The master's waiting for you and his guests are expected soon. Follow me." The footman stepped back to allow her entrance into the warm, cavernous basement that smelled of herbs and cinnamon.

"The master wishes to see me?" Struck by the oddity of the situation, she handed over her sodden bonnet, muddy cape and umbrella. Damp patches spotted her gown and a rip marred the hem. Water from her wet hair trickled down her temples and the back of her neck. "You must be mistaken. I'm in Baron Malbury's employ. Mrs. Pickles sent me to help with the shortage of kitchen staff this evening. Why should your master wish to see the likes of me?"

Robert shrugged. "It's not my place to ask, miss."

"Does he interview all the temporary help?"

"Not to my knowledge."

As she followed the footman, she noticed the copper pots bubbling on the wood stove and the variety of roasted meats resting on the chopping blocks. Kitchen maids buzzed about doing chores and putting the final touches on the sauces and desserts. Unlike the Malbury townhouse, or even Hopewell Manor at times of late, this kitchen seemed well staffed—perhaps overly so.

A flight of stairs delivered them to the ground floor

where a checkered pattern of black-and-white marble anchored the central hall. Massive paintings of somber individuals looked down on her from ornate, gilded frames hung on walls covered with blue-watered silk.

Until now, she'd found Hopewell her ideal of refinement, but the grand manor where she'd worked for the past several years seemed like nothing more than a pretty house compared to the opulence on offer here.

"This way, miss."

The faint sound of servants discussing the proper placement of cutlery filtered out of the dining room as Rose trailed the footman past marble busts, cut-crystal vases filled with hothouse flowers and a massive etched mirror. She cringed at her ghastly reflection of bedraggled hair and cold, blue-tinged lips.

Robert stopped in front of a door and rapped on the dark wood.

"Enter," came a muffled order.

The flash of pity that crossed Robert's expression gave her pause. "He'll see you now."

Trepidation snaked through her as he opened the door. The peculiar situation couldn't be discounted. Employers usually took as much notice of their lower servants as a fallen leaf in the park.

With nervous fingers, she brushed damp tendrils off her face and tried to smooth the wrinkles from her skirt before she hesitantly crossed the threshold.

The scent of lemon polish and leather greeted her. Despite the glow from the fireplace, shadows lurked in the corners of the masculine room. Shelves crammed with books lined the walls and her exhausted brain began to ache at the thought of trying to decipher even the simplest among them.

"That will be all, Robert."

Gasping, she spun in the direction of the deep voice. Sam's voice.

Disbelief coursed through her. Her heart clamored in wild abandon even before she found him standing behind a wide, polished desk at the head of the room.

"Hello, Rose."

Chapter Two

Rose blinked rapidly as she struggled to form a sensible reply. How she wished Mrs. Pickles hadn't gotten the name wrong and had given her time to prepare for being face-to-face with Sam. "Hello…"

"It's been a long time."

"Yes." Her lips wooden, she stared helplessly as simultaneous joy and agony overwhelmed her. Her gaze roved over Sam's face in a frantic, failed attempt to take in all the details of him at once.

Time had erased the last traces of the boy she'd known. His face was leaner, his features sharper, his jaw more defined than when he'd left Ashby Croft. As tall as she remembered and even more handsome, if possible, with his thick, black hair and chocolate-brown eyes, he was dark for an Englishman. As children they'd fancied he must have gypsy blood since his sun-warmed complexion set him so far apart from the many pasty-faced boys of the village.

"What are you doing here, Sam?" Registering the smoldering fury in his dark eyes, she took a self-protective step back. "How…how did you find me?"

"Funny thing, that. I saw you on the street this morning and followed you to Malbury's."

"This morning?" Even as she noted his polished accent, her eyes widened with sudden recollection. "You're the man I saw in the square. The one speaking to the paperboy."

She took his silence as confirmation. His anger spread to her like a contagion. A multitude of questions swirled through her brain until she felt lightheaded. Praying she wouldn't fall apart in front of him, she swallowed the sob of emotion lodged in her tight throat. "Where have you been all these years? *Why* did you never come back?"

A silky, black eyebrow arched with unconcealed derision. "Where have *I* been? Why, here in London, of course. Right where I said I'd be."

Sam's frigid tone dripped with enough scorn to penetrate Rose's dazed senses. Her Sam had never spoken to her in such a fashion—as though he loathed even the faintest knowledge of her existence.

"The better question is—" his square jaw tightened "—where have *you* been?"

A shiver rippled through her that had nothing to do with her damp garments or clammy skin. Any hope she'd ever cherished for a pleasant reunion vanished. This severe man looked like Sam—albeit a more mature version—but he bore no resemblance to the lively, brash and indomitable boy she'd loved. He might as well be a stranger.

The tick of a mantel clock marked the silence. Her shock began to fade. Other emotions raced through her in quick succession. Anger and confusion gave way to disbelief, then fear as she pieced together the truth of

the situation. Sam had arranged this meeting to knock
her for six and he'd succeeded. She didn't understand
his apparent loathing, but his intentions were clear.
He'd always wanted to shine. Obviously, he'd made
his fortune and sought to rub her nose in the fact that
he'd forgotten her without so much as a by-your-leave.
Why else would he plot to bring her to this magnificent house to act as his servant when he'd ignored her
for the past nine years?

The meanness of his scheme tweaked her pride and
renewed her anger. She had nothing to be ashamed of.
She did honest work. How dare he treat her so shab-
bily? He was the cad who'd lied to her, abandoned her,
ground her heart into dust. If he expected her to rant
and rave like some forsaken fishwife, he'd be disappointed. She refused to give him the pleasure of seeing
her make a fool of herself, especially when he deserved
nothing but contempt for his selfishness. He may have
been amassing a mountain of money all these years,
but she'd been seeing to the important task of raising
their son.

She straightened her shoulders and lifted her chin.
"If you must know, I was in Devonshire until two days
ago. Just as I said I'd be."

Dark eyes fringed with thick, black lashes narrowed
with disdain. "You're such a good liar. You'll have to
forgive me if I don't believe you straightaway."

"*Me,* a liar?" She lifted her chin. "That's rich coming from you, Sam."

"Mr. Blackstone, if you please. Kindly remember I'm your employer at present. Nothing more."
He rounded the desk and moved toward her. Instinct

warned her to run, but she held firm. She'd done nothing amiss, but he had much to answer for.

Bristling with tension, she focused on his shirtfront
for that seemed the least threatening spot. Dressed
in formal attire of black and white, he looked like a
seething tiger with an elegant bow tied round his neck.

He stopped before her, close enough to touch. She
breathed in deep, taking in his scent of soap and the
subtle hint of sandalwood cologne. Desperate to feel
indifferent, she detested the traitorous way her heart
refused to calm.

"Stay away from me." She clenched her trembling
fingers into fists to keep from reaching for him. She
prayed he'd maintain a proper distance, but then again
he'd never been the least bit proper.

A sly grin tugged at his firm, sculpted lips. "Make
me."

The whisper-soft touch of his fingertips along her
jaw silenced her. Tremors raced down her spine and
her feet grew roots to the floor. A sigh feathered in her
throat as he lifted her chin.

Their eyes met. Instantly ensnared by the rich,
brown depths of his gaze, she lost track of time and
all sense of good judgment. Blood rushed in her ears
and her knees began to quiver like an aspic left in the
sun. She swayed toward him. The fleeting thought
of how much their son resembled him evaporated the
same moment his thumb caressed her full bottom lip.

He leaned closer. His warm, mint-scented breath
fanned across her cheek and tickled her ear. "You want
me to kiss you, Rosie. Admit it."

His smug expression rubbed her raw and restored
some order to the chaos of her senses. How could she

have let her guard down? Sam may have embodied home and safety for her nine years ago, but no longer. In fact, no one seemed more dangerous to her body, livelihood or peace of mind.

Please Lord, give me strength.

She released a shaky breath. "Is that an order, Mr. Blackstone? Am I to understand that although you're my employer I'll have to be concerned about untoward advances from your corner?"

He laughed. "Untoward? Debatable. Unwanted? I think not."

Her cheeks burned. She wished otherwise, but she'd never had any strength of will when it came to Sam and she hated that he could see her weakness while he was the picture of strength. "Think what you like, sir. If I may, I'd like to return to work."

She turned, desperate to leave, to regain her breath and her bearings. Somehow she managed to navigate halfway to the door before he stopped her. "There's no use for you in the kitchen."

She stumbled midstep, then whipped around to face him. Sheer panic seized her. "Are you sacking me?"

He studied her for such a long moment she squirmed like a butterfly pinned to a board.

"That depends on if you're nice to me or not."

"I've never been cruel to you, Sa…Mr. Blackstone. Unlike you and how you're treating me at present."

"Is that so?" He returned to his desk and sat in his imposing leather chair. "Then I suppose you thought you were doing me a favor when you ran off and married another man?"

Her knees buckled and the room tipped to an unnatural angle. Only God's mercy kept her upright. She gripped the back of a chair, her fingers digging into the soft leather. Had she heard him correctly? How did he know about her marriage? Did he know about his son?

Fear invaded the deepest recesses of her being. Having inhabited a lower rung in society all her life, she was used to being powerless. More than once she'd seen the rich get away with all sorts of evil simply because they had the means to buy their own justice. Was that why he'd brought her here? To show her he had the wealth to bend the law to his will? Was he simply funning with her before he revealed his knowledge of Andrew and that he meant to snatch their son from her care?

Nausea soured her stomach. How could she live without her child?

"How...?" She cleared her throat. Voices in the hall competed with the rush of blood in her ears. "How did you learn about Harry?"

He shrugged. "Does it matter?"

"It does to me."

"What is he? A footman?" His lip curled. "No, my money's on a groomsman. You always did want a horse."

"He was a farmer, if you must know," she said, irked that he didn't answer her. "A good and godly man. He deserves your thanks for helping me, not your scorn."

He surged to his feet. All six feet two inches of lean, hostile muscle. "I'll be flayed alive before I thank the likes of that clodhopper. You were my girl, Rosie! You promised to wait for me forever if need be. Those were your words, not mine. Imagine my surprise when I went to fetch you in Ashby Croft and learned your definition of forever meant less than eight measly months."

In the wake of his outburst, a hush fell over the room. "You came for me?" she whispered, unable to accept he told the truth.

"Of course."

"Of course?" She balked at his arrogance. "There's no *of course* about it. You said you'd return in a few weeks."

Color scored his high cheekbones. "Settling in and learning my trade took longer than I expected. Stark had me working eighteen hours a day for months… I wrote to you. I hoped you might get your friend, Lizzy, or that layabout of an innkeeper you worked for to read my letters."

"Letters? As in more than one?"

He weaved a letter opener between his long, elegant fingers before letting the ivory-handled implement clatter to the desktop. He cleared his throat. "The post isn't always reliable. I wanted to be certain you heard from me."

Her heart plummeted. If he was telling the truth, where had those messages gone? Had they truly been lost or had someone stolen them? How different their lives might have been if she'd received even one. "None of them reached me."

He shrugged. "Water under the bridge now that you're wed."

She flinched at the accusation in his voice. Whatever he knew of her marriage, he mustn't be aware that she'd been widowed within weeks of saying her vows or that Harry's wounds had made it impossible to make a true union. Was it possible he didn't know of Andrew's existence, either?

Hope buoyed her for the first time since she'd entered the study. "I did wait for you, but I'd been ill and—"

"Are you ill now?"

"No, but—"

"Then details aren't worth a farthing as far as I'm concerned. What it boils down to is you didn't have enough faith in me and you ran off with the first available chap to come along. But don't worry. It didn't take me long to get over you, either. As you might expect, a city as lively as London offers countless diversions." His smile didn't reach his eyes. "With a little imagination a body can't be bothered to wallow in the past for long, and it didn't take much for me to realize I'd be better off without you."

She gasped at the spike of pain that pierced her heart. "I see." Hating that her eyes misted with tears, she glanced out the window. Gas lamps glowed along the street, alleviating the darkness and eerie wisps of fog.

Bitterness welled inside her at the unfairness of the situation. While he'd been playing away in London, uprooting her from his heart, she'd been expecting his child, terrified and lonely to her bones.

She closed her eyes and took a deep breath. Honesty insisted she tell him he was a father since he'd given no indication he knew about their son, but for now Andrew seemed to be her secret. She planned to keep it that way until Sam proved he could give her a fair hearing. Since he harbored such ill feelings toward her, he would no doubt use Andrew as a weapon to punish her for her supposed wrongs, and she'd be mad to give this wrathful, unforgiving stranger such a powerful means to ruin her life.

Besides, her heartache demanded she let him stew for a little while longer. All of his indignation was for show. He may have been disappointed when he learned of her marriage, may have even convinced himself he'd been heartbroken for a time, but unlike her, he'd recovered from their separation with far too much ease to claim his love had been of the eternal variety.

What a fool she'd been to believe they'd shared something special. She'd been no more to him than a habit he'd easily broken. She hated that she'd missed him when he didn't deserve such sentiment almost as much as she loathed the inviolate hope that whispered time was all they needed to clear the air.

Yet, how could they become reacquainted when they were no longer equals? To others they were as different as gold and rust. She'd grown up in a small village, but she wasn't completely ignorant of the ways of the world or society's expectations. Sam's wealth placed him head and shoulders above her. She couldn't see him coming to the kitchen to chat while she peeled potatoes.

No, he was one of the privileged now, a fact he must realize given how easily he'd used his higher status to intimidate her.

"Since you're over me, why did you bring me here?" she asked past the lump in her throat. "To make a display of yourself and show me what a fool I've apparently been for not pining for you all these years?"

"That's part of it," he answered flatly.

"Then I didn't miss a thing." The chiming of the clock almost drowned out her strained whisper. "You're petty and coldhearted. I'm fortunate I never tied myself to a cad like you."

His dark eyes shimmered with thinly veiled rage. She teetered on a knife's edge, stunned by her outburst when she had so much to lose. Certain he'd send her packing, she felt every nerve in her body clench with dread.

A knock on the study door shattered the tension.

"What?" Sam snapped.

Robert opened the door and took a hesitant step into the room. The shiny, brass buttons of his uniform glistened in the lamplight. Although he seemed a bit winded, his sallow face had been wiped clean of emotion. "Forgive me for interrupting, sir, but Mr. Hodges sent me to inform you Lord Sanbourne and his daughter, Miss Ratner, have arrived. Mr. Hodges installed them in the drawing room, but Miss Ratner—"

"Has declined to wait," a feminine voice announced from the corridor. A petite beauty with light brown hair breezed past the footman and into the study without further introduction. Artfully wrapped in a silk lavender gown, she made her way straight to Sam and kissed him in greeting. "I think it's positively ghastly to suggest I do so when you should at least *pretend* to be on pins and needles waiting for your hostess to arrive."

Aggravated by the brunette's pawing of Sam, Rose noted he didn't untangle himself with any haste. Obviously, he approved of Miss Ratner's brazen ways.

At the end of her patience, she headed for the exit without waiting for Sam's permission to leave. Robert withdrew first, but she managed a narrow escape just before the door clicked shut in her wake.

Sam watched Rose dart for the door and checked the impulse to call her back. The newspaper boy might as well have stabbed him in the vitals when he confirmed that Rose Smith did, indeed, work for Baron Malbury. Used to dealing with the 'Change's unexpected variables, he rarely suffered from surprise. However, the knowledge that Rose lived within striking distance had knocked the wind from his lungs and he had yet to catch his breath.

How dare she act as though she were the injured party? He'd done nothing wrong. He'd sought to make a better life for them. She had forgotten him like week-old rubbish the moment someone new came along.

"Sam?"

"What?" He blinked and focused on Amelia. Glad for the distraction of her arrival, he detested the noxious mix of resentment and regret coursing through his veins.

"Are you listening to me, darling?"

"Of course." Using all his powers of concentration, he forced Rose from his mind, although she refused to go without a fuss. "You'll have to forgive me. I'm more than a little overcome by how lovely you look this evening."

She smiled and angled her trim body to show her gown to best advantage. The shining silk and lace belonged on a duchess instead of the daughter of an impoverished viscount, but Amelia wasn't one to burden herself with such pesky distinctions. The bright blue ribbons framing her oval face and the sapphire gems at her throat reminded him of Rose's eyes. He gritted his teeth. Everywhere he looked today, Rose was there to taunt him.

"You seem distracted." As was her wont in private, Amelia dismissed propriety and sank gracefully into one of the leather armchairs. "I saw you on Oxford Street earlier today. You looked rather harassed. I had my driver hail you, but you quite had your head in the clouds."

"I've been preoccupied with a personal matter." His gaze drifted to the door. How was it possible that Rose was even lovelier than he remembered? Over the years he'd forgotten the blueness of her eyes and the natural blush of color in her smooth, fair cheeks. Worse, no one made him feel more invigorated than she did. The moment she entered the room he lost track of all else. "It's nothing to be concerned about."

She glanced at him from under downcast lashes. "It's not financial difficulties, I trust? After the grandeur you've become accustomed to, one doubts the Marshalsea would suit your tastes in the least."

Compared to the squalor he and Rose had lived in once the orphanage closed its doors, the notorious debtor's prison qualified as a palace. "I'd manage."

"I'm certain you would. I find it excessively appealing that you've remained a scrapper beneath all the polish you've acquired, but I'm quite certain I'd die if I ever found myself in such a hideous place." Her gloved hand soothed the silken folds of her gown. "If you are in dire straits, I hope you will remember you can come to me should you ever need a confidant—"

"I'm much obliged, but you needn't fret."

"As long as you know I'm always here for you."

He tamped down the cynical suspicion that her loyalty depended on the sum of his bank accounts. "Your friendship is dear to me."

She smiled. "As you're aware, I want very much to be more than just your friend."

Still rough from his confrontation with Rose, he leaned back against the desk. His fingers clutched the lip of the desktop, his right ankle crossed casually over the left.

This wasn't the first time Amelia had made her wishes known. Just as she'd hinted on several occasions, he should probably marry her. In truth, he'd been considering a proposal for weeks. Her father's hapless investments had made her family desperate enough for funds to overlook his guttersnipe background, and Amelia would make the perfect wife for a man who had everything except a permanent place in society.

"My father agrees we'd make a splendid couple," she continued, undaunted by his lack of comment.

"I'm certain he does," he said drily. In fact, he could think of a million reasons why.

The provocative gleam in her dark eyes faded. "Darling, what's gotten into you today? You're too sullen by half. I wish you'd reconsider and come shooting with us at the Digby estate in Devonshire next month. A nice long holiday would do you good."

"It wouldn't be much of a holiday, I'm afraid. I grew up in Devonshire. The area is filled with memories I'd rather forget."

"Even more reason to come with us." She stood and moved close enough to brush up against him. Her perfume, though subtle, carried a powdery scent that made his nose twitch. "It will give us a chance to replace those bad memories with fond, new ones."

He gave her a cool half smile. "I'll consider it."

"That is all I ask. Her gloved hands reached for his cravat and began to refashion the knot. "You are quite a catch, you know. You may not be a peer, but you are divine to look at, charming when you choose to be and—"

"Rich."

She pouted. "I've told you before, it's vulgar to mention money, but since you have, yes, your wealth is, shall we say, one of your finest assets. It saddens me greatly because I am so fond of you, but without your fortune to make up for other things…"

"You wouldn't be seen within a mile of me."

"You needn't be harsh. You're aware of my circumstances." She patted his chest. "Nor must you be unfair in your judgment of me. My family expects me to wed, if not well, then at least lucratively."

Her snobbery both amused and revolted him. "And why should I want to marry you?"

"You must be joking. I'm the daughter of a peer."

"You can also be a crick in the neck."

"True, but you're a philistine." She laughed. "We've been dancing around an agreement for weeks, so since we're being honest, let's face facts. An alliance between us is a most sensible option. You have everything except a family to carry on your name and eventually squabble over the fortune you've amassed. I, thanks to my father's missteps, am in need of… protection, shall we say. We understand each other and get on well most of the time. You can help my family, and I can open doors for you that your background prohibits you from entering on your own."

"You assume I want to cross those lofty thresholds."

She frowned as though she'd never heard such a ridiculous notion. "Of course you do, Sam. You don't have to pretend with me. Everyone, even those who deny it, want to be part of the crème de la crème."

"I don't lack for invitations as it is."

"Yes, however, these invitations will be from people who matter, not those boorish tradesmen or stuffy politicians with whom you usually conspire. All I ask is that you contemplate the possibilities. Imagine I'm a new stock and consider your potential rate of return."

He already had. The Ratners' decline in circumstances may be recent, but their title and mortgaged properties were centuries old. To a man whose own roots went no deeper than the day of his birth, buying a branch on the Ratners' lauded family tree held a certain appeal.

Best of all, he wasn't in any danger of falling in love with Amelia, nor did she expect him to. Their union would be little more than a mutually beneficial business arrangement. No deep emotions to make him feel helpless or dependent on anyone but himself for happiness.

"I'm always calculating variables."

"Brilliant." Voices passing in the corridor drew Amelia's attention. "I'd best see to the dining room before our guests descend. Everything must be perfect tonight."

"Speaking of variables—" he opened the door to help usher her out "—something popped up today and we're short a footman this evening."

Amelia paled. "How can that be?"

"I've made other arrangements with Hodges."

"That old fossil you call a butler should have been put out to pasture a decade ago. I gave him strict instructions to send word to me if the slightest mishap occurred."

He refrained from mentioning that Hodges had been

in a dither himself when he'd informed the older man that he'd given Frank the night off and that Rose would fill his position.

"I can't believe this is happening," she moaned. "I've planned every detail and now all is ruined!"

"Hardly. A kitchen maid has already been found to replace him."

"One of the *maids?*" Amelia's hand fluttered to her chest as though she might faint. "I'm aware you're not fully educated in these matters, but a woman serving... are you mad? That will never do."

Amused by her dramatics, he wondered vaguely if there were any smelling salts on hand just in case she keeled over. "It's already been decided."

"I'll send for one of ours—"

"There's no time." The first muffled notes of a violin being tuned bolstered his point. He led her to the door. "We'll have to make due. You are the one interested in all the latest fashions. Perhaps we'll usher in a new one."

Chapter Three

Once free of Sam's study, Rose followed the footman into the servants' stairway. Shaking uncontrollably, she reached toward the wall for support as she made her way down the steps.

In the kitchen, the chaos before a dinner party was a situation with which she was well acquainted. Already at a fever pitch from her confrontation with Sam, her senses seemed unusually sensitive to the clamor of voices, banging pots and the aroma of roasted meats and exotic spices.

"Miss Smith?" An aged man with a bald pate ringed by gray hair called from the doorway. "Miss Rose Smith?"

"Yes, sir." She made quick strides across the room. The man's formal ensemble and somber mood marked him as the butler. With trepidation, she wondered what she'd done to be called out by the likes of him when it was the housekeeper's duty to oversee female staff. "I'm Rose Smith."

"I'm Mr. Hodges, Mr. Blackstone's butler. Robert

tells me the other girl on loan tonight suffered an accident on the journey here."

"Yes, sir."

Mr. Hodges's bushy, gray eyebrows pleated together into a straight line. His faded green eyes peered at her through thick spectacles, sizing her up from head to toe. His sigh of exasperation didn't speak well of his impression of her. "Follow me."

He led her to a small, oak-paneled office at the end of the corridor and motioned toward a mirror in the corner. "Have you seen yourself? You look as though you've been dragged by a runaway mount. How in the world am I to make you presentable in time?"

"In time for what, sir?" she asked, mortified by how mussed and messy she looked compared to the radiant Miss Ratner.

"Mr. Blackstone insists you serve tonight."

Dismay choked her. "*Me* in the dining room? But I work in the kitchen."

"He doesn't care. He wants you."

He wants to humiliate me, more like. He no longer loved her and intended to hammer home the point. There was no other reason to toss convention to the four winds just to have her wait on him and his self-important friends. She didn't remember Sam being such a vindictive swine, but apparently nine years in London had hardened his heart to granite. That ruthless quality terrified her.

"Stay here," Hodges said. "I'll have one of the other girls fetch you a cap and something more acceptable to wear."

Left alone with her untidy reflection, she longed to return to Devonshire and Hopewell Manor. She'd never been this far from Andrew, and her arms ached to hold her son. Exhaustion pressed in on her and hunger pangs cramped her stomach. The entire day had been one foul kettle of fish after another with the worst being the superior way Sam looked down his nose at her. The more she thought about how he'd ambushed her, the more indignant she became. He'd had no right to call her on the carpet, berate her and deny her the chance to explain. Who did he think he was? A pompous nobleman?

And yet...he *had* returned to Ashby Croft to collect her as he'd promised. He must have done or he wouldn't have known about Harry. Regret pierced her like a thousand knives. If only she'd found the strength to wait for him a little longer.

The knowledge they were both to blame for losing one another helped to cool her temper. His love may have withered with more ease than she cared to admit, but he had not abandoned her without cause as she'd long believed.

"Lord," she whispered, taking a moment to pray. "I need Your help again. I feel like David facing Goliath without a sling. How can I defend myself when Sam has already made up his mind? Please, soften his heart. Convince him to give me a proper listen and accept the truth for Andrew's sake if not for mine."

Moments later, an older kitchen maid with dark hair and merry blue eyes appeared in the doorway. "I'm Abigail," she said as she closed the door behind her. "Our 'ousekeeper, Mrs. Frye, sent me." She extended a short stack of fresh garments. "You'll 'ave to change quick, dearie. We may 'ave to pin up the 'em a bit, but it's the best we can do on short notice."

Unfortunately, the skirt's length wasn't the problem. The tightness of the bodice and waist made it nearly impossible to breathe. "I can't wear this."

"You must." Abigail surveyed her with a critical eye. "Tomorrow's wash day and this is the last acceptable garment we 'ave that might fit you. The skirt is shorter than I expected so at least you won't take a tumble."

"Don't you find it a bit peculiar I'm to serve tonight?"

"I'd say. Especially since the master usually likes things jus' so. Some say 'e's extra fussy cause 'e used to be a nobody 'imself and 'e don't want those lofty new friends of 'is to ream him out behind 'is back."

Rose doubted Sam cared much about stray opinions, but he had always been a man of detail. His ability to notice what others failed to see had made him restless as far back as childhood. While growing up in Ashby Croft, he'd been unable to ignore the injustice of their lot and be content. Little wonder Mr. Stark's promises had stolen him away in a blink. After seeing just a glimpse of what Sam had been able to accomplish in London, she marveled that she'd ever dreamed she might be enough to hold his interest.

"There," Abigail said as she finished tying the strings of Rose's long, white apron. "Try lifting that stack of receipt books on the corner of the desk. Were I to fancy a guess, I'd say they're as 'eavy as most of the trays you'll be expected to carry."

Rose reached for the pile of books and hefted them into her arms. The dress's seams protested, but none of them gave way.

"Thank the Lord for small mercies." Abigail smiled

with obvious relief. "After the way Mr. Blackstone stormed about in a temper this afternoon, he was liable to dismiss us all if anything else went wrong this evening."

"Don't be surprised if does. I don't have the faintest idea about the proper way to serve. I'm afraid I'll be so nervous I'll knock over a glass or drop a dirtied plate in someone's lap."

Abigail chuckled. "You'll do fine. Jus' be sure to steer clear of Miss Ratner's father, Lord Sanbourne. 'E's been known to make free with his 'ands when he thinks no one'll notice."

"I'll keep that in mind." Rose tugged at the tight material bunched at her waist. The clang of pots and pans filtered down the hall from the kitchen. "Anything else I should be aware of?"

"Well," Abigail said after a thoughtful pause, "I 'ope you won't think I make a 'abit of carrying tales about Mr. Blackstone or his friends, but if I was you, I'd be careful of Miss Ratner, as well."

"She and Mr. Blackstone seem very close."

"Indeed. Tonight is 'er debut as 'ostess 'ere. She's been in a rumpus all week, giving orders and bragging about 'ow much the master would be lost without 'er. By bringing you on, 'e's given 'er efforts a punch to the nose, to be sure. She won't be 'appy about her plans being tinkered with, and she's the kind to seek revenge on you, not 'im."

"I'm only here to do my job. If I have my way, I'll be gone for good before midnight."

"That's probably for the best." Abigail finished pinning Rose's cap into place. "You've got the prettiest 'air. What a pity it 'as to be 'idden under this silly article."

The rare compliment gave her spirits a boost. "I've been a servant most of my life. I know how important it is to blend with the walls."

"Especially since Miss Ratner searches for things to complain about."

"She must have something to recommend her. You told me yourself, Mr. Blackstone is taken with her," she said, denying the sudden ache in her chest had anything to do with Sam and stemmed from her inability to take in enough air.

"I suppose so. 'E's been with 'er six months—longer than any of the other women 'e's kept company with in all the years I've worked for 'im, more's the pity. But rumor 'as it she's angling for marriage, and a clever woman knows nothing is final until she 'as a ring on 'er finger or one in 'is nose."

A loud clatter and a long stream of angry French drew Abigail's quick retreat to the kitchen. Rose pressed her fingertips to her throbbing temples. Armed with more information than she'd bargained for or wanted, she fought back a dark cloud of depression. Even if she hadn't been convinced Sam had well and truly moved on without her, she was now.

"Are you presentable?" Mr. Hodges called from out in the hall. "Only ten minutes until it's time to announce the dinner service. We must go up this instant."

She took as deep a breath as the gown allowed and whispered a prayer for mercy. Her rattled nerves refused to settle. With one last glance in the mirror, she saw an ordinary servant sausage-wrapped in black wool and starched, white cotton. There was nothing special about her, hopefully nothing to draw Miss Ratner's ire.

"Robert is managing the soup course, but I shall oversee the fish and carve the roasts," Mr. Hodges informed her on the way to the first floor. "Hold the platters within easy reach of each guest and allow them to serve themselves. By all means don't speak to anyone unless you're spoken to first. If that should happen, keep your responses to a minimum. Some of the ladies and gentlemen present are of noble stock and won't take kindly to being addressed by a lowly subordinate such as yourself."

The melody of a violin grew louder as they reached the top step. Both of them were out of breath by the time they paused on the landing. Rose tugged at the tight material bunching about her waist, certain she must be blue in the face while the warm glow of the gas lamps cast Hodges's wrinkled visage in a golden hue.

From the corner of her eye, she saw the violinist standing in a small circular alcove off the main hall. The somber melody he played added an extra layer of formality to the high, curved ceilings and dark, paneled walls.

The low rumble of conversation signaled the direction of the drawing room and the current location of the party. Hodges lifted an index finger to his lips, warning her to keep silent. He pointed to an open set of sliding doors on the left side of the corridor. Rose nodded gravely and followed him to what seemed like her doom.

In the drawing room, a fire flickered in the hearth and the aroma of savory herbs wafted across the hall from the dining room.

Aware he should be pleased with the early success of the gathering, Sam could not dismiss his impatience to send everyone home. The laughter and light conversation that flowed freely from the assembly of his guests failed to hold his interest when the possibility of renewing his discussion with Rose beckoned him.

By design, he'd left the double doors open and chosen a seat with a clear view of the corridor where Rose would have to pass by. He'd tried to deny his longing to see her, but the simple knowledge that she was somewhere beneath his roof tormented him beyond all good sense and reason.

The music took a somber turn. He stood, intending to request a more cheerful tune, but Rose chose that moment to appear and everything ceased to exist except the slim column of black slipping into the dining room on the butler's coattails.

To his annoyance, the sight of her eased his restlessness and improved his floundering mood with an immediacy that disturbed him. After all the years they'd been separated and the way she'd broken her promise to wait for him, how was it possible she inspired anything in him except contempt?

Amelia moved to his side and linked her arm with his. "The evening is going swimmingly well, don't you agree, darling? Just as I predicted, the Ellistons are impressed with the vintage on offer and are already imbibing their second sample."

"How marvelous for them. I'm going to see about dinner."

"I'm the hostess. I'll go."

"No, stay here and charm your pigeons. I'll return in a few minutes." He untangled his arm from hers and moved to the hallway where he caught a glimpse of Rose by the sideboard helping Robert ladle soup into porcelain bowls.

A glossy, blond tendril had escaped her ruffled cap and fallen in a gentle wave between her shoulder blades. An intense longing to touch the soft strands, to touch *her,* swept over him. He didn't know what he wanted more: to usher her back into his study and continue demanding answers for jilting him or to kiss her senseless where she stood. He could not have guessed when he first saw her this morning that her nearness would be akin to having a severed arm reattached to his body or his heart returned to his chest.

He must be going mad.

In desperate need of a diversion, he dragged his gaze from Rose and glanced about the dining room. He had to tip his hat to Amelia. For a woman who found it vulgar to speak of money, she possessed a talent for spending his. The trio of crystal chandeliers had been cleaned and reassembled the day before, causing the room to sparkle. No expense had been spared in the crisp white linens, the ornate candelabras or arsenal of silver flatware flanking each set of china. The multiple towers of tropical fruit and hothouse flowers must have cost the earth if they'd cost a farthing.

Had Rose been impressed by the finery on display? Had it dawned on her that, had she waited for him a short while longer, all of this would have been hers?

Behind him, the chatter in the drawing room grew louder and the music progressed into an elegant melody he'd heard somewhere before but didn't quite recognize. Hodges approached, his weathered features crinkled into an anxious mask. "May I help you, sir?

We're almost ready. Miss Ratner gave strict instructions to announce seating at precisely nine o'clock. We have six minutes remaining."

"Fine, fine," he said, waving the older man back to work. Rose had yet to look his way, and her inability to sense his presence when every nerve in his body was fixed on her cut deep. He wanted to rattle her air of efficiency, to make her feel as disjointed as he did. The hour since she'd quit his study had dragged on like a week, and the need to see her face had grown with every tick of the clock.

He willed her to turn around, but she continued her task for an age before finally pausing to glance his way.

She froze the moment she saw him. Triumph surged through him as her dark-blue eyes widened in response and color scored her cheeks. The soup in the ladle she held missed the bowl and puddled atop the sideboard without her notice.

He moved toward her, but Hodges stepped in to scold her, breaking the connection. "What do you think you're about, you clumsy girl? Look at the mess you've caused!"

"I'm so sorry." She glowered at Sam before dismissing him to focus on the butler. "I'll tidy up straightaway."

"See that you do and be quick about it." Hodges consulted his pocket watch. "Four minutes until we must announce the meal. Miss Ratner—"

"Hodges." Sam joined them at the sideboard. "Is everything well?"

"Everything except this simpleton, sir. She's bound to be a detriment. I did try to explain that she's never served at table, but—"

He dealt his usually mild-mannered butler a quelling glance before motioning toward the table and the flawless crystal goblets sparkling in the candlelight. "There are fingerprints marring several of the glasses."

"Fingerprints on the glasses? Oh, dear! I just wiped them down. I don't know how I missed them, sir."

"A tragedy to be sure. I trust you'll see to the matter straightaway."

"Certainly, sir." The butler shuffled away with all the meager speed he could muster. "Robert, come quickly. It seems renegade fingerprints abound on the tableware."

Sam turned back to Rose once Hodges passed out of earshot. "Look at me, Miss Smith."

"I have to see to this soup you caused me to spill," she said as she searched the drawers in the sideboard for a cloth.

"I caused you?" He smiled at the dig. She'd always been cheeky, especially when her ire was up. "I was nowhere near you." He took a clean square of linen from his pocket and mopped up the hot broth. "All better. Now look at me," he insisted.

She tossed her head back. Eyes bright with hostility glared at him. "Why are you hounding me?"

"Is that any way to speak to your employer?" He placed the damp linen on a nearby tray of used items bound for the kitchen.

Her lips tightened into a thin line. "You are not my employer, Mr. Blackstone. I work for Baron Malbury. I realize you have the power to see that I'm dismissed if you choose, and I sincerely hope you will not, but I was sent here to help in your kitchen, not endure humiliation just because you want to teach me a lesson."

"How have I humiliated you? You're a servant. I've tasked you to serve." Noticing Hodges and Robert glance his way, he lowered his voice. "I've made you a footman for the evening. If anything, you've been promoted."

"We both know what you've done and why." She located an extra cloth and shut the drawer with a not so gentle shove. "There are rules to these sort of functions, Mr. Blackstone. I may be a simple cook's assistant, but even I understand your guests won't see me as anything but a mistake that will make your hostess appear inept. I'm not trained to serve at table. Most likely I'll commit one blunder after the next."

"And that will humiliate you? Who cares about the opinion of a bunch of uppity toffs?"

"Don't you? They're your friends."

"Hardly. They're an experiment."

She frowned. "And Miss Ratner?"

"She's my concern, not yours."

She used the clean cloth to wipe excess drops from the edges of the steaming bowls of soup. "That may be, but from what I understand she's put a good deal of effort into making this dinner party a grand occasion. It seems small of you to mar her arrangements just to show me what I've missed."

His eyebrow arched in vexation. It had been years since anyone had dared to bring him down a peg. Even longer since he'd conceded he was in the wrong, but he did now. When Amelia first brought up the idea of tonight's engagement, he'd considered it a lark, the first move in a game to see if a low-born weevil such as himself could worm his way into the upper crust. Little wonder he'd found it easy to change the rules the moment something more interesting came along.

He cupped her shoulders and turned her to face him. She looked up, her blue eyes pleading with him to understand something he didn't quite grasp. Her soft lips tempted him without mercy, but as much as he wanted to kiss her, she belonged to someone else.

Bitterness burned him. His hands dropped back to his sides. "Despite our past association, don't think you know me well enough to lecture me. What I do with Miss Ratner is my business. You know nothing about our arrangement."

"You're right, except that I don't know you at all. The Sam I knew was loving and kind. As far as I can tell, that Sam is nowhere to be found. It seems London's made you rich, but it's also made you heartless."

"Rich, yes, but heartless? You can't blame London on that score," he scoffed. "That honor belongs to you, nothing and no one else."

The clock chimed nine. From the corner of his eye he caught sight of Hodges ringing his hands. "Mr. Blackstone—"

"It's time, Hodges." An agitated Amelia stood in the doorway. "What did I tell you about being prompt? Where has Mr. Blackstone gone? Oh, there you are, darli—"

The word died as her eyes narrowed on Rose. "Why are you consorting with this…this housemaid?" she asked Sam.

Ignoring the question, he stepped in front of Rose. "All seems to be ready. Hodges has outdone himself just as I suspected he would do. If you're ready, let's begin."

Chapter Four

Thankful the first two courses had kept her too busy to ponder Sam's cryptic accusation that she had somehow made him heartless, Rose picked up a heavy tray of seasoned beef from the sideboard and returned to the six couples seated around the long table.

If she were the hostess, she would be pleased by the evening thus far. The lovely smells of dish after dish filled the dining room. Piano music drifted in from the drawing room, having replaced the violin sometime during the first course. The merriment of the diners and the ease of discussion among them proclaimed the party a triumph. All the while, Sam sat at the head of the feast like a lord to the manor born.

The rough and tumble youth she'd loved had been replaced by a fine-mannered gentleman whose tailored waistcoat probably cost more than Andrew's school tuition. Had she not known he'd spent the first fifteen years of his life in an orphans' asylum and the next four gambling, stealing and doing whatever else it took to scrape together the barest of necessities, she would never have believed he hadn't been weaned on wealth and privilege.

She lowered a tray of beef for the gentleman she'd heard referred to as Mr. Winters. Deeply unimpressed by the change in Sam after the foul way he had treated her, she was not proud of how her gaze sought him out time and time again or that she found him so handsome she had to keep reminding herself that outward beauty was of no consequence when the core of the man was rotten.

"If I were you," Mr. Winters said quietly, "I'd find something besides Blackstone to marvel at before Miss Ratner goes apoplectic."

Marvel? At Sam? Was that how she appeared? She balked at the idea of Sam thinking he had her moonstruck. She glanced toward the hostess, whom she had already served.

Miss Ratner appeared to be having a cozy chat with the honored lord to her right, but her eyes were devoid of mirth and throwing daggers in Rose's direction. Rose shrank from the malice fixed on her and went quickly back to her work.

"Thank you," she whispered to Mr. Winters, a rakish gent with dark hair and green eyes who'd flirted with her each time she brought a new offering to the table. She wished she had the opportunity to say more, but after the butler's warning to speak to guests as little as possible, she didn't dare give Miss Ratner another excuse to take offense with her.

"I be…believe you're correct, Winters," slurred Lord Sanbourne from across the table.

"Of course I am, milord." Winters winked at Rose

as he speared a piece of beef with his fork. "But might I inquire as to why you think so?"

"That tempting do...dove beside you." He picked up his goblet and signaled toward Rose. "Quite a lovely little bird Blackstone has caged there. Wouldn't mind having one in my own parlor to sing for me whe... whenever I like."

His suggestive laugh brought heat to her cheeks, but Rose kept her face expressionless as she swiftly moved on to the next guest. After making her way down the table, she came to Sam, who was listening to Lady Fulton rattle on about her trio of dogs.

With no way to avoid him, she held the tray while he took his time to choose a selection. Miffed that he ignored her except to make her stand there overlong, she was tempted to drop the lot in his lap and bully the consequences.

"I wouldn't if I were you," he warned under his breath. Their eyes met in challenge. She ground her teeth, hating that he still knew her well enough to make an accurate guess at her thoughts.

An hour passed and Rose silently rejoiced in the arrival of the last course. Her feet and lower back were on fire. The tightness of her dress pinched her middle and her empty stomach mourned the inability to sample the array of cheeses, fruit and confections on offer.

As she arranged steaming cups of coffee and tea on a small trolley, she prayed the next hour would fly by without incident. Except for the constant distraction of Sam, she'd survived the evening intact, and once the meal concluded her services would no longer be required. If all went well, she'd be able to head back to the Malbury townhouse by half past one. Not only did she need a few hours of rest before beginning work in the morning, she planned to avoid another confrontation with Sam by escaping while his guests kept him too occupied to notice she'd gone.

After serving the Nesselrode pudding, a complicated iced dessert that Rose had seen only twice before, Robert fetched a silver platter of strawberry charlotte russe and returned to the table. Rose followed him with the hot beverages. Careful not to spill a drop, she started with Miss Ratner before working her way up one side of the table, past Sam, who took his coffee black as she'd known he would, and back down the other. As she served Miss Ratner's father, he placed his hand on the small of her back, holding her captive despite her best efforts to extract herself without drawing attention.

"I wasn't aware Blackstone meant to marry anytime soon," Mr. Winters said.

"Oh, yes, we're ess…pecting a proposal any day now, aren't we, poppet?"

"Papa, you weren't supposed to mention our little secret, don't you remember?" Miss Ratner said coyly. To the rest of the company within earshot, she added, "I trust all of you will be more discreet than my dear father has been. Mr. Blackstone and I intend our joyous news to remain private for a few weeks longer before we announce the occasion in the *Times*."

Rose's stricken gaze flew to Sam. Winded, unable to catch her breath, she lost all sense of her surroundings. The chatter faded to silence as though she'd been sealed in an airless glass box. Blissfully unaware that Miss Ratner had just dealt her heart a savage blow, he continued to listen to Lady Fulton with a glazed expression and tolerant half smile.

The prospect of losing Sam forever sickened her to the core. Through all their years of separation, even after she'd lost faith he'd ever return, a long-buried part of her had hoped she might be wrong. The cup rattled against the saucer she held, but she remained incapable of movement. Even Lord Sanbourne's hand creeping around her waist failed to elicit a response.

Sam's indolent gaze turned her way. He quit speaking midsentence and a question of concern furrowed his brow. He mouthed the words *What is it?* but she could do no more than shake her head.

Sanbourne's hand stroked her hip. Outrage thawed her frozen state. She jerked, splashing hot coffee against her palm as the hubbub of the party filled her ears in a rush.

His expression fierce, Sam motioned for Mr. Hodges. The butler shuffled to him, bent forward to listen then started in her direction. Intent to be away before the butler reached her, she squirmed to be free of Sanbourne, but the old man's fingers tightened into a claw that dug into the layers of her garments and pinched painfully into her skin.

Mr. Hodges didn't speak to her as she'd thought he intended. Instead, he stopped on the other side of Lord Sanbourne and leaned over to whisper in his ear.

The viscount's wandering hand dropped from her waist as though she'd caught fire. She scuttled away and took a place next to the sideboard, her back to the wall. Grateful the scene had transpired without causing so much as a ripple of interest among the guests, she longed to rub the sore spot where the painful stamp of Sanbourne's fingers lingered on her hip.

She daren't look at Sam. His outrage had been palpable a few moments earlier. Did he believe she'd caused the incident with his future father-in-law? She'd seen maids held responsible and dismissed for the improper advances they were subjected to, and given Sam's dissatisfaction with her, she wouldn't be surprised if he didn't delight in placing the fault at her door.

Without making a to-do, Mr. Hodges instructed her to leave and wait in the corridor. Worry followed her into the hall. Surely being sent away like a naughty child spoke ill of her performance as a footman.

Outside the dining room, the heightened volume of the piano music veiled the clink of glasses and cutlery as a pair of maids stacked the dishes for their return to the kitchen.

A huge oil painting graced the wall above a tufted velvet bench. The landscape reminded her of a meadow on the edge of Ashby Croft that she and Sam used to visit.

Her feet aching, she ignored her training and sat down. Beside her, a chest of drawers offered partial concealment from anyone not intent on finding her.

The need for rest demanded she sleep. She fought the urge to kick off her tight shoes and leaned her head against the chest of drawers, promising herself she'd close her eyes for just a moment.

Sam waited ten excruciating minutes before excusing himself from Lady Fulton and the endless account of her madcap pugs. He didn't usually make tactical errors, yet he'd failed spectacularly today when he'd come up with the harebrained scheme of having Rose brought in to serve. He'd been an idiot to imagine watching her from across the room through several long courses of rich food and vacuous conversation would be anything less than torture. Not that she'd suffered the same ill effects.

If her behavior this evening was anything to go by, he was no more than a nuisance to her, a relic from the past that she'd best like to forget. His reappearance and the unusual task he'd given her tonight may have knocked her off-kilter, but she'd handled every demand with a reserve and poise not found in someone that was overly upset.

Ignoring the annoyed glances Amelia cast his way, he strode into the corridor. The maids clearing the dishes stopped their task and bobbed a curtsy. He looked to his right. The warm, yellow glow of several gas lamps lit the long hallway, but he saw no sign of Rose.

Had she disappeared again? Unreasonable panic gripped him. Had he been such an ogre she would risk the danger of leaving this late at night without an escort? If anything ill happened to her, the fault would lie with him.

So far the pendulum of his emotions had swung between disbelief and anger to desperate, irrational longing. His need to feel indifferent warred with a base desire to hurt her as deeply as she had wounded him. Why her sudden appearance troubled him after their many years apart and all he'd accomplished was an enigma that demanded attention. If he believed God had the slightest interest in him, he might even pray for the answers.

A small movement on the far side of an antique chest filled him with relief. He raked his fingers through his hair. He hated the way she made him feel every emotion—good or bad—like the blow of a hammer, but at least she hadn't left him.

He reached her in three strides. The shadows guarded her. Encased in black as she was, he could barely see her slumped against the large piece of furniture, her head tipped against the wood. Her cap was askew and her eyes were closed. Fast asleep, she sighed softly, drawing his attention to the full curve of her bottom lip and the delicate point of her chin.

He watched her, afraid to touch her because he wanted so much more than she cared to give. If only he'd married her before coming to London, she might still be his. She wouldn't have had the chance to forget him or fall in love with someone else. Did her husband have any inkling how fortunate he was to have stolen her heart?

Desperate for a distraction from such gloomy thoughts, he settled on the memory of Sanbourne touching her. How he would love to smash the old leech. In their younger years, he'd been too poor and powerless to protect Rose from the vultures who'd reckoned paying for a room at the inn where she worked included the right to grope her. How many times had he promised that when he made his fortune, he'd see her treated with respect?

Yet, here he was, the master of the house and she'd been subjected to the same foul behavior. Worse, in his study earlier he'd given her the impression she wasn't safe from him, either, that he would treat her in any fashion he saw fit.

Guilt assailed him. As lovely as she was, she'd never been a stranger to male interest. As far back as the school yard, her sun-kissed hair, bright blue eyes and delicate stature had drawn admirers like honeybees to a wildflower. Without knowing how many times he'd warned those same blokes away from her, she'd been mindful of their feelings and treated each of them with kindness—a far cry from how he'd treated her this evening.

He crouched in front of her and took hold of her hand. Unlike Amelia's, her palms were dry and rough from a lifetime of labor. How long had she worked today? From what Hodges had discovered for him at Malbury's this afternoon, she served as a between maid. He gave little notice to household management, but he knew most of the maids were up before dawn and it was now a quarter past midnight. Little wonder she'd fallen asleep the moment she sat down.

Amelia's voice reached him from the dining room. "I know you gentlemen must be anxious for us ladies to retire to the drawing room. No doubt Mr. Blackstone will return in a moment."

The undertow of irritation beneath her words promised she would come in search of him soon. With no wish to cause a scene that might disturb Rose's slumber, he eased her into his arms and lifted her gently. He thought he heard something rip, but he had no time to find the tear. Her cap fell to the floor and he kicked the scrap of evidence beneath the padded bench.

As she settled against his chest and shoulder, his arms tightened around her. He gritted his teeth as a tide of longing swept over him. He headed for the stairs, her soft hair tickling his throat and the line of his jaw. Aware of the absurdity of tiptoeing around his own home like a thief, he carried her to the second floor. Using all his self-control, he passed his bedchamber and conveyed her to one of the guest rooms.

After a bit of maneuvering, he managed to open the door without setting her on her feet. He relied on the light from the hall to guide him to the massive four-poster bed festooned in velvet and covered in silk.

Reluctant to let her go, he held her several moments before laying her down. As she sank back against the mountain of pillows, she opened her eyes. Certain he'd been caught, he froze. He was bent over her, his hands sinking into the mattress on either side of her narrow shoulders, his face so close to hers he could feel her warm breath on his lips.

A drowsy smile curved her mouth. "Sammy?" she whispered as she reached up and caressed his cheek. "Is it already time to wake up?" She curled onto her side and clutched at his arm. Her eyes drifted shut. "So tired. Sleep…joost a few more minutes."

He smiled at the slip in her accent. Unable to resist and fearing he'd never have another chance, he pressed a kiss to her forehead before standing upright and easing his arm from her grasp.

He removed her battered shoes and frowned at the dampness of her threadbare stockings.

The door creaked behind him and the slice of light from the corridor fanned wider. He turned, irritated by the intrusion and certain he'd been hunted down.

"Oh, it's you, sir," said the chambermaid in a rush to back away. "I didn't mean to interrupt."

"Come back," he demanded in a whisper. "Just be quiet."

The maid's tentative steps brought her across the room. Her eyes swept over the slight mound in the bed. "Is she unwell, sir?"

He shook his head. "I don't believe so. What's your name?"

"Prudence Lively, sir. Mrs. Frye thought the guest rooms should be prepared in case some of yer visitors wish to stay until morning."

"I applaud Mrs. Frye's dedication, but I assure you no one's staying over except this lady here. Her name is Miss Smith and I don't want her disturbed so I'll be leaving her to your care. I expect you to see to her every comfort. Let her sleep until she wakes and make certain she has a hot bath drawn in the morning if she'd like. Do you understand?"

"Yes, sir."

He pulled the counterpane across Rose's hips and legs, careful not wake her. "Her gown seems too tight."

"It's borrowed," Prudence whispered. "There was talk of it downstairs. Seems she got caught in a tussle with some gent on her jaunt from Cavendish Square. Her own frock got soiled in the mud and rain."

"What kind of tussle?" Had she been harmed? It would be just like her to keep an injury quiet. "What happened? Was she hurt?"

"I dunno know, sir, but the girl who was supposed to come with her twisted an ankle and fled back home."

He glanced back to Rose, whose sound sleep seemed well overdue. "See that she has something new to wear."

"Her frock's been washed. It just needs to finish dryin' a bit."

"Fresh stockings, then. Hers are wet."

The faint gong of a clock in the hall announced half past twelve. He didn't want to leave, but his guests were waiting. "I'll see that you have extra time off to rest tomorrow."

She brightened. "Thank you, sir. That's very kind."

He turned to go. At the door, he paused. "Don't tell anyone about this. Especially Miss Smith."

She grinned. "Tell her about wot, sir?"

He nodded curtly. "Send someone to inform me when she awakes."

At the top of the stairs, he leaned against the plastered wall and drew in ragged breaths. He despised this helpless feeling of being set adrift on a stormy sea. His reaction to Rose was inexplicable, irrational, futile. Years ago, he'd believed they were two halves of the same whole, but no longer. He'd chased after a pot of gold, only to realize too late he'd lost his rainbow.

He groaned. What utter rot and nonsense. Obviously, he'd been subjected to too much of Amelia's insipid poetry. He started down the stairs, determined to overcome his renewed obsession with Rose. "Pull yourself together, Blackstone. You're not the first bloke to be rejected and there's no profit to be gained from mooning over another man's wife."

Rose stretched and opened her eyes. Used to awaking in the darkness just before daybreak, she blinked at the shadows dancing on the high ceiling above her. Edged with ornate plaster moldings, the panels were painted with an elaborate motif of colorful flowers and vines. The last dregs of sleep evaporated. She was not in the servants' quarters as she ought to be. With growing unease she realized someone must have placed her in a guest room by mistake.

As she mentally calculated how she'd come to her current location, she remembered being sent from the dining room, sitting on the bench, closing her eyes. Everything after was blank. What had she done, walked in her sleep?

Horrified by the possible consequences of being found where she did not belong, she sat up and pushed back the silk bedcovers with care. Some kind soul had loosened her dress. She took a deep breath, drawing in the faint scent of lavender that clung to the soft linen sheets. The thick mattress she'd slept on felt like a cloud after the hard, narrow cots she was used to.

A copper tub sat before a fire that flickered in the hearth. Waking up to warmth was a luxury as foreign to her experience as the decadence of a morning bath. She hoped none of the servants got into trouble when the housekeeper realized so much effort had been wasted on one of their own.

Her bare feet touched the floor and sank into carpet as soft as a spring meadow. Where were her stockings? Her shoes? Her own clothes?

The porcelain clock on the mantel had yet to be wound. Had she done the unpardonable and slept overlong? Was she late for work two days in a row? Mrs. Pickles's warning rang in her ears. She sprinted past delicate chairs with spindly legs and thick seat cushions to peer out the window. Pushing aside the cream velvet drapes and layer of lacy sheers, she took in the ominous gray sky and driving rain. A few carriages passed by in the street below, but there was nothing else to indicate the hour.

Fearful Mrs. Pickles would dismiss her on principle, she moved to a small seating area done in cream, light gray and soft yellow. Bereft of her own clothes, she was a prisoner.

A light knock sounded on the door. "Who is it?" she called hesitantly.

The door opened. "My name is Prudence, Miss Smith. I'm the chambermaid. May I come in?"

"Yes, please," she said, relieved someone knew she was there.

Prudence closed the door without entering, then pushed it open a moment later. A pretty blonde with dark eyes and a full figure, she crossed the room with a breakfast tray in hand, a black dress folded over her forearm. "I thought you might be hungry."

The delicious aroma of hot tea and fresh scones made her mouth water. "I am, indeed, but I think there's been a dreadful misunderstanding."

"No mistake, miss." She set the tray on the low table in front of her. "I hope we didn't disturb you when we brought in the tub. I had it set by the fire to keep the water warm."

"The bath is for me?" Her bewilderment deepened. "But I'm a kitchen maid, not a guest."

Prudence placed the black garment over the back of a chair. "This is the dress you arrived in last night. It's laundered and mended. I hope you find it to your liking."

"Thank you. I'm sure I will."

"I almos' forgot." Reaching into her pocket, Prudence pulled out a neat ball of white cloth. "This is a new pair of stockings. Your shoes are by the fire. Is there anythin' else I can fetch you? I reckon you should eat."

"No, you've been too kind already."

"I'm happy to do it, but it weren't my idea."

"Did Mr. Blackstone have me brought here?"

The maid turned sheepish. "I'm not supposed to say."

That was answer enough. "Do you know the time?"

"Twenty past ten," Prudence said on her way to the window.

"Twenty past *ten?*" She'd never slept so late in her life. Why, today of all days, had she slept like she had no worries? Her heart sank. She sat heavily on the settee behind her, anxiety making her head pound.

"The hall boy, Timmy, winds the clocks," the maid continued, oblivious to her distress. "But he hasn't been in here as yet this morning. You weren't to be disturbed." She pulled back the drapes. Rain beat against the windows. She turned around. "What's the matter, miss? You've gone a bit pale."

"I believe I've lost my job."

Prudence gasped. "Oh, no! Why would you say so?"

She told the girl about Mrs. Pickles's warning. "I'm usually much more punctual."

"I shouldn't be alarmed," Prudence said in an effort to cheer her. "If it comes to that, no doubt you can count on Mr. Blackstone to have a word with your employer. He'll make everything right as rain. Just you wait an' see."

"I doubt it."

"Oh, no, I'm certain he will if you tell him wot's happened. He's an excellent master. More than fair."

It seemed so foreign to hear Sam referred to as master.

"Perhaps he'll hire you here," Prudence offered. "I think he's rather fond of you."

From the frying pan into the fire. "I promise you, Mr. Blackstone's regard for me is anything but fond."

"Pardon my saying so, but now I think you're mistaken. He's still here, dontcha know."

"Shouldn't he be?"

"He leaves every morning at half past seven like clockwork. I've never once known him ta be late."

"Last evening's party. Perhaps he needed a lie in?"

Prudence shook her head. "There have been other late nights and gatherings. None of them kept him from his work before you came along."

It was useless to debate the young woman whose loyalty to Sam appeared unshakable.

Prudence checked the bath. "The water's still warm. Shall I help you undress?"

"I'm afraid I don't have time," Rose said, wishing she did. "It was very kind of you to go to the trouble."

"Again, it weren't my idea, miss."

Seeing the other girl's face fall and aware of how much work it took to haul the necessary buckets of water to fill the tub, she almost relented. "Mr. Blackstone put you up to this?"

Prudence smiled. "Again, I'm not at liberty ta say."

Wondering if Sam thought she smelled bad, she cast a longing glance at the tub. How wonderful it would be to wash off the travel dust of the past few days.

"You're already late," Prudence cajoled. "Wot's a few more minutes?"

She worried at her bottom lip. She might never have

another opportunity to enjoy a private bath. "I suppose it wouldn't hurt if I hurry."

"That's the spirit, miss."

Twenty minutes later, clean, dry and clothed in her own spotless dress, Rose sat before a mirror, combing the knots from her waist-length hair as quickly as she could. Her queasy stomach was at peace since she'd eaten a scone with clotted cream and sweet blackberry jam.

Prudence had run an errand, leaving her to bask in a rare moment of solitude. Used to the few rushed minutes she was able to bathe twice a week on the servants' wash night, she'd found the warm bath a luxury, and the lack of a line before or after her almost as grand.

"Are you decent, miss?" Prudence asked through the door.

Rose called her in.

The younger girl closed the door behind her and crossed the room. "You weren't joking when you said you'd hurry. If I was you, I'd have soaked till I grew scales." She took the comb and began to arrange Rose's hair into a tidy bun at the nape of her neck.

"Have you seen my cap by chance?" she asked Prudence. "I seem to have mislaid it."

Prudence picked up the wet towel Rose had folded and hung over the edge of the tub. "I haven't, but I'll inquire. There may be an extra one in the cupboard."

"Thank you." Her gaze met Prudence's in the mirror. "Do you suppose he's gone by now?"

"No, miss, I'm fairly certain he'll still be here tomorrow if that's how long you make him wait."

Chapter Five

Downstairs, Rose stopped before Sam's study door. The clock in the hall marked half past eleven. Prudence had wished her well before parting from her on the stairs. Her palms damp from nerves, she prayed for guidance and knocked on the heavy wood portal.

"Come in," Sam called after several long moments.

She turned the shiny brass knob and forced one foot in front of the other. Rain beat against the window-panes of the large, masculine room, but a fire in the hearth dispelled any chill brought on by the inclement weather.

She located Sam seated behind a massive walnut desk, a wall of tomes behind him, their spines different sizes and colors.

Clean shaven, his glossy, black hair too short to be fashionable, he wore a crisp, white shirt and tailored, silver-brocade waistcoat. Soulful, dark eyes, as deep and inscrutable as the sea at night, latched on to her and the very air between them began to hum with a vibrant energy she found intoxicating. He stood and bowed, displaying a politeness usually reserved for proper ladies, not unimportant kitchen maids. She curt-seyed and aimed for a respectful tone. "I'm leaving, but Prudence mentioned you wished to have a word with me before I go."

"Yes." He motioned to one of the tufted, green wing chairs in front of his desk. "Won't you please have a seat?"

"If it's all the same to you, Mr. Blackstone, I think I'd rather stand." All too aware she found him more irresistible than was good for, she tried to sound stoic, but her voice quivered, betraying her inner turmoil. "Last night you made your opinion of me as clear as crystal. From what I can tell nothing has changed and I'm tardy for work enough as it is."

"If you're worried about Malbury, don't be. I'll have a word with him on your behalf and sort things out if there are any difficulties."

"Thank you." Although wary of his kindness, she was relieved she hadn't had to ask for the favor when she had no idea what he might demand in repayment. "It's his cook, Mrs. Pickles, that concerns me most. We started out on the wrong foot from the moment we met. She's got a penchant for promptness and the longer I'm here, the more I test her goodwill and mea-ger patience."

"I shouldn't be anxious about her, either. She'll do what Malbury dictates."

She moved to the chair but remained on her feet. "Yes, and I'll be grateful to keep my job, but if she dislikes me I doubt she'll be pleasant and I've had my fill of the scullery."

"Then I won't take much of your time. Are you sure you won't be seated?"

She shook her head.

He paused before turning grave. "Last night was a mistake. I want to offer an apology."

"Pardon?" Struck by surprise, she sank into the chair behind her. "What's brought about this sudden change?"

"Seeing you yesterday…it knocked the wind out of me." He combed long fingers through his coal-black hair. "I felt as though I'd drunk a jug of insanity that went straight to my head."

Speechless, she stared at him, afraid to move in case she spooked him. She could not believe this was the man who'd hunted her down, frightened her and conspired to humiliate her all in the course of one day. Had the Lord intervened as she'd asked? Had He helped Sam to see her in a different light? Or was Sam being insincere and this was some sort of test or new form of trickery?

"I can see that I've shocked you."

She nodded.

"I'm not excusing my behavior—"

"Good."

He stiffened imperceptibly. She doubted he'd been treated with anything less than deference in ages. Where she got the brass to be cheeky she didn't know, but remembering he had the power to alter her life for the worse, she thought better of acting outright insolent.

His lips tightened, but he soldiered on. "I had hoped you might consider forgiving me on account of our past…association. We were good friends once, or don't you remember?"

Her fingers tightened into the arms of the padded leather armrest. As far as she was concerned, the word friend was an insult to what they'd shared. He'd been her reason to wake up each morning and her last thought before she went to sleep. Even now, there were nights when he filled her dreams. Without him she'd been wretched. The world had been fierce and frigid. If not for the Lord and His guiding hand, she didn't know where she'd be.

"How could I forget?" she whispered.

"I wouldn't blame you if you refuse me a second chance, but truth to tell, I hope you will because I've missed you all these years."

Her nose stung and her heart hurt as though it were being torn into pieces. Oh, how she'd missed him, too, but after yesterday she'd be a fool if she weren't leery. His first instinct upon seeing her again had been to threaten and humiliate her. Those were not the actions of a kind or loving man. There was no doubt he'd changed during their years of separation, both inside and out. Just how much was the question.

"Perhaps we might begin afresh? You, me and, of course, your husband, Harvey."

The derision behind *husband* stopped her cold. "His name is Harry," she said, ever more suspicious of the true sentiment behind his words. "And that won't be possible."

"I don't see why not. Perhaps I might even help him."

"How so?" she asked, intrigued by his sudden generosity.

He shrugged. "I could show him a thing or two about investments. Perhaps give him an interest-free loan."

"He won't care about your money, I assure you."

"Everyone cares about money," he scoffed. "It makes the world go round." Absently, he spun a pen in a circle on the desktop. Its metal nib flashed as it caught the light on each successive turn.

"I don't agree," she said. "Money may make life more pleasant, but it's not the be-all and end-all."

"Spoken like someone who doesn't have any." He stood and ventured around the corner of the desk. Leaning against the front of the heavy piece of furniture, he crossed his arms over the broad expanse of his chest, his wide shoulders testing the seams of his fine linen shirt. "If there's something more important, I have yet to find it."

"That saddens me. It does," she insisted, seeing his lip curl. "What of love, and friendship and fam—family?" She tripped on the word, remembering too late that just as she had been before having Andrew, Sam was alone in the world.

"Love is for the naive and those too young to know better. I've learned true friends are few and far between. As for family—" he offered a grim smile "—you know as well as anyone, you can't miss what you've never had."

Needing more space between them, she stood and moved to the window. The faint scent of lemon polish and leather suggested a recent cleaning of the bookshelves flanking each side of the glass.

She hated that she'd spoken with so little care. As an orphan, she understood that discussion of family was the same as poking a raw nerve. "I'm sorry—"

"You needn't be. I've never been as thin-skinned as you are."

Conceding the point although she could argue, she recognized bravado when she heard it and it hurt her that she'd hurt him. "Since we parted, I've come to know Jesus as my Savior. If you want something better than money, you'll find it in Him."

He scowled. "A load of religious rubbish, if you ask me. Everything I have is thanks to my own hard work and cunning. Don't forget I prayed all the right prayers as a child. What did it get me? A God that keeps His distance—always has. That's what."

She ached for his soul to the recesses of her being. *Lord, if there's a way, help me lead him to You.*

Turning, she pressed her forehead against the windowpane. The coldness of the glass helped to clear her thoughts. The driving rain had relented to a drizzle and the sun struggled to shine from behind a string of faded, gray clouds. Beyond the townhouse's gated front garden, pedestrians had started to trickle onto the street, their umbrellas unfurled like small, black tents.

"I used to feel the same way you do." Her fingertip followed the trail of a raindrop as it slid down the window. "You know how I hated when our headmaster forced us to church when we were children. The way the congregation looked at us—as though they were growing a patch of thieves beneath their roof."

"Yes, in their unforgiving eyes we'd committed a crime by being born. Then again, if our own mothers didn't want us, why should they?"

"I used to think God saw me in the same light as they did, but I've learned I was wrong."

"What changed your mind?"

"I learned God has a true love for orphans. I thought if He could love me, perhaps I'm not so bad."

"Not bad at all." His arms dropped from his chest, and his hands gripped the desktop. "Where did you learn this good news?"

"Harry to begin with, bless him."

"Ah, yes, the paragon. I should have known," he said, his dismissive tone as dry as toast.

"You needn't be a snit." Certain to rile him, she added, "Someone might think you're jealous."

"So what if I am?" he asked in such a way that she couldn't decide if he was teasing or serious. He angled to sit on the desk, his left foot on the floor, his right leg free to swing at the knee. Big and dark and unfairly handsome, he flashed her a heart-stopping grin. "You and I aren't finished. I doubt we'll ever truly be."

She struggled to catch her breath. He had a knack for catching her off guard. "I thought you only had friendship in mind—you, me and, of course, dear Harry?"

"I've reconsidered."

"You have?" she said, crestfallen that he'd changed his mind and a touch leery he'd revert to his vengeance. "You don't want to be my friend?"

Dark, fathomless eyes bore into hers. "I don't want you to be married."

Her heart began to race. Good conscience urged her to tell him the truth, but her mind warned her not to be hasty. The past few moments had eased the strife of yesterday and dispelled a small measure of their discord, but only a fool would believe all their fences were mended. She didn't want to be ungenerous or unforgiving, but she feared putting her hand out again when he'd bitten it already.

And yet, hadn't she prayed for a way to reach him?

Not only for her sake, but more so for Andrew. How would they ever find a common ground if they didn't begin to clear the acres of confusion between them?

She closed her eyes as frightened as though she were about to jump off a cliff. "I shouldn't think that will be a problem. I... That is to say... I mean...I'm not."

"You're not...what?" He stood, his wide shoulders straight, his dark eyes incandescent with interest. "Tell me," he urged as though she had to speak the words to make them true.

"I'm not married," she choked, stepping out in faith and choosing to believe God must have had a plan when He allowed Sam to find her.

Except for the sudden loss of color beneath the natural warm tone of his skin, he showed no sign he'd heard her. "You should have told me."

She bristled at the accusation. Far from being contrite, he seemed to blame her for deceiving him. "When? The moment after you ambushed me here in your study or later when you were breathing fire down my neck?"

Dark color spread across his high cheekbones. "You should have told me to shut my gob and *forced* me to listen."

"Don't you dare blame this on me, Sam Blackstone! You meant to knock the wind out of me and you succeeded with a flourish. I was so shocked to see you again I could barely string two words together. Even so, I tried to explain, but you declared my side of things made no difference to you."

He started to speak, but his lips snapped together. A small muscle ticked in his jaw. He reached for her, then reconsidered. His hands balled into fists at his sides. "I told you…temporary insanity."

"And I'd be insane to forgive you."

Dark eyes searched her face. "Tell me this. Were you ever married or was I completely bamboozled?"

"What do you mean?" Her forehead pleated with confusion. The spicy scent of his cologne filled her head and even in the midst of their turmoil she longed to throw herself against him. "Bamboozled by who?"

"Just answer my question." His voice was gruff. "I never had the chance to ask you in person. I was forced to take the word of others."

"I was married for a short time," she admitted, unable to tell him the whole story without confessing about Andrew, which she was unprepared to do until she was convinced of Sam's sincerity. "As you know, his name was Harry. Harry Keen. I already told you he was a good and godly man. I truly don't know where I'd be if the Lord hadn't brought him to me."

"What happened to him?"

"He died," she said quietly.

Without a word, Sam began to pace. He was no more than a few feet away from her, but he might as well have moved to China. Finally, he stopped in front of her and pinned her with a hostile glance. "Did you love him?"

Not like you. Never like you. "How could I not love a gift from the Lord?"

"How could you not, indeed?" His beautiful mouth twisted. "And there's been no one else?"

"May I ask you the same question?"

"You can ask."

"All right, last night I overheard Lord Sanbourne announce your plans to wed Miss Ratner. Is that true?"

As cold as a winter's day, he returned to the imposing chair behind his desk. "I'd be a fool not to, don't you think? She's beautiful, well-connected, educated...she'd make a perfect wife and hostess for a man like me."

In other words, Miss Ratner was the exact opposite of her—a common scullery maid who would never be accepted into his rarified world.

Tormented by the thought of him married to anyone but her, she glanced at the clock on the mantel. Unshed tears blurred the long hand approaching the twelve. As much as she hated to admit it, he was correct. A sophisticated woman like Miss Ratner would make the ideal mate for a man as exceptional and successful as Sam had become. "No doubt the two of you are well suited."

"As well suited as you and your husband?"

"I couldn't say. I know very little of your intended bride and...and you and I might as well be strangers."

"I think you might be surprised at how little I've changed." He gave the pen another spin on the desktop. "How did you know that Keen fellow was the right man for you?"

Because I was pregnant and alone...and terrified. "He was the kindest, most selfless man I've ever met. He cared about my soul as much as my person. Never once did he look down on me. He invited me into his life without restraint, and right to the end he put my needs above his own."

Sam frowned. "In other words, he was perfect."

"As perfect as they come." The clock chimed noon

and she jumped at the excuse to leave. "I must go. I've been here too long as it is."

"Let me call for my coach." Far from trying to keep her, he seemed eager for her to go.

"That's not necessary. I can walk."

"No, it's pouring out. You'll catch your death."

"And you? Don't you have somewhere to be?"

"My office." He went to the door and called for the footman. "I'll wait until the vehicle is returned before I go." She followed him into the hallway and waited while he gave Robert instructions. Once they were alone again, he reached for her hand. His grip was warm and firm, yet gentle. She'd missed his touch more than she cared to admit. So much so, even this most basic of gestures shot an arrow of desperate longing to the depths of her soul.

"Let's part as friends, shall we?" he said. Contrary to the light note in his voice, his dark eyes bore into hers as though he meant to uncover her deepest secrets.

Painfully aware she had yet to tell him about Andrew, she wrestled with her conscience. "I doubt your fiancée would be pleased if we did."

Robert returned to announce the coach's arrival, and she tugged her hand from Sam's grasp. "I wish you well and I'll keep you in my prayers."

"You needn't waste your time," he said as she made her way out the door. "As far as I can tell the only thing God's given me is a wide berth, and I steer well clear of Him."

Chapter Six

Impervious to the thrash of rain just east of Newgate, Sam stared out the coach's window as he rode toward his city office. Men of business in somber black attire dashed along Oxford Street clutching their hats and umbrellas to keep from losing the articles to the driving wind. Rag women, food sellers and bare-footed street urchins huddled in the doorways of well-to-do shops as they waited out the storm.

Glad he was no longer one of the poverty stricken, he closed his eyes and leaned his head against the headrest. Possessed of every convenience from embossed leather seats and foot warmers to a hidden beverage cabinet in the side panel, his well-sprung coach and team of four were amongst his favorite possessions. Yet today, nothing he'd amassed seemed to matter now that he knew Rose had been free and might have been with him all these years.

Furious with the world at large and eaten up with jealousy, he struck the seat with his fist, needing to break something or someone. He could not bear the fact that Rose loved another man, nor could he set aside the sensation that he had been robbed of an irretrievable fortune.

As the conveyance rolled along, he reached into his pocket and removed the cap Rose had lost the night before. He'd fetched it from under the bench and meant to give it back to her this morning, but he found he liked having a tiny piece of her with him too much to let it go.

Irritated by the weakness, he shoved the scrap of material back into his coat pocket. He refused to love her again. Overcoming the loss of her nine years ago had been a torment-filled process he would not survive if he was forced to do so a second time.

His head fell back against the seat. He should let matters lie. He'd gone out on a limb to admit he'd missed her, but she had not returned the sentiment. Indeed, she could not have quit his presence fast enough. Had he been wise he would have squelched his compunction to follow her yesterday. Life had taken them in divergent directions and it was clear that although her husband was dead she had yet to extinguish the torch she carried for him.

The coach turned a corner and hit a bump in the road. Fighting the host of bad memories descending upon him, he scrubbed his hand across his eyes. Her defection all those years ago had ruined him in countless ways. She had not merely broken his heart; she'd shattered him and danced on the pieces. Learning she'd married someone else had reduced him to a wreck of a man. He'd spent years afterward in a haze of work and debauchery that had left him with nothing but compounded regrets.

He hated to admit just how much Rose appealed

to him. When it came to her, all good sense evaporated and he'd be a fool not to cut his losses and walk away when she so obviously cared not a whit for him in return.

A thump on the roof and the stillness of the carriage alerted him to his arrival. The carriage door swung open, revealing his firm's grand facade of windows and shiny, brass fittings. A large, black placard with gold block lettering hung above the establishment proclaiming the name of Stark, Winters and Blackstone.

Rain poured from the eaves, splashing on the footpath. His driver filled the space, rivulets falling off his wide-brimmed hat. "We're 'ere, sir."

Ducking his head, Sam pulled the collar of his coat up around his neck and dashed into the office. He heard the doorman's greeting as though from a distance. The familiar smells of ink and wood polish surrounded him as he entered the sober, dark-paneled workroom where more than a dozen clerks pored over mountains of files and open account books. Engraved brass nameplates marked each door of the firm's three partners. Jake Winters and Ezra Stark's offices remained firmly closed against the incessant hum of activity.

Sam's staid assistant, Cecil Haverty, approached him. The circular frames of his spectacles perched low on his nose. "Is all well with you, sir? We were quite worried when we received no word concerning your absence this morning."

Lost in his thoughts about Rose, Sam turned without comment toward the older man to hand over his dripping hat and frock coat. A chill pervaded the office. Ezra, the miser among them, didn't care to waste money on coal.

"Are you ill, sir? You don't seem yourself. May I fetch you something to eat or a cup of hot coffee?" Haverty's usually implacable expression slipped a notch to expose his concern. "Perhaps your coach to convey you back home? It might do you good to get a bit more rest."

"Add some coal to the fire," he said absently. "It's too cold in here." Ignoring the startled looks of several clerks, he continued to the large office where, out of habit, he was most comfortable and spent the better part of his waking hours.

Desirous of being alone, he shut the door behind him with a backhanded motion that gave little regard to anyone who may have followed on his heels. He pushed aside the pile of correspondence demanding his attention on the ornately carved desk he'd had imported from India, and dropped into the revolving chair that served as his throne.

He grabbed up a report concerning the annual sugar crop of the West Indies, but for once the ways and means of making money failed to hold his interest. Tossing the report aside, he swiveled to the wide expanse of windows behind him and stared blindly at the pouring rain.

A knock sounded on the door, but he ignored the intrusion, hoping whoever it was would take the hint and go away. He should have stayed home. He'd earned a day off. No, more like a year.

He shook his head, wondering where such a peculiar thought had come from. He lived to work. Thrived on the constant cut and thrust of making a deal or calculating what stocks to invest in next. Just two days ago, he would have scoffed at the idea of missing a minute let alone a whole morning.

The door opened. His friend and business partner, Jacob Winters, stuck his head inside the room. "Blackstone, where have you been, man? Marks and Camden both made a fortune at the 'Change this morning. Seems benefits of the Nanking treaty are already paying in spades. They intimated you missed the festivities."

Sam swiveled the chair to face his friend. "I had some personal business to attend to."

"Then it's true?" Winters asked, incredulous. "Tell me, are you ill?"

Did being heartsick count as an illness? If so, he was on death's door. "No, I'm as hale and hearty as always."

Jake, a tall ox of a man with a broad, thick chest and powerful arms and shoulders, settled into one of the armchairs facing his desk. "Since you're not about to keel over, I'll hazard a guess that your personal matter had something to do with your party last evening and the pretty blonde serving maid you couldn't stop staring at."

"Why are you here?" Sam asked irritably. "Isn't there a degenerate gentleman somewhere with a property in need of foreclosure?"

"As a matter of fact, there is." Jake grinned. "You know how fond I am of seeing the gentry suffer." As the head of the firm's real-estate holdings, Jake found nothing suited him better than snapping up the homes and overextended properties of arrogant landowners who'd fallen on hard times or, better yet, into disgrace. "I'm leaving the day after tomorrow to take care of a rather fine property in Hampshire. Seems a baron or some such drank himself into oblivion, then died without paying his debts."

"Not very sporting of the fellow," said Sam.

"No, indeed. The daughter, a real harpy, or so I'm told, has chased off all the agents I've relayed to handle the matter."

"Perhaps she has nowhere else to go."

"That's her concern, not mine," Jake said without compunction. "I'll be gone a fortnight, give or take a day or two."

"I'll tell Ezra when he gets back from Edinburgh on Friday."

Nodding, Jake stood. "I'll be closing the file on Sanbourne when I return…that is unless his announcement last night is correct and congratulations *are* in order."

"Nothing's final."

"But you are considering the prospect?"

"I think marriage to Amelia is the most profitable option."

"That depends on the choices. Personally, I thought you had more sense than to chain yourself to that frozen-hearted viscount's daughter."

Sam almost laughed at the snide comment. Jake had never warmed to Amelia. She was many things, some of them not so pleasant, but to Jake her greatest flaw was that her ignominious father bore a title.

"If nothing is official why is Sanbourne blabbering?"

"I assume he's starting his own gossip to keep his creditors at bay. From what I understand, Amelia's other guests are all well connected and rather loose-lipped. If word gets out he'll have a rich son-in-law to buoy the family fortune soon, the bloodhounds will bide their time before they run him to ground."

"Sounds like just the sort of man you want in an in-law," Jake said drily. "However, it's your decision and I'll wish you the best. Now," Jake said, grinning, "let's get back to something worthy of my attention. If you plan to waste yourself on Amelia, what of the pretty blonde maid?"

He shrugged, feigning disinterest. His friend loved a competition and if Jake sensed he wanted Rose for himself, he'd chase her for amusement if nothing else. "What about her?"

"I've never seen her at your home or in your company before and you have to admit it was rather odd to have a woman serving at such a formal occasion. I'm surprised Miss Ratner allowed you to break with almighty tradition."

"It's my home. I'll decide what happens there."

"We'll see about that once you're leg shackled." Jake leaned forward in his chair, his face animated with curiosity. "So? Are you going to tell me the chit's name or is it some great secret?"

"How should I know? I don't fraternize with servants."

"We all know I do," Jake said with a decadent smirk.

"She isn't available."

"How would you know when you don't even know her name?"

Jake's confidence rankled Sam. "She just isn't," he said tightly.

"With the right incentive, I've found almost any woman can be available."

"This one won't be around very long. She'll be away

to Devonshire long before you arrive back in London."
He flipped open the nearest file and reached for a pen.
"Now, if you'll excuse me, I'd best make up for my absence this morning."

"No need to be testy, but your reaction does make
one wonder." Jake made to leave but stopped at the
door and glanced over his shoulder. "For two people
supposedly as unacquainted as you are, you both seem
to suffer an odd response when the other is mentioned."

Sam sat back in his chair. His interest piqued to an
unbearable degree, he feigned boredom with the topic.
"What are you prattling on about?"

"I'm sure you won't care, since you haven't fraternized with the girl…but I found it intriguing last night
that she looked like she might faint when she heard
Sanbourne announce your impending nuptials. I think
she might fancy you. I never saw anyone pale faster
in my life. For a moment, I feared she might fall in a
heap where she stood."

Sam fumbled his pen, splashing ink across the
page's neat row of figures. He might as well have been
kicked in the stomach. "Wait—!"

He surged to his feet. Too late. Jake had already
gone, his knowing laughter trailing behind him as he
shut the door with a firm click.

Rose entered the Malburys' servants' entrance at a
loss concerning her status. She'd done nothing wrong;
she'd merely done as instructed, but considering she
should have returned twelve hours earlier, Mrs. Pickles may not be inclined to be generous in her assessment of the situation.

The small entry was empty, but a dispute between

two maids could be heard from the kitchen beyond the stone archway. The spicy-sweet smell of gingerbread scented the air. She slipped out of her coat and hung it to dry on a peg by the door.

"There ye are. Where have ye bin?"

Rose wheeled around, a hand clutched to her heart. "Ina!" she exclaimed with a startled laugh. "You gave me such a fright."

"That's th' leest of yer worries." Ina glanced over her shoulder covertly and lowered her voice. "Pickles was lookin' fur ye early this morn an' she was none to pleesed when she couldna fin' ye."

"I was detained...by the bad weather." She groaned inwardly. Although partly true, she wished she'd come up with a more convincing reason.

Ina limped toward her. "What's a wee bit ah rain?"

"How's your ankle?" she asked, hoping to divert the conversation.

"Nah too well. It's still swollen."

If there's anything I can do to help—"

"Actually, there mi' be somethin' tae help us both."

"How so?"

"The baron's fancy lady, Mrs. Leighton, jist rang from the first-floor guest room. Seems 'er fire needs relit an' she's th' demandin' sort. Wi' this ankle, Ah willna git there until dinner. But if ye go, Ah can tell Pickles yer here if she asks. Mebbe she'll forgit she was angry wi' ye once she knows yer back tae wark."

Rose bit her lower lip in indecision. "Perhaps I should speak with her? If she doesn't like my explanation, Mr. Blackstone, the man who hosted the dinner party last evening, said to contact him if there were any difficulties."

"That's a good idea. Yoo've seen what a reasonable woman Pickles is."

"Where are the billets?" she asked, thinking better of drawing the cook into the mix.

"I'll hae Landon show ye. Landon," she called down the empty corridor. "He's the second footman an' he knows where we keep the goods yoo'll need. Speakin' ah things we need, where's yer cap?"

"I seemed to have misplaced it."

Ina nodded. "I'll fin' ye another."

"Thank you."

"Afore Ah forgit, a letter cam fer ye in lest evening's post. Ah put it on yer bed."

Before she could ask who'd sent the letter, Landon arrived. A gangly, ginger-haired young man of about nineteen, he loped down the corridor in front of her to the storeroom. Once armed with a pail of billets, old newspaper for kindling and a box of matches, Rose climbed the servants' airless stairway past the ground floor and up to the first-floor guest rooms.

Concerned the letter might have news about Andrew, she longed to go to her room and fetch it. Since she wouldn't be able to read the correspondence on her own, she set aside the notion and entered the elegant hall where porcelain sconces and large oil paintings hung on dark burgundy walls. Heavy, gray velvet curtains dripping with lace flanked the closed windows on either end of the long corridor.

The muffled sound of weeping drew her to the third door on the right. She frowned, hesitant to interrupt, but afraid of the consequences if she failed to complete her task. She knocked, quietly at first, then louder when she didn't receive a reply.

"Come in," a tearful voice wailed from the other side of the door.

As Rose entered the opulent room, the heavy, sweet scent of perfume caught her off guard. Painted in a deep shade of plum, the chamber boasted a large, canopied bed draped in purple-and-gold-velvet brocade. The carved, cherrywood furniture spoke of ageless refinement and feminine flair.

Mrs. Leighton, the room's lone occupant, sat before the dressing table. Clothed in a delicate pink gown with embroidered white flowers on the sleeves and satin-edged hem, she was hunched before the oval mirror, her elbows on the tabletop, her face held in her hands. Dark, flowing hair rippled down her back and pooled on the striped seat cushion. Her weeping beckoned Rose to offer comfort, but she denied the urge. Servants didn't trespass into the lives of their employers.

Eyes averted to the thick, floral carpet, she bobbed a curtsy. "Good day, ma'am. I'm here to light the fire you requested."

Mrs. Leighton waved her pale, slender hand in the general direction of the marble mantel and continued to weep.

Rose set down the heavy pail of cut branches and knelt to clean the grate. The strong odor of charred wood and smoke blotted out the room's sweet cloy of perfume. Ashes dirtied her gloves as she swept them up with a small broom and dustpan.

The lady spoke but, with her head and upper half buried in the fireplace, Rose didn't hear more than an incoherent mutter. She sat back on her heels and brushed a fallen tendril of hair from her eyes as she turned toward the dressing table.

"I beg your pardon, ma'am?"

Mrs. Leighton didn't answer, just stared at her reflection of perfect skin, reddened cheeks and wide, bloodshot, blue eyes filled with misery. Her full lips trembled. "He used to love me."

Rose strained to hear. "Ma'am?"

The woman turned on her chair. Her tearful gaze latched on to Rose. "Have you ever been loved and rejected?"

Still topsy-turvy from her encounter with Sam earlier in the morning, she fought to keep her face expressionless. Until an hour ago, she would have answered yes without a doubt, but now she wasn't certain. "I've loved and lost, ma'am."

Mrs. Leighton appeared not to hear. Her gaze dropped to the floor. Rose began to wonder if the beauty was demented or simply foxed.

"I used to be a nobody like you," the lady finally said. "Reggie used to love me then. Now he wants nothing more to do with me thanks to that heiress in the country he plans to wed."

So, like most toffs, the baron planned to correct his money shortage through matrimony. She'd been told few upper-crust marriages were based on affection, but her heart went out to the woman, whoever she was, that he planned to marry solely for profit.

A brisk rap on the door startled Rose. The portal swung open, revealing a young, well-dressed gentleman with wispy, blond hair and bright green eyes. Judging by his regal bearing and the chamber he'd just sauntered into, he must be her employer, the new Baron Malbury. Although she'd never seen him in the flesh before, gossip around Hopewell Manor claimed he was as appealing as a spring day in December. That description didn't do his striking features and lithe frame a single ounce of justice.

"Why are you still here, Lucinda?" The baron's coldness made Rose shiver. She hurried back to the fireplace, intent on fading into the background and finishing her task although she doubted even a roaring blaze could dispel the frosty chill that accompanied the man's arrival. "I told you to be gone by noon," he said. "It's now two hours past."

"And where am I to go?" Mrs. Leighton cried out.

"How is that my concern?"

"How is it not? You seduced me, brought me to London—"

"As I recall, you were willing to do anything necessary to escape Mr. Leighton's hovel. Perhaps your rum-soaked spouse will oblige us both and welcome you back with open arms."

Rose banged the pail, rattling the handle by accident. The conversation paused, making her wince.

"You used me!" Mrs. Leighton recovered first.

Rose's hands trembled in her haste to layer the paper, wood and coal into place. Desperate to escape the escalating argument before it exploded, she reached for the matches.

"We used each other, m'dear."

"You used to love me—"

"Hardly." The baron laughed. "You're comely, to be sure, a beauty, in fact, but you act like a barmaid and have the tastes of a strumpet."

A high-pitched screech erupted from Mrs. Leighton, drawing a backward glance from Rose. The scorned woman sprang to her feet, her fingers clutched into claws. "You filthy, lying swine—!"

"Enough!" The baron fended off her attack by grabbing each of her wrists before she chanced to mark his face. He gave her a shove, sending her reeling into the dressing table. Perfume bottles and cosmetic containers went flying. He adjusted his waistcoat and dusted off his lapel. "Now that my plans are coming to fruition, m'dear, you are no longer counted among them. Why, pray tell, not save us both this unpleasantness and leave with some grace and dignity—assuming you have any?"

Rose struck a match, lit the paper and dropped the flame between the logs. Unwilling to witness more of the horrible scene, she jumped to her feet without waiting for the fire to catch. She bobbed a quick curtsy, although she doubted either of the embattled occupants noticed her as she raced from the room.

In the hallway, she leaned against the door, trembling. The row escalated. A chambermaid stepped into the hallway from another guest room.

"Mrs. Leighton needs help," she said to the girl.

"The twit's on 'er own, same as we all are." The maid scurried to the stairway to avoid being drawn into the fray.

Rose wished she could aid the poor woman, but the fact was the chambermaid was correct. Like so often in life, she was powerless to do as she wanted. Interfering would see her dispatched from the premises posthaste, and Mrs. Leighton's lot would go unchanged—or might be made worse—if Baron Malbury was the kind to punish others when someone pointed out his wrongs.

Inside the servants' stairway, she said a prayer for the other woman. She may not have the power to help Mrs. Leighton, but the Lord was more than able.

She lifted her skirts and raced down the stairs as fast as the narrow space allowed. The ugliness of the encounter she'd witnessed might as well have jumped straight from her nightmares. Although not a servant, Mrs. Leighton was as dependent as Rose and any of the staff whose livelihoods were pinned to the baron's good graces. She was a perfect example of how easily one's fortunes could change with little or no warning. One day, a body could have a position somewhere, the next, she might find herself on the street.

So far, she'd been saved from the dilemma of choosing between scruples and starvation due to the Lord's mercy and His gift of her pleasant arrangement at Hopewell Manor. But after witnessing the new master's coldhearted cruelty firsthand, she understood that changes were in the wind whether she managed to keep her job or not.

Clearly, the new baron was of a different cut altogether from the old. The room she'd been allowed to share with Andrew instead of one of the other kitchen maids and the expense of her son's schooling had both been kindnesses from her previous employer that her fifteen pounds per annum would never suffice to afford.

If the scene she'd witnessed with Mrs. Leighton was the baron's standard of behavior, and if the rumors were true that he'd inherited the title but no fortune, then Andrew's days at school were numbered.

How was she to tell him he could no longer return to his studies? Smart, attractive and amiable, her son deserved a better lot in life than she would ever be able to give him.

Thankfully, he suffered none of her learning deficiencies and, like his father, possessed an uncanny talent for numbers. If any child deserved a proper education, Andrew did.

The heavy weight of failure pressed down on her. She missed a step and almost stumbled. She had done her best to provide Andrew with a home and to give him all the love she herself had been denied, but she and her efforts were not enough.

She supposed she should be grateful that Sam had reappeared in her life when her job was at its most precarious, but she found it hard to be gleeful when he planned to marry another woman. News of Andrew's existence was bound to disrupt Sam's well-ordered life. What if his new fiancée resented Andrew's sudden appearance? She knew of children who'd suffered horribly because they were considered a nuisance. Just as bad, what if Sam wanted Andrew and tried to take him away from her?

Considering Sam's wealth and obvious importance, she doubted there was anyone to help her stop him.

If that were to happen, she didn't know how she'd survive, but as much as she would miss Andrew, she had to consider his best interests. Opportunities for her kind were as rare as diamonds falling from the sky. She would not stand in the way of the full life Sam could offer their son.

Deep in the throes of inadequacy, she made her way back to the kitchen. The smell of fish being cleaned for the evening's second course turned her stomach. Needing to be alone, she trailed into the scullery and began to scrub the pots already piled high from the day's meal preparations.

She was almost finished, her hands and forearms red from the hot water and harsh soap, when she heard footsteps in the corridor. Her instinct warned the heavy gait belonged to Mrs. Pickles. The fine hairs rose at the back of her neck.

"There you are, Smith."

Picking up a towel to dry her hands, she turned slowly to face the rigid woman who seemed intent on causing her strife. "Yes, Mrs. Pickles, I'm here. Is there something you have for me to do?"

"Come with me," she said stiffly. "We wish to have a word with you."

Anxious to learn who the *we* included, her worry grew with each step. Once they reached the small office Rose had been shown the previous day, Mrs. Pickles stepped aside and indicated she should precede her. A crisply dressed woman in a burgundy gown with a white collar sat behind the old table that served as the room's small desk.

Mrs. Pickles closed the door with enough force to rattle its small panes of glass. "Smith, this is our housekeeper, Mrs. Biddle. We've been made aware of your shameful behavior last evening and we're both distressed that you're associated with this house."

"Shameful behavior?" Rose wrung her hands, afraid her worst fears were upon her. "I must protest most sincerely. Who made such a claim?"

Mrs. Biddle cleared her throat. "Back chat will do you no good. It has been decided your services are no longer required here or at either of the Malbury country estates."

Rose braced against the desk for support. Light-headed, she wondered how many more shocks she could bear. The past day and a half had been filled with one right after another. Terror for her and her son's future threatened to swallow her whole.

Her thoughts tangled. Disbelief, anger, fear, sadness—all threatened to send her to her knees to beg for mercy, but their condemning stares and tight, unforgiving lips kept her on her feet.

"There's been an awful mistake." Her voice was low and trembling as she gathered her dignity. "If you'd be so kind as to contact Mr. Blackstone, I'm certain he'll explain."

"Who do you think offered the complaint?" Mrs. Biddle asked. "No decent maid would throw herself at her employer or his dinner guests or fall asleep in the middle of her labor."

"Throw myself?" Seized by disbelief, she gaped at the housekeeper. "I did no such thing!"

"Not according to Mr. Blackstone."

"And his word takes precedence over yours," Mrs. Pickles added with a smirk.

"Why? Because he's rich and I'm poor?" she demanded, unable to register or accept that Sam would seek to destroy her so viciously. During their discussion earlier that morning, she'd been right to be suspicious of his apology and his supposed change toward her when clearly the need to punish her ruled his heart.

"I've worked for the Malburys eight years," she said in an effort to make them see reason. "Never once have I been reprimanded or caused the faintest hint of trouble. I've worked hard and to the best of my ability. If you don't want me here, why, at least, can't I return to my position at Hopewell Manor?"

"There is no place left for you there." Mrs. Biddle's craggy face showed a hint of humanity at last. "Baron Malbury has graciously allowed his ward to stay there whilst she's in mourning for her parents. Since he won't be taking up residence there and Miss Malbury is no longer in need of full staff, the unnecessary positions are being suspended due to a need for economy."

After all her years of service, she'd been deemed unnecessary—just as she'd been by everyone else throughout her life.

Except Andrew. He needed her. "I have a child—"

"As do some of the other maids employed by his lordship," Mrs. Biddle chided. "Perhaps you should have thought of your son when you behaved as you did last evening."

"A worm can't be turned," Mrs. Pickles inserted. "Once a woman of low morals always—"

"I'm not—"

"Enough the both of you," Mrs. Biddle injected. "It is not our fault, Miss Smith, that you do not have a husband to help with your responsibilities and we are not obliged to treat you with favoritism because of your circumstances."

"No, of course not." Her eyes settled on a chopping block atop a small table beneath a rack of drying herbs. Numb and painfully aware of the irony, she asked, "What about my wages? And the fare I'll need to return to Devonshire?"

"Such insolence," Mrs. Pickles condemned in a huff. "You no longer work for Baron Malbury, therefore his lordship is no longer responsible for your expenses—travel or otherwise. As for your wages, do you have any idea what you might have cost him with your salacious behavior last night? Do you even care?"

A knot of panic tightened in her belly. Without her wages or coin for travel how would she get back to Andrew? Believing she'd collect her wages before she returned to Hopewell Manor, she'd spent the little money she'd brought with her to London on the carriage needed to transport Ina after she hurt her ankle. The roads were dangerous and walking to Torquay would take a fortnight or more, if she managed to survive the trek at all.

She straightened her shoulders and tipped her head back in an effort to mask her rising anxiety. The pair of old dragons had made up their minds about her and wouldn't be moved by pleas for mercy. "I behaved right and proper, Mrs. Pickles, no more, no less. To deny me my wages is outright thievery—"

"How dare you?" Mrs. Biddle exclaimed. "This is an honest house."

Her head began to pain her as though nails were being hammered through her skull. "Then give me what's owed me, I beg you. I have no wish to offend you or anyone else, but I *must* return to my son and I need the funds to do so. Do you want to be responsible for keeping an innocent child from his mother?"

Mrs. Pickles opened her mouth to argue, but Mrs. Biddle raised a weathered hand to interrupt. "Let no one be able to accuse us of a lack of Christian charity. Go and pack your things, Miss Smith. I'll have the stipend ready by the time you leave. As for the other matter, I'll ask our butler to consult with Lord Malbury. Any wages he feels you're due will be sent by post to Hopewell Manor, which you can collect in a few weeks' time. That is the most I can promise you."

Embarrassed by their accusations, she wanted to plead her case, but she recognized the best offer she was likely to be extended. Returning to Andrew was most important and she didn't dare give them the excuse to revoke their concession.

She turned and, without permission to leave, sprinted from the room before she disgraced herself with a flood of tears. She hitched her skirts and took the stairs two at a time. Once she reached the room she'd been meant to share with Ina, she sat on the narrow bed, still unmade from the previous day, and wept.

"Lord," she prayed, hanging on to her faith by her fingernails. "I believe You will light my path and make a way where there is none. But forgive me, because at the moment I can't see anything but darkness and I fear there's a trap up ahead. What am I to do? Where am I to go? Without a job, how will I be able to take proper care of Andrew?"

Sam's face swam into her mind's eye. She wanted to push the vision aside, to forget she'd ever met him again. Far from regaining her trust or renewing her sympathy, he'd proven to be a snake in the grass. Yesterday he'd planned her downfall and today he'd pushed her off the cliff. She considered going to him to demand he pay her fare home, but she could not— would not—give him the satisfaction of seeing her at her lowest ebb when his lies were the reasons behind her ruin.

Why would he go to such lengths to hurt her? His life was golden. He claimed God had forgotten him, yet he possessed everything he'd ever wanted and more.

Grateful she hadn't told him about Andrew, she could only imagine what he might do to wrest him from her if he believed taking him might cause her pain.

She brushed the tears from her cheeks and began to pack her belongings. Her fingers brushed the portrait of Andrew she'd sketched with a piece of charcoal last week. Missing her son more with each passing minute, she unfolded the wrinkled piece of stationery she'd rescued from a pile of Miss Malbury's discarded first drafts.

Andrew's smiling face peered up at her in black and white. The edges of the charcoal were faintly smudged, but his bright eyes and sweet smile bore a clear likeness. She pressed the rendering to her chest, wishing with all her heart she could hug him. Except for the dark months following Sam's departure to London, she'd never missed anyone quite so much.

She'd returned the drawing to her valise and packed the last of her garments before noticing a folded piece of paper at the end of her bed. Remembering the letter Ina mentioned, she tried to make out the sender, but the script rearranged into a garbled mess. She broke the red wax seal and unfolded the sheet of paper. Again, she couldn't make out more than a few words and none of them were in any particular order. She assumed the note was from Andrew or Harry's mother, Mrs. Keen. The dear woman was the closest person to a grandmother Andrew would ever have and she was keeping him while Rose was away in London.

Frustrated more than usual by her deficiency, she refolded the paper and stuffed the precious piece of home deep into the pocket of her gown, hating that she would have to find someone who could read before she was able to learn the contents of the letter.

After fastening her valise, she lugged the heavy piece downstairs. In the kitchen, the herbaceous scent of rosemary, thyme and garlic surrounded her. She'd eaten little in the past few days and her stomach growled with hunger. Mrs. Biddle had left the funds for her travel expenses with Ina, who awaited her at the servants' entrance.

"Ah would have come upstairs, but mah ankle is killin' me." The Scottish lass held a small covered basket in her hands.

"Come, sit." She helped Ina hobble to a chair at the foot of the stairs.

"Ah jist heard th' terrible news. Ah think it's a right shame wha' they done tae ye."

"Thank you. I wish I could make them listen to me, but they're deaf to my pleas." Rose pulled the letter from her pocket. "Do you happen to know how to read?"

Ina shook her head. "Loch ye, Ah ne'er had th' chance tae learn."

"That's quite all right. It won't be anything dire. My son, Andrew, and his grandmother promised to write cheerful thoughts from home, but they knew I'd have to find someone to read them to me." The paper crackled as Rose slipped the letter back into her pocket. She didn't dissuade Ina of her assumption that she'd never had the chance to learn. Many people of their class couldn't read, but unlike them, she had had the opportunity to go to school. She'd just been too deficient to take advantage of the blessing.

Unlike most orphans' asylums, the one where she

and Sam had grown up believed in the virtue of a rudimentary education for the less fortunate. After five hours in the workhouse each morning, they attended school for two.

Sam had thrived, not only learning to read and write, but to cipher. He'd done his best to help her, but her inability to master the written word made her lag further and further behind the other children her own age. Their instructors had used punishment to try to motivate her, but even a ruler slammed across her knuckles or long mornings spent with her nose in the corner had failed to help her make sense of the shifting letters. It hadn't seemed to matter that she picked up the spoken lessons with ease. Whispers that she was simply ignorant had hurt and embarrassed her.

Ina hung her head for a moment before she spoke. "Ahm sorry fur th' way Ah treated ye when ye arrived yesterday."

"There's no need to apologize."

"But there is. Ye were so kind tae me after Ah hurt mah ankle las' night. If Ahd bin there Ah could vouch for ye. Ahm th' one who shoulda bin sacked."

"No, it's not your fault." The reminder of Sam's duplicity renewed her resentment. "The blame for that lies entirely with someone else."

Ina looked skeptical as she handed the basket to Rose. "Ah have no way tae repay ye fur th' hackney ye called tae brin' me home lest night, so Ah prepared ye a baskit of food fur yer journey."

"How thoughtful of you, Ina. I'm much obliged." Rose accepted the gift, grateful she would have something to eat for the next few days. The stipend would compensate for the locomotive's fare to Reading and the stagecoach to Torquay, but not much else. "I'd best be on my way or miss the last departure. Would you be so kind as to give me directions to Paddington Station? When I came to town yesterday, everything was such a jumble I didn't have a chance to find my bearings."

A few minutes later, she left the house. Ina stood in the doorway, waving goodbye. Armed with directions she carried in her head, she held the valise and small basket in one gloved hand, an old umbrella in the other. Fear for the future weighed her down, but her faith kept her from drowning.

The wind made her umbrella next to useless and transformed the rain into bullets that struck her face with stinging force. She soldiered on, aware that if she missed the day's last train, she'd spend the night on an unprotected bench in the railway station rather than a relatively safe bench in third class.

Huddled beneath her umbrella, she walked into the storm, barely able to see through the sheets of rain.

She ducked her head and pulled the collar of her cape up to her chin. Much of her was soaked before she reached the first corner and she was shivering from cold before she'd traversed the short distance to Wigmore Street. The footpath was slippery and more than once she almost fell. Sludge, horse droppings and other rubbish littered the ground and flowed along the curb, making it nigh impossible to go without soiling her shoes or the hem of her gown.

A break in the downpour sometime later gave her the opportunity to assess her whereabouts. Somewhere along the way she must have gotten turned about. The fashionable area surrounding Cavendish Square had disappeared in favor of a narrow, dingy lane lined with rundown shops already closed for the day. Simple row houses boasted peeling paint, overgrown front gardens with sagging gates and the occasional cracked window, but at least she hadn't stumbled into one of London's many notorious rookeries. Here, there were few private conveyances or other signs of prosperity, but there was no air of menace or abject poverty, either. Not that she could take her safety for granted or put down her guard for a moment.

Fearing she was lost, she retraced her steps the way she'd come. A blast of thunder ended the rain's short reprieve. The foul weather made for a dark afternoon and the smell of smoke tinged the air as people lit fires to ward off the increasing chill.

Hollow-eyed street urchins scattered like mice as they looked for somewhere to take cover. Lamps began to shine in a few windows, their glow glistening on the wet, cobblestone street. She endeavored to stop the occasional passerby to ask for directions, but everyone either waved her away or ignored her, the need to find shelter challenging the most basic of manners.

The dull ache in her head still throbbing, she searched for a way back to the main thoroughfare. It couldn't be that difficult. She hadn't walked *that* far, had she? But the more she looked, the more the slick streets and ancient lanes merged into a maze of confusion.

A faraway church bell tolled six o'clock. The howl of the train's whistle followed soon after. The hope of reaching the station in time to leave London began to give out. She beseeched the Lord for protection and direction, but it wasn't long before her unfamiliar surroundings forced her to admit she was utterly lost.

Footsteps clapped on the cobblestones behind her. She glanced back, but saw nothing in the rain and darkness except the lanterns of a passing hack. She laughed, realizing she'd been spooked by the sound of horse hooves. She continued walking, hastening her pace to the next cross street. The queer feeling that she was being watched filled her with unease. She remembered a trick Sam had taught her ages ago and just to be cautious she decided to use it. If she feared she was being followed, she picked up speed and listened for her hunter to do the same.

The footsteps increased in time with hers. Fear gripped her. She looked for an open shop or church to duck into along the deserted street, but there were none to be found. The footsteps came closer. She broke into a run. Just as she feared, whoever was stalking her gave chase. Her heart kicked against her ribs and a sheen of perspiration broke out on her upper lip.

A hand clamped on her left elbow. "Help!" she screeched as a man spun her around. She whacked the attacker with her umbrella, over and over until he managed to wrench the makeshift weapon from her white-knuckled grasp.

Calling her a string of foul names, he slapped her across the face. A trail of fire burned across her cheek. The taste of blood filled her mouth. Stunned, she tried to scream but could force no more than a squeak past the panic clogging her throat.

Her attacker pressed a dirty hand over her mouth and dragged her protesting body into a nearby alley. He yanked her to his chest. His arm was an iron bar imprisoning her against the wet stink of his coat. "We can do this the easy way, lassie, or the 'ard way, it's up to you. But either way, you're goin' to lose."

Chapter Seven

Rose balked at the rotten odor of the man's breath in her face. "What…what do you want?"

"Wha' do you fink? The goods…and maybe a kiss or two."

She closed her eyes and tried to pull away from the brush of his dirty fingers across her cheek. She shivered in disgust and her thoughts ran rampant with the need to escape. "I have nothing of value, I promise you. My valise has a few clothes. The basket has a bit of…of food."

"Put them down nice and slow. I'll decide wots got werf or not."

The valise and basket hit the ground with a thud. She tried to knee the blighter in the groin, but he twisted away before she caused him the damage he deserved. He shoved her. A rip in her dress rent the air. She careened into the wall on the opposite side of the narrow alley, yelping in pain as she slammed her shoulder and hit her head against the rough, uneven, brick building.

"You're livelier than you look, I'll give you that,"

he said with a snicker. "Be glad it's rainin' or I'd fancy more 'an a kiss from such a comely wench as you." His footsteps raced away, leaving her alone and huddled against the wall, trembling. Shaken, she pressed her forehead to the cold, wet bricks. Rain ran down the back of her neck and under the edge of her cloak. Her lungs pumped like bellows and her blood raged with indignation. Heat scored her sore cheek where he'd slapped her. She could feel her face swelling, and her head throbbed without mercy.

This wasn't the first time she'd been robbed and she'd known friends who'd been attacked far worse. She needed to leave in case the thief came back, but her feet refused to budge.

As her shock began to recede, she tested her jaw. It wasn't broken, thank the Lord. Unsteady, but calm enough to force her wobbly legs into movement again, she confirmed her bags were gone. The louse had taken her clothes and food, but…

She reached into her pockets. Her damp hands found the letter in one and her railway fare in the other. Relief rescued her from weeping. *Thank You, thank You, Lord!*

Cautious and still frightened, she approached the entrance of the alley. A rat scurried across her toes. Disgust pushed her out onto the footpath. She ran half a block before she slowed down. Convinced she'd missed the last train, she had nowhere to go and no one to take her in. Even if she considered swallowing her pride and went to Sam, she feared she'd never find him.

She was utterly lost.

Please direct my path, Lord.

Clinging to her favorite scripture, she didn't know

what else to pray. Alone, in pain and lost in a strange city, she pulled her cloak tighter around her, her faith slipping to its lowest ebb in years.

Shorn of her umbrella, she trudged through the rain for what seemed like miles, until her feet had blisters from her soggy leather shoes. Eventually, she reached a narrow, well-kept lane in a less tatty part of town. Streetlamps at regular intervals surrounded what appeared to be a small garden square and several covered benches that offered respite to the weary.

Concerned the absence of others meant she'd stumbled into someone's private park or grand back garden, she decided she'd meet any further difficulties as they arose, instead of worrying about them before they arrived. Grateful for any small mercy on offer, she collapsed rather than sat on one of the bench's hard, slatted seats.

Her teeth chattered, sending constant shocks of pain through her cut and swollen lips. She couldn't stop shivering. The cold and delayed reaction of the attack had set in with a vengeance. She pulled her cloak tighter around her and leaned against the chilled, metal post that held up the covering above her. At the end of her tether, she was too enfeebled to muster the energy required to be properly afraid of the dark and its countless dangers.

Rain beat against the cover, disguising the usual sounds of night. In the distance, small, hazy rectangles of light glimmered from windows and glowed from the streetlamps or passing coach lanterns.

She closed her eyes and clamped her jaw to keep her teeth from chattering. Her hand reached for her pocket to make certain her letter remained safe in the thick folds of her gown. Satisfied she hadn't lost the correspondence, she thought of Andrew and how good it would be to see his sweet face again. She prayed for him and Mrs. Keen and even grudgingly for Sam. As much as she disapproved of him and the cruel man he'd become, she worried for his soul and his eternal salvation.

Time slipped by at a snail's pace. Exhaustion tugged at her, tempting her to let her guard down and give in to sleep, but she'd done that last night and the mistake had cost her more than she cared to count. She shifted on the park bench, desperate to stay awake and alert. Tomorrow, once she was on the train, she could rest.

"Rose!"

The distant call of her name startled her. She listened for a moment, but all she heard was the steady beat of the rain. She scoffed at her wishful thinking and shook her head. In all of London, she knew of no one who cared enough to look for her or be concerned for her welfare.

"Rose!"

This time the voice sounded closer. She stood and moved to the edge of the covering, straining to see through the darkness. The streetlamps were too far away to offer much assistance and it was difficult to hear anything over the rain's incessant cascade. She gave up and almost sat down until she noticed the faint glimmer of a lantern that assured her the voice wasn't just in her head.

A boy appeared at what seemed to be the small rise of a hill, not far from where she waited.

"Hello?" She winced from the pain in her swollen lip when she spoke. "I'm over here."

As the boy drew near, she took stock of the youth's gaunt appearance. Most likely a street urchin of twelve or thirteen, he wore wet, grubby clothes and a cap that had seen better days. He held the lantern at arm's length above his head. His skin looked bone-white in the candle's glow. Rain poured off the tip of his nose and chin. Wide-eyed, he stared at her as though he'd won the grand prize at a country fair. "Rose? Are you Rose Smif?"

"Who are you?" she asked.

"I'm a friend...or at leas' I know wanna yours." He held out his hand. "Come wif me."

"No, I—"

"Stay 'ere then, I'll be righ' back."

"Wait, young man, who is this friend?" He was already gone, the shrinking dot of light as he retraced his steps along the path the only proof she hadn't imagined him.

How had he known her name? Her acquaintances in town were few and far between, yet he'd claimed she had a friend?

The temptation to follow him fought with the self-preserving instinct to flee or, at the very least, hide in the shrubbery until she learned the identity of her rescuer, but her feet were swollen and her raw blisters burned. Even if she tried to run, she wouldn't get far.

She racked her pained head for clues to the identity of anyone who might wish to find her. Except for Ina, none of the Malbury servants would bother to search for her. Sam came to mind, but she discarded the notion. He couldn't be aware she was gone. Besides, lying about her and having her sacked were not the actions of a friend, but a villain.

"Rose!"

Sam's deep voice washed over her. She crushed the instantaneous frisson of joy that surged through her and searched the night for his appearance. "I'm here."

She saw the boy with the lantern first. Then, like a prince from a fairy story, Sam emerged from the darkness. He took the boy's lantern and aimed for her with purposeful strides that ate up the spongy ground between them. Tall, lithe and so breathtaking, he seemed otherworldly. She could not imagine how he'd learned she was lost or why he had come for her. As much as she'd like to throttle him for the lies that had put her out on the street, she could not deny the wave of relief she enjoyed from having him near.

"She's there," the boy pointed out needlessly since Sam was already headed straight for her.

His expression inscrutable, he set the lantern on the bench and without warning pulled her into a bone-crushing embrace. "Thank You, God," she thought she heard him murmur.

Just as quickly, he set her free and shrugged out of his coat. In one smooth movement, he wrapped the heavy garment around her and drew it tight. The heat of his body permeated the layers of her clothes, cocooning her in warmth and the subtle scent of his spicy cologne.

He drew her toward him, but she fought the foolish desire for his comfort when he was the source of her troubles. It was one thing to accept his coat to keep from freezing to death, another entirely to follow him as though she were some mindless mule.

She returned to her place on the covered bench. He studied her a moment before crouching in front of her, his hand on her knee to steady him. Oddly, he wasn't wearing a hat. A lock of wet hair fell across his brow and her fingers itched to comb through the thick strands. Raindrops dripped down his temples and into the shadow of whiskers along the chiseled line of his jaw.

Gradually, her teeth stopped chattering and her shivering eased. "Where are we?"

"Paddington Green. It's over two miles from Cavendish Square. If you were coming to me, you went the wrong direction."

She glanced away. "How did you find me?"

"I hired a clutch of street urchins. They find information or people for me from time to time. Charlie over there is their leader. They're much faster than the police and twice as reliable." He searched her face. Anger clouded his piercing dark eyes as he took in her battered visage. "Who did this to you?" he demanded, his voice husky and deep. "Where else are you hurt?"

"I was robbed in an alley. I turned down the wrong street and got lost. The louse pinched my belongings. He said I had the rain to thank that—" her voice cracked "—that he took nothing else."

He muttered under his breath and reached for her chin to examine her face.

She jerked back. "Don't touch me."

His hand dropped away.

"Why are you here?" She could not allow herself to be drawn in by his supposed concern. "I doubt it's a pang of conscience so it must be to gloat."

His eyes narrowed. "I beg your pardon?"

"As well you should after the way you ensured I'd be sacked."

The plains of his face hardened to stone. "You're a madwoman. Do you know that, Rose? I did no such thing."

"Then how did you learn I'd gone?"

"I went to Malbury's. I worried you might be upset about something Jake mentioned, but that's neither here nor there. Malbury's butler informed me you'd quit in a huff."

"Not true!"

"I figured as much. You were never impulsive." He stood. "Malbury said *I* wanted you gone?"

She nodded. "Of course Mrs. Pickles and the house-keeper relished performing the deed."

"They're liars, the both of them."

"So you say."

"You doubt me?" He scowled. "Then tell me this. If I despised you enough to see you chased from your job, why would I be out scouring this wretched city for you in the dead of night and freezing rain?"

"As I said—to gloat." To her own ears the explanation sounded feeble, but she was in no mind to be reasonable. "Last night you were clear in your desire to punish me."

"And this morning I apologized."

"Or did you pretend to?"

He dashed a hand across his brow. A thunderclap rattled the small covered structure. "Bother this infernal weather." He scooped her into his arms, startling a shriek from deep in her throat. "Charlie, bring the lantern with you."

He headed out into the rain and started back the way he came. "If all you're going to do is bicker, Rosie, I'll be more inclined to listen in the comfort of my coach."

"Put me down this instant."

"Fine, if you'd rather sit out here and catch your death, so be it." His arms loosened.

"Wait!" She threw her arms around his neck. "I've reconsidered. I'll go with you."

He readjusted her weight in his arms. She felt him smile against her wet hair. "I thought you might."

"Only because my feet are blistered and I can barely walk." Behind them, Charlie hooted with laughter. She pressed her brow against the chilled curve of Sam's throat and closed her eyes.

"You know you don't want me to leave you."

She didn't, but she would never tell him so. She was angry and confused by the events of the day, but she wasn't stupid enough to sit out in a storm merely to prove her point. More, she wanted to hear his explanation. She desperately needed him to convince her he wasn't the heartless scoundrel he'd been made out to be.

"Charlie," Sam called to the boy who'd been following close on his heels. "You and the others take the hack back to my townhouse. I'll have my housekeeper arrange a hot meal and gather some fresh clothes for each of you. Anyone who needs a place for the night can sleep in one of the empty servants' quarters or in the stables if he likes. Either way, I'll have your pay ready whenever you choose to leave."

Sam picked up speed. His swift steps crunched along the gravel path. He ducked his head against the wind and cold autumn downpour. His lips were close to her ear and the warmth of his breath fanned her cheek. Inside the coach, a small lantern cast a golden glow over the leather seats and tufted, velvet walls. Sam's missing hat hung on a hook beneath the window, as though he'd left in too much of a hurry to remember to take it with him.

Once they were seated and the door was shut, Sam knocked on the roof. The driver snapped the reins and the vehicle lurched into motion.

Sam reached into a box under the bench and extracted several soft blankets. Ever since he'd arrived at Malbury's and learned Rose was alone on the streets, he'd been in the throes of panic. "Where were you going?"

"I don't see how my whereabouts should matter to you."

He covered her with the blankets, grateful he'd found her before she came to irreparable harm. He'd imagined every possible scenario, each of them worse than the last. London was dangerous enough in the daylight, but after dark the city became a vipers' nest where wickedness reigned. He'd nearly gone mad searching for her. "You don't, do you?"

"No, I don't. I haven't been your concern for years now."

His jaw tightened. If only that were true. Believing she was married had kept him from her life, but a day rarely passed without him thinking of her in some form or fashion. "Nevertheless, I'm your only friend in London—"

"Friend?" she scoffed. "At this moment, you're my enemy."

"Based on the lies of two old biddies?"

"You haven't convinced me they lied."

He'd forgotten how distrustful she could be. He took

a deep breath and restocked his patience. She'd endured a string of ordeals today and anyone in her position was bound to be less than amiable. "I assume you weren't coming to me."

"You always were too quick for your own good, but if you must know, I was headed to Paddington Station."

He absorbed the announcement like a knife slipping between his ribs. He glanced swiftly out the night-darkened window to cover the flash of pain he was certain he couldn't hide. She'd planned to leave him without a word. Given their backgrounds, the action spoke louder than a fire bell. Any hope that she might bear him even the slightest bit of affection withered and died.

"Where are you taking me?" Color marked her cheeks as though she realized she should have considered that succinct question long before now.

"Since you've missed your train and foul weather is bound to have filled every inn for miles, I'm taking you home with me...that is unless you'd rather make camp with the ruffians that lay claim to Paddington this time of night or prefer the park bench to one of my guest rooms."

"What will your fiancée say if she learns you've taken me in?" she asked stiffly. "Aren't you afraid she'll think we've been up to no good?"

"I have a house full of servants to vouch for my virtue. Their word will have to prove enough for her."

She colored. "I assure you, your virtue is safe from me."

A swarm of sweet memories from their past tormented him. He quickly pushed them aside. "Pity."

"Don't," she said quietly.

Buoyed by the realization that she suffered from similar memories of her own, he promised, "I'll take you to Paddington in the morning—when it's safe."

"I don't see that I have much choice."

"I don't, either," he agreed. She didn't trust him, but he hoped the evening might offer a chance to change her mind. He may not be willing to trust his heart to her keeping again, but for some reason he didn't care to examine, he didn't want her to walk out of his life despising him, either.

"If you're not the one who complained about my work or demanded I be dismissed, then someone did in your name," she said, drawing him out of his thoughts. "Mrs. Pickles and Mrs. Biddle were quite clear on that point. Do you know who the culprit might be?"

"I have a few suspects in mind, but I don't know for certain."

"You do realize that's a very vague and unhelpful answer, don't you?"

"You might try trusting me."

Her gaze dropped to her lap and she picked at a small nit of wool in the striped blanket covering her legs. "I wish I could, but that doesn't seem likely. Each time I begin to believe I can, something happens to convince me I'd be foolish to take the chance."

He hadn't expected such a telling admission, but her belief that she was the more trustworthy half of their couple rankled when he bore as many scars from their past as she did. "I understand. I'm on trial with a judge and jury of one."

"You needn't think of it that way—"

"How else is there to see it?"

"That we've been separated for nine years and times

have changed between us. We used to be equals, now we're anything but. Surely you realize you possess all the power and I have a need to be…careful."

Intrigued by her choice of words, he realized she wasn't the only one who needed to be careful. In terms of the money, influence and social standing she spoke of, he did have more clout, but in matters of the heart he was quickly coming to realize the balance of power was shifting in her favor, and he didn't like it one bit.

Chapter Eight

The coach slowed to a stop. Voices Rose didn't recognize mixed with the sound of the rain beating on the roof. Sam turned the latch and opened the door.

A uniformed footman awaited them with an umbrella. He offered his gloved hand to help Rose down the coach's steps as though she were some grand lady. Unused to assistance of that nature, she flushed, but managed to make a graceful exit despite the sting of her blisters when she stepped onto the footpath.

Her gaze drifted to the servants' entrance out of habit. She felt like a fraud when Sam took hold of her elbow and escorted her through the front door.

Rose saw the butler and the flash of disapproval that crossed his weathered face when he spotted her. Pretending not to notice, she shrank behind Sam as he rattled off instructions for a meal to be prepared.

"Is there anything in particular you'd care for?" he asked, catching her off guard.

"Whatever's most convenient," she said, hating to be a nuisance.

As Sam continued to speak with Hodges, she took

in the entryway, which she had not seen the previous evening. A fire in the hearth filled the massive, circular room with warmth. The walls were painted a soothing shade of pale green. Glossy, white molding edged the arched windows and a wide-arched doorway that opened to a grand staircase beyond.

An intricate, scrolled pattern of white-on-white plasterwork finished the domed ceiling and provided the perfect backdrop for the glistening chandelier. In the center of the open space, a round table crafted of polished chestnut held a tall urn spilling with a profuse rainbow of fragrant, hothouse flowers.

To her recollection, she had never seen a room quite as lovely. As she stood there dripping on the polished marble floor, part of her was in awe while the other part wondered how long it took to clean such a magnificent space. She knew the entries of fine houses were usually the grandest, being that guests were supposed to be impressed when they first arrived, but not even Hopewell Manor, the most beautiful home she'd been in, could hold a candle to this one.

"And where is Mrs. Frye?" Sam continued. "She should be here."

"I am, sir." A slim, older woman with gray-streaked black hair hurried around the corner from the next room, narrowly missing the footman. "I sent Robert to fetch a stack of towels. He'll be here in a thrice."

"Excellent." Sam pulled Rose forward. Dismay flashed across the housekeeper's face before she managed to hide her disappointment. Rose suspected both of the upper servants were thinking she'd done something brazen to catch Sam's notice and how affronted they must be considering her lower station.

"Miss Smith is an important guest of mine," Sam said. "I expect her to be treated as though she's Queen Victoria come to stay. Do I make myself clear?"

Hodges nodded stiffly. "Very good, sir."

"Of course, Mr. Blackstone," Mrs. Frye agreed at the same time.

A footman arrived with the towels.

"Miss Smith has had a frightful night." Sam explained as he slipped his coat from her shoulders and handed the garment to the butler before offering her a towel.

Mrs. Frye stepped forward. "Shall I show her to a room, sir? Perhaps arrange a hot bath and a fresh gown?"

He turned to Rose and smiled. "Anything she wants. Make sure she has it."

Disconcerted, she hadn't expected Sam to introduce her to his staff, let alone acknowledge her as a friend and see to her comfort. As she followed the housekeeper up the main staircase, she caught him watching her with an intensity that was both intimidating and strangely stimulating.

They reached the first floor, then the second before walking down a long corridor that she recognized from that morning. The housekeeper had yet to speak to her and although it was none of the woman's business, she preferred to clear the air. "Mrs. Frye, I realize how untoward my being here must look to you."

The housekeeper stiffened. "I'm not paid to have an opinion on Mr. Blackstone's deeds, Miss Smith."

"Nevertheless, I know you have one and I'd be more comfortable if you'd let me explain."

Mrs. Frye opened the door to the room Rose had

used the previous night and waited for Rose to enter first. "There's nothing to explain, miss. I'm not innocent to the world. The master's rich and handsome. You're doing what most girls would if given half a chance."

"Then he does this often?" Rose couldn't resist asking.

Mrs. Frye turned up the lamp. "No, he's a decent fellow. Head and shoulders above most. I've never known him to take advantage of his subordinates and from time to time he's helped each one of us. We're all very protective of him," she said in clear warning.

Rose smiled. The woman's coolness stemmed from her care for Sam, not from judgment toward her. To Rose's way of thinking, it meant a great deal to have his servants vouch for him. "I'm glad he's earned your good opinion. You see, Mr. Blackstone and I grew up together. We were quite close, but we lost touch when he came up to London. We met by chance when I came to help with the dinner party last evening. I was on my way to Paddington Station when I was assaulted tonight. Thankfully, Mr. Blackstone found me or I'd have passed the night on a park bench."

"Oh, dear," Mrs. Frye exclaimed.

"I'll be leaving for Torquay to return home soon," Rose continued. "Mr. Blackstone's been kind enough to offer me a room until I go."

Pity filled the housekeeper's eyes and she began to thaw. "I'm relieved to hear it. Being in service yourself, you know how some of these modern girls work to catch their master's eye. They get some foolish notion he'll marry them or at the very least, become a wealthy benefactor."

She also knew that many masters were happy to take the maids up on those schemes, but she didn't say as much. "I'm not one of them, I promise."

"I'm glad to hear it. I've been praying for him for years. It's my hope he finds the Lord and a suitable woman who loves him, not some fly-by-night who seeks to use him for his hard-earned fortune." From then on, Mrs. Frye treated her with kindness and a budding respect. She had a bowl of cold water and a cloth fetched to help bring down the swelling in Rose's cheek and cut lip, then called for a hot bath before leaving to find her something fresh to wear.

Rose finished her bath, the first time she'd ever taken two in one day, and pulled on the velvet dressing gown Mrs. Frye had placed across the bed for her use. She was basking in the warmth of the fireplace and combing her hair when Mrs. Frye returned.

"I have a surprise for you," the housekeeper said with a bright smile. She held up a fashionable gown made of rich turquoise silk and edged in matching lace.

"Oh, my! You can't possibly mean for me to wear that."

The housekeeper colored. "It wasn't my intention to offend you, miss."

"No, no, you didn't. Indeed, I'm much complimented. I'm afraid I couldn't possibly wear something so fine."

"Of course you can." Mrs. Frye relaxed. "I think this color will make the most of your fair skin and lovely blond hair."

"I've never worn anything so pretty." She touched the cool silk with hesitant fingers. A gown such as this would cost more than she earned in a year. "Wherever did you find it?"

"I forgot we had it until I left you to bathe. It belonged to the wife of one of Mr. Blackstone's business associates. She discarded it a fortnight ago when she dribbled wine down the bodice. I had it cleaned, thinking it would make a nice gift for my niece when I venture home for a visit next month."

"And you don't mind if I borrow it?"

"Of course not. If anything, I expect it'll be a mite too big for you. I brought a packet of pins just in case."

Once she'd dressed, Rose stood before a cheval mirror. Somehow Mrs. Frye had given an ordinary duck the look of a graceful swan. Secretly, she admitted she wanted to be beautiful for Sam, to knock him off his feet and make him forget Miss Ratner, but she barely recognized herself and the transformation was a bit intimidating.

Mrs. Frye stood back to judge her handiwork. "I'd say you look like the cake and the icing, too, miss."

"Thank you," she said full of sincerity. Her hair had been pinned into a loose twist at the nape of her neck with soft, curled tendrils falling freely from her temples. The gown fit her well due to two extra petticoats that held out the tiered, bell-shaped skirt. The cut of the bodice was lower than she was used to, but a froth of lace protected her modesty. The fashionably puffed sleeves sat below the shoulder and ended with a snug ribbon a little above each elbow.

She'd never imagined wearing a gown of this quality or delicacy. She liked the movement of the fabric and the way the silk shimmied in the lamplight. Women like her were meant for rough wool or coarse cotton, not silk and finery. She rarely saw herself in anything except serviceable black or dour, dark gray, but Mrs. Frye had been right. Even she had to admit the turquoise did wonders for her pale skin despite the bruise marring her cheek and cut bottom lip.

"Shall we go downstairs?" Mrs. Frye asked. "Your dinner should be prepared by now. I should think after your ordeal this evening, you'd be rather hungry."

Freshly bathed and shaven, Sam paced from one end of the Oriental carpet to the other while he waited for Rose in the parlor. The dining and drawing rooms had seemed too formal for a simple meal. He'd had a table set for two, which his servants had contrived to turn into a romantic setting of fine china and candles. The bouquet of red roses had been plucked from various arrangements throughout the house.

"Mr. Blackstone?"

He looked up to find his butler a few paces away. "What is it, Hodges?"

The butler placed a piece of folded paper on the table. "Gibson found this in the coach. It's addressed to Miss Smith. She must have dropped it."

"I'll see that she gets it when she comes down."

Hodges shuffled out. Sam reached for the missive. It was damp and wrinkled. The ink was smudged in places but the black, one-penny stamp and Rose's name were legible. He turned it over to identify the sender. The seal had been broken and the flap torn, but the name and part of the location were clear: Andrew Smith, Keen Far—

His brow pleated with confusion, as though someone had shouted at him in a foreign language. Smith was the moniker given to Rose by the orphanage. If the writer were a relative, he wouldn't bear the same name. But one thing was certain: Rose loved the name Andrew. She'd pinned it on him as a middle name when the two of them decided to change his original moniker from Jones to Blackstone and she'd always claimed that's what they would name their son if they had one.

His heart began to pound. Insatiable curiosity goaded him to read the letter. He ignored the pang of conscience that warned he shouldn't and began to unfold the delicate paper. He despised the way his hands shook, as though he already knew what he'd find. The damp paper stuck in places. Frustrated, he slowed himself to keep from ripping it in his haste to have it open. Eventually, the paper unfurled. His eyes frantically sought out the first words:

18 September, 1842

Dearest Mummy...

Chapter Nine

Sam doubled over. The letter slipped from his fingers and floated to the floor. Lightheaded, he grabbed the lip of the table, his legs unsteady and threatening to buckle. The room spun out of control. He drew in deep breaths of air, desperate to choke back his rising nausea.

He stood there, frozen by agony. His mind, usually so reliable in a crisis, swirled with disjointed thoughts and snatches of jumbled memories. Pieces of conversation began to make sense. No wonder Rose had claimed the need to be careful. Like a thief hiding stolen treasure, she'd meant to keep his son from him.

Unaware of the passage of time, he heard faint voices down the hall. By sheer force of will, he gathered his wits, determined to confront her. Rising anger and vast disappointment grappled for control.

His hand still trembling, he retrieved the letter and scanned the childish scrawl:

18 September, 1842
Dearest Mummy,
Granny and I are well. Today I milked Hester

the cow and gathered eggs. One of the roosters chased me around the yard, but I outran him. We took a walk down the lane and made scones to go with our tea and cream. I miss you. Come home soon.
I love you,
Andrew.

Through misty eyes, he read the note three more times before he refolded the paper as he'd found it and slipped it into his pocket.

He wiped his eyes with the back of his hand. He had a son! Not for a moment did he believe the boy wasn't his. Rose would not have gone out of her way to keep Andrew a secret otherwise.

The idea that she planned to return to Devonshire without telling him the truth was beyond abominable. She must despise him. There was no other excuse. No matter what she thought he'd done she had no right to withhold his son's very existence from him. He would never have believed her capable of such selfish deception, but perhaps he should have given how faithless she'd proven to be nine years ago.

He poured a drink at the sideboard and downed the bitter contents in a single swallow. The realization that somewhere another person existed that shared his blood filled him with elation and erased his lifelong sense of isolation. Now that the initial shock was beginning to pass, his curiosity abounded. He wanted to know everything about Andrew: his likes and dislikes, the color of his hair, his eyes. Was he big or small? When was his birthday?

He went out into the hall to wait for Rose. Schooling his features, he strove to adopt an air of normalcy when he really wanted to shake her and demand the truth. He'd always thought of Rose as honest and devoid of guile, but she'd proven to be a better actress than he remembered and more than willing to cheat him. Up to know, she'd been playing her hand without telling him the rules of the game, but he'd spent the past nine years outwitting craftier opponents than she would ever be. Now that he was aware their son was at stake, he'd play by his own rules and not necessarily fair.

Mrs. Frye's voice drifted down from the upper floor. "I'll have your frock mended and laundered by tomorrow morning."

"Thank you for everything you've done already, Mrs. Frye," Rose said, still out of sight. "But I do have one more favor to ask. There is an important letter in the pocket of my dress and coins in the other that I'll need to pay my fare home. I should have removed them myself, but I didn't think to do so in all the commotion."

"Don't worry, child. I'll retrieve the items and put them on the bedside table."

The women appeared on the landing. Seeing Rose, Sam's fury flared. How dare she look so beautiful and innocent when he'd just learned the depths of her wickedness.

A smile lit Rose's face until she winced and her hand flew up to cradle her split lip and bruised cheek. Laughter sparkled in her bright blue eyes. "Judging by his silence, I don't think he recognizes me, Mrs. Frye."

"I'd know you anywhere," he said. Just yesterday, the mere color of her hair had been enough to lead him on a merry chase through half of Mayfair. She was the mother of his child and the woman who'd caused him more pain than should ever be allowed.

With pride-crushing force he realized even her duplicity wasn't enough to prevent him from longing for her. Somehow he had to overcome this irrational weakness. He would never trust her again.

"Shall we?" He offered his arm once she reached the bottom step and escorted her into the parlor. Seeing that Hodges had already been there, he dismissed Mrs. Frye.

Candles flickered on the table and across the mantel. Chilled beverages awaited them in cut-crystal goblets. With the rain falling in earnest outside, the rich aroma of savory meat pies and herbed potatoes transformed the refined room into a cozy and intimate haven.

"How wonderful, Sam." Rose's voice was soft, just like he remembered it when she was happy. She turned to him, the silk of her gown rustling with the movement. Her expression was an equal mix of pleasure and perplexity. "Is this your handiwork or did Mr. Hodges make assumptions?"

"It was a joint effort. I told him what I wanted and he embellished."

"Well, then, cheers to you both on a job well done."

"You're the only woman I know who gives a thought to the servants."

"That's because I am one."

"Not tonight," he reminded her.

Her light mood dimmed a notch. "I suppose that's true. For the first time in years I'm out of a job."

And yet she'd still preferred to keep Andrew a secret rather than come to him for help.

"Don't dwell on that now. We'll sort it all tomorrow." He pulled out her chair. "Won't you have a seat?"

She eyed the delicate piece of antique furniture with uncertainty. He understood her hesitation. She was a fish out of water and unused to finery. He'd suffered the same insecurities the first several times he'd been invited to formal occasions with their endless rules of etiquette and rarified manners. To him, it all might as well have been gibberish.

"You needn't worry," he said, determined to keep her at ease before he demanded the truth about Andrew. "It's just you and me. There's no one here to judge you or make you feel insignificant."

"I didn't think you would," she said in earnest. "It's this beautiful gown. It's a loaner from Mrs. Frye that she intends as a gift for her niece. I can't stop fretting I'll ruin it somehow."

"It's just a dress, one in a thousand and a snap to replace."

The pleasure on her face faded noticeably, but he refused to feel guilty. She moved to the chair and they managed to seat her close to the table without any harm to the many layers of her skirts. He leaned in to place a serviette across her lap. The frantic beat of her pulse at the base of her throat, the gentle slope of her shoulder, the clean fragrance of her skin all conspired to enflame his traitorous senses.

He hastened to his side of the table before she made him lose sight of his plans. They had much to discuss and he could not afford any further distractions.

He served them both. Steam rose from the rustic pastries stuffed with choice beef, root vegetables and thick, brown gravy. Rose closed her eyes and she breathed in deep. "These smell delicious."

Aware of how hungry she must be, he let her finish most of the meal before he sat back and hooked an arm over his chair.

He felt for the letter in his pocket and welcomed the renewed surge of injustice that goaded him onward. One way or the other she was going to tell him the whole truth before he finished with her this evening.

He watched her sip from her goblet. "I hope you won't find me too forward, but I've been wondering. Did you and your husband have any children?"

She choked on her water and her hand trembled. She just managed to slip the goblet back onto the table before she dropped it. "I beg your pardon? I don't think—"

"It's a reasonable question." He leaned in and smiled to allay her misgivings. "Surely not one with a great need for secrecy."

She looked as hunted as a treed fox. "No, we didn't. Harry died before we had the chance."

"What a pity." He reached into his pocket and extracted the letter. "Are there any other children you wish to tell me about?"

He held the tattered piece of paper under the table, waiting for her to admit the truth. Her eyes widened and the color slowly seeped from her face. Her bottom lip quivered. "You already know somehow, don't you?"

Anger sizzled through him. He tossed the note on the lacy tablecloth between them. "Know what, Rose? That I have a son you've denied me?"

The facial muscles began to twitch and without

warning, she burst into tears. Shocked, he'd expected defiance or cheek as were her customary reactions, not these heartrending sobs.

She swiveled away from him, the back of her hand pressed to her mouth, her eyes squeezed shut. Her chest heaved with the effort to suppress her weeping.

His instincts urged him to comfort her. His usual opponents were hardened men of business, not vulnerable young women. He'd overplayed his hand in his own grief and need to win, but how much had his momentary victory cost him?

With a groan, he left his seat and sank to his knees before her. "Don't cry, Rosie. You needn't cry."

Her hands dropped to her lap in a defeated motion. He grasped her fingers and held them tight in one of his. With the other, he used the serviette to gently blot her damp cheeks.

She sniffed. "Where did you get my letter?"

"Gibson found it while cleaning the coach. You must have dropped it."

She snatched the folded rectangle from him and pressed it to her chest as though the smudged piece of paper were a rare and precious gift. "And of course you had to read it when you had no business doing so."

His eyebrow arched at the complaint when he had more than enough of his own. "Under normal circumstances, I wouldn't have, but yes I did once I saw Andrew's name. Fortunately for me I did or you would have gotten away with your plan to steal my son."

Her stricken gaze swung to his face. "Unfair!"

"What else would you call it except thievery of the worst kind? By your own admission you were leaving London with no intention of telling me about him."

She fidgeted with the serviette in her lap. "How could I come to you, believing as I'd been told, that you were the one responsible for having me tossed from my job?"

"What stings the most about that course of reasoning is that I didn't merit a single benefit of a doubt. You intended to leave me as I would never have left you—without the slightest consideration or a word of farewell."

"I'm sorry," she said, her voice strained with emotion. "You frightened me with your threats of revenge last night. I thought I was protecting him."

"From me, his own father?"

"He's never been yours."

"Are you truly claiming Andrew isn't my son?"

"No...there's been no one else, but—" Her mouth clamped shut as she realized what she'd admitted.

Primitive satisfaction surged through him, even as instant questions about her marriage occurred to him. He set them aside until later. "Then how is he not mine?"

"You don't know him from Adam. You can't pretend to love him...at least not like I do."

"How dare you presume to know how I feel?" He stood and glared at her. "He's my flesh and blood. You of all people must know what that means to me. I do love him. If not like you as yet, it's because I haven't had the chance."

"No, it's because you left me—us."

"I wouldn't have gone had I known you were expecting."

"And then you would have resented us."

"Don't be an idiot. I *loved* you."

She glanced away as though he'd struck her. "Yes, but you can't deny you'd dreamed of leaving Ashby Croft for years. You were made for grander things, Sam. You've proven that here in London. Had you stayed, you would have been miserable."

"I reckon we'll never know." What he did know was that he'd been wretched without her. So much so, he'd never been able to trust or love another woman.

She held out the letter. "Will you read this to me?"

He unfolded the paper and read the message before handing it back to her. "Our son sounds delightful."

"He is," she agreed with pride in her voice. "He's a darling. Smart and as sweet as plum pudding." Her eyes teared up again. "He looks just like you."

Pride expanded in his chest. A thousand questions came to mind, but Rose looked exhausted and he had plans to make.

"I want to hear every detail about him, but for now I think you'd best get some sleep. We're leaving for Devonshire in the morning. I've missed eight years with my son. I think it's time I finally meet him, don't you?"

Chapter Ten

Rose awoke before dawn the next morning. Despite her prayers, she'd slept fitfully, once she'd slept at all. Sam's reaction to Andrew was both a blessing and a curse. Andrew needed his father and she wanted what was best for him, but the future with Sam and what his presence meant to their lives remained a quagmire of questions.

To make matters more complicated, she'd admitted to herself that she'd never stopped loving him. As much as she'd tried to banish him from her heart through the years, she'd failed at every turn.

Not that her epiphany would do the slightest bit of good. She had no doubt Sam would adore Andrew, but he had made it clear the love he'd once felt for her was buried in the past.

As she wrestled with her agony, predawn turned to first light. The townhouse began to stir and she listened to the faint bang of a pot in the kitchen and unintelligible voices of delivery men outside on the street below the window.

Eager to begin the journey back to Andrew, she

pushed off the heavy covers and slipped from the canopied bed. She straightened the counterpane and stoked
the fire before using the pitcher of water and basin to
wash for the day.

She pulled a dressing gown over the night rail Mrs.
Frye had left for her use and pushed her feet into a pair
of soft slippers. Without her own garments to dress in
there was nothing for her to do except wait for someone to bring them. She considered putting on the turquoise gown, but the intricate buttons down the back
required an extra set of hands. Besides, Mrs. Frye had
let her borrow the frock for an evening, not indefi-
nitely. She didn't want to take advantage of the good
woman's kindness.

With nothing to pack, she went to the window. The
morning sun rose higher. The storm had cleared, leaving slick, wet streets and puddles along the curb to bear
witness to its passage.

Sam's coach and matched black horses pulled up in
front of the townhouse. The driver set the brake and
jumped down from his perch to inspect the wheels
while the footman unlatched the garden gate at the
end of the walkway.

Gusts of wind rustled the trees in the square and
along the street, littering the ground with bright autumn leaves in shades of red and gold.

A few moments later Sam appeared on the steps.
A severe, aloof figure in a black frock coat and trousers, silver cravat and top hat, he reeked of wealth and
command. He stopped long enough to issue clipped,
indiscernible instructions to his driver before climbing into the luxurious vehicle.

Rose knocked on the window to draw his attention, but none of the men seemed to hear her. The driver took his place in the box and unfurled his whip. Through the coach's glass panes, Rose watched Sam settle into the black leather seat. He removed his hat and tossed it onto the empty place beside him. His expression was somber to the point of melancholy. Had he changed his mind about meeting Andrew? After a few hours of contemplation, did he feel trapped? Had he considered that having an illegitimate child might derail his situation with the lofty Miss Ratner?

Distressed by the prospect, she prayed she was wrong.

"Miss Smith?" Prudence's voice accompanied a light rap on the chamber door.

A last glance at Sam found him watching her, his intent, dark eyes causing her heart to flutter. His carriage rolled forward. With a nod and a half smile, he was gone.

"Miss Smith, are you awake?" Prudence asked through the door. "May I come in?"

"Give me a moment," she called, shaking her head to refocus her thoughts, but the image of Sam's grave expression refused to leave her alone.

She opened the chamber door. Prudence held a breakfast tray with a steaming teapot, cup and covered plate.

"I brought you a bit of breakfast." The maid crossed the threshold and placed the tray on the table in front of the settee. "Shall I call for a hot bath?"

"I took one last night."

"If you'd like somethin' else, I'll be happy to fetch it."

"Thank you. I have everything I need, except for my clothes and shoes."

Prudence glanced at the turquoise gown hanging neatly from a hook on the back of the door. "Mrs. Frye thought you might prefer to wear this gown today as your black dress isn't quite ready."

"I couldn't," she said. "I'm leaving London today. I'd have no way to return it to her."

"Bring it with you when you come back."

"It's unlikely I'll return to London anytime soon."

"Wot a shame." Prudence poured a spot of tea and handed the steaming cup and saucer to Rose. "You'd make a kind mistress."

Rose blinked, caught off guard by the compliment. "Thank you, but I'm a servant, the same as you are."

"Uh-huh." Prudence picked up the brush on the dressing table. "Mr. Blackstone sent Mrs. Frye on an errand early this morning. She's supposed to return by half nine. I imagine that gives us almost an hour. Shall I arrange your hair?"

She took Prudence up on her offer and sat down before the mirror at the dressing table. The bruise on her cheek wasn't as inflamed as before and the swelling of her lip had gone down by at least half. "I saw Mr. Blackstone leave. Do you happen to know where he's off to?"

"I believe he's gone to his office, miss."

"Oh." She wished he'd taken a moment before he left to inform her of his intentions. If he'd changed his mind about leaving today, he should have told her. Her plans remained the same and she had to find a way home somehow.

"And I heard it mentioned he's visiting his solicitor before coming back here."

His solicitor? She closed her eyes and absorbed the

bad news. Were her worst fears coming true? Did he mean to take Andrew away from her? Or was it simply a coincidence that Sam sought legal counsel the morning after he learned of his son?

"I shouldn't worry." Prudence pinned a section of Rose's blond hair into place. "I expect he'll return soon. Mr. Hodges and Mr. Blackstone's valet are like two old crones bickering over what he'll need for your journey."

Relief coursed through her. If he hadn't reconsidered leaving, then she'd have several days of travel to learn what he was up to…and to try to change his mind if need be.

Mrs. Frye joined them earlier than expected. The housekeeper was effervescent with excitement. "Before I begin, Miss Smith, I must tell you I did my best to rescue your dress and shoes, but both items were damaged beyond repair."

"Oh, no," Rose said, sincerely distressed. "My other dress was in my stolen valise and those were my only shoes."

"Mr. Blackstone and I suspected as much given the robbery that occurred. In light of that event, he sent me to the modiste this morning in hopes of finding something decent for you to wear. I took your belongings to ascertain the proper size. I felt certain I'd find very little on such short notice, but happily I was wrong. It seems a young lady came into the shop a few days ago and declined several ensembles she'd ordered. The colors she chose turned out to be too springlike for her tastes, but I think they'll suit you very well. A few minor alterations were performed and now any of them should fit you." She turned to Prudence. "Help me fetch the packages. I had Frank leave them at the chamber door."

Rose didn't know what to say. She offered a prayer of thanks to the Lord for always providing for her needs. And she would remember to thank Sam as well for his thoughtfulness and generosity.

She went to help the two women with the boxes, but they gently shooed her away. Overwhelmed by the sheer number of packages, she couldn't imagine what all of them contained.

"The shoes aren't here as yet." Mrs. Frye placed a large box on the settee. "I explained the need for haste and the shoemaker promised he'd have two pairs delivered before you're away with Mr. Blackstone. Given the limited time, I think they'll be more plain than fashionable, but they'll be of good quality and comfortable, at least."

The good woman sounded as though she were apologizing, but she needn't. Considering Rose chose her shoes by price and serviceability, the thought of a comfortable pair seemed grand.

Twenty minutes later, the room was littered with box tops, lavender-scented tissue paper and a wealth of colorful fabrics. There were six gowns in all, four day gowns and two for evenings. Matching bonnets, shawls and reticules were perched upon the bed pillows. Frothy shifts, layer upon layer of petticoats, fresh silk stockings and garters made of embroidered strips of cotton rounded out the bounty. Every piece was expertly crafted from the finest silk, cotton or softest velvet. The delicate undergarments were edged with lace or satin.

Marveling at the sheer number of items, Rose focused on the four day gowns lying neatly across the bed. She brushed her fingertips across one of yellow-and-white brocade. "They're all so beautiful. I don't know which one to choose."

"Which one?" Mrs. Frye looked perplexed. "Whatever do you mean, child? All of these are yours. I'm glad you like them so well, because they cannot be returned once they've left the shop. If you hadn't cared for them, I don't know what we would have done, but… Oh, dear, I almost forgot," she continued happily as she picked up a large, unopened box off the floor. "When I saw this I knew it had been made for you."

The housekeeper removed the lid and pushed back the paper. She shook out the garment within, revealing a cape crafted of rich, blue velvet. Lined with silver silk, the cape's collar, edges and hem were an intricate pattern of silver thread embroidered on deep blue satin.

Speechless, Rose moved the short distance to Mrs. Frye. With gentle fingers, she caressed the cape's soft material. "I can't believe Mr. Blackstone meant for you to purchase all of this for me."

"He told me to find whatever you need. This is a good start, but—"

"A good start? I've never owned above three dresses at once in my life and that includes my two for work. Sa—Mr. Blackstone's going to think I'm a greedy baggage who's trying to take him."

"Is that what's got you concerned? Don't worry. I didn't spend half as much coin as he sent."

Rose paled at the fortune he must have spent. "That isn't the point. All of this is too much. I could never repay him for one of these gowns, let alone…" She sat down at the dressing table. She hung her head, hating that she was worth so little. "I'm sorry, Mrs. Frye. I don't mean to seem ungrateful."

There was a rustle of fabric and the sound of a box top being replaced. "Prudence," Mrs. Frye said, "there are several portmanteaux in the attic. Enlist Frank to bring two…no three of them here."

The door clicked as the maid left. Mrs. Frye began to fold one of the shifts. "Miss Smith, I hope you won't think I'm being too forward or speaking out of turn, but I believe I know what's distressing you. It's not these fine clothes, it's your own fear that you're not good enough to merit them."

She gave the housekeeper a sidelong glance. "How transparent I am. I must seem very silly to you."

"Not at all." Mrs. Frye folded another article. "I've been on the bottom of society for a long time, but I have my dignity. I'm grateful to have honest work and a good master, but I also know how difficult it is to believe you're valuable when you've been taught all your life you mean next to nothing."

Rose nodded.

"Are you a Christian, Miss Smith?"

"Yes," she murmured. "I strive to serve the Lord with all my heart. I know I have value in His eyes, but I'm also aware that in the opinions of other people I might as well be invisible. Ever since I came to London I've been plagued by fears I can't seem to rise above."

"Whenever I'm fearful, I read my Bible."

"I can't read," Rose admitted quietly. "But I hear the Word at church on Sundays and my…my son reads passages to me every night."

The housekeeper's eyes widened at the mention of

the child and sudden understanding dawned on her weathered face. "A son? You and his father are blessed, indeed."

"Yes, yes we are." She reached for a petticoat, intending to help Mrs. Frye fold the garments, but the housekeeper swatted her hand away.

"Well, since your boy reads to you, perhaps you know the passage of Jeremiah 29:11?"

"It's one of my favorites." She leaned back and tried to smile. "For I know the plans I have for you, declares the Lord, plans to prosper you and not to harm you—"

"—plans to give you a hope and a future," Mrs. Frye finished with her. "Or how about 1 John 3:1, 'How great is the love the Father has lavished on us, that we should be called children of God.'"

"I love that one," Rose said, greatly encouraged. "I'm an orphan. Ever since I came to the Lord, it's been a source of strength to know I have a Father who cares for me."

Mrs. Frye straightened the skirt of a yellow silk gown. "Has the Lord ever forsaken you?"

"No, never."

"Do you believe He wants to bless you?"

"Yes." She glanced at the new wardrobe that had yet to be put away. "But I'm not convinced His blessings have solely to do with material things."

"All good things come from the Lord, both material and spiritual, I believe." Tissue paper crinkled as Mrs. Frye packed away another petticoat. "Has He ever led you down a wrong path?"

Rose shook her head.

"Then perhaps you needn't fear this new road, either."

"It's not that simple," she said, thinking of Sam. She didn't belong in his polished, London world and she didn't believe he'd be willing to leave his exciting life for the quiet domesticity of a small, country village.

"It's a rare day when life is simple." The housekeeper gave her a soothing pat on the shoulder. "But since you know God loves you, that He wants to bless you, that He has great plans for your life and never steers you wrong, why not see yourself as He does and follow Him wherever He happens to lead?"

Sam returned home by eleven. He'd given Hodges orders to have everything packed and ready to be loaded in time for departure at noon. No mean feat considering preparation for a journey of this scale usually took a full day or two.

A footman opened the front door. "Welcome home, Mr. Blackstone."

He handed over his coat and hat and was met by the sweet scent of the floral arrangement filling the circular entryway. A stack of large trunks awaited transport to the coaches outside. "Where are Hodges and Mrs. Frye?"

"I'm here, sir." Hodges's slow gait clapped on the marble floor. He carried a leather-bound journal in one hand, a fountain pen in the other. "May I have a word with you?"

The two of them went to the study a few doors down. The heavy, velvet drapes had been drawn back. Light streamed through the series of open windows along the far wall and rain-freshened air whipped the sheer, white curtains. Outside, the trees swayed in the wind and the ground was covered in a golden carpet of fallen leaves.

Sam motioned to the chair across the desk from him. "Have a seat." The old boy looked done in, with dark circles under his bespectacled eyes and the lines in his craggy face deeper than usual.

"I couldn't, sir." A former clerk in Sam's city office, Elliot Hodges had been kind and invaluable to him when he first came to London. Failing eyesight had made figuring long lists of numbers day after day an impossibility as he grew older, but Sam hadn't had the heart to boot him out into the street. For the past six years, he'd served as a loyal butler whose penchant for formality amused Sam more often than not.

"I'm the master here and I say you shall. You look dead on your feet. As usual, you've gone above and beyond my expectations."

Clearly delighted by the commendation, Hodges hesitated, but sat down. "I'm glad of it, sir, but I have a few minor matters to discuss with you."

Sam opened a leather satchel and began to peruse the wall of books behind his desk. "Discuss away. I'm listening."

Hodges adjusted his spectacles and opened his journal. "Everything is going to plan. As you instructed, riders have been sent to arrange lodgings at each point along your journey."

"Good." Sam chose a book from the shelf. "What of the wild-goose chase I sent Mrs. Frye on this morning? Any success in finding Miss Smith a suitable wardrobe?"

"Yes, sir. The exercise was quite beneficial. Miss

Smith's been outfitted with several acceptable garments."

Pleased, Sam chose an additional book.

"On another note," Hodges continued, "Mrs. Frye reminded me that Miss Smith has no lady's maid," Hodges said. "I'm not certain of your intentions, but if you mean to engage one for her may I suggest Prudence Lively? At present, Miss Lively is a chambermaid with no formal training as a lady's maid, but she comes from a large family and does possess some of the necessary skills. She should do well until a more acceptable candidate can be found."

"Prudence, you say?" Sam recalled the chambermaid from the night of the dinner party. "Does Mrs. Frye believe Miss Lively and Miss Smith will get on well? I won't abide anyone making Miss Smith uncomfortable or looking down on her in any way."

Hodges peered at him over the rim of his spectacles. Usually impassive, the butler failed to hide his surprise or curiosity. "I shouldn't think Miss Lively is capable of either of those activities. She's a good and affable girl. Mrs. Frye thinks highly of her."

Sam considered the limited time frame and difficulty of finding a trained lady's maid. "Fine. Arrange for Miss Lively to accompany us this morning, but tell her the position is a temporary one. We'll leave the final decision to Miss Smith."

Hodges closed his journal. "If there's nothing else, sir, I'll be about my business."

"By all means."

Hodges reached the door at the same moment Rose

arrived. The two nearly collided. Both exclaimed an apology before Hodges backed up to allow her entry.

Fixated on Rose, Sam put down the book he held and watched her cross the room. Dressed in a yellow-and-white brocade gown, she looked like the lady he'd always known she was. Except for the bruise marring her cheek, her skin was as pale and creamy as a pearl. Her glossy hair had been fashioned into an elegant bun at the nape of her neck. His mouth went dry at the prospect of unpinning the arrangement and running his fingers through the silken strands of gold, wheat and honey.

"Sam? Do you have a moment?" Blue eyes as bright and clear as a day in June looked at him quizzically. "Have you taken ill? You have the oddest expression."

He'd made another tactical error. He was supposed to resist her, not provide her with weapons like this gown to aid in his downfall. He cleared his throat and gripped the back of his chair. "I'm fine. What do you want?"

Her hands went to the skirt and held out the fabric. "I'd like to thank you for the beautiful clothes. I can't imagine why you went to the trouble, but I'm grateful. Mrs. Frye outdid herself. Each piece is lovelier than the next…and I expect more expensive."

If this gown was any indication, it was coin well spent. "You might as well get used to finer things, Rose. As the mother of my son, you'll be provided for. You needn't worry about your expenses ever again."

She took a step back and eyed him suspiciously. "So you think to keep me, do you? If so, be warned. I—"

"I'm not going to keep you as you imply. I'm going

to marry you. As my wife, you can't very well dress in servants' togs."

Her mouth dropped open. *"What?"*

"It's the only sensible option. I thought you'd be pleased by the prospect considering the drastic change marriage to me will bring to your circumstances."

"So I'm supposed to be happy to marry you for your money?"

Amelia and countless other women would be, why not her? He shrugged. "Consider my wealth an added benefit. We have a child. A child who deserves what we never had—parents and a family, a comfortable home and a first-rate education. I don't want my son to have to bear the stigma of our mistakes any longer. Surely, you don't want that for him, either."

"No, but what of your understanding with Miss Ratner?"

"My son's welfare is my main concern."

"I appreciate that, but—"

"No excuses. Will you marry me and do what's right for Andrew or not?"

"I... We have things to consider—"

"Fine, consider all you like until we reach Torquay. I'll expect an answer by then."

She turned to go as though she couldn't leave fast enough. Her reaction pained him beyond bearing and bolstered his belief that she no longer cared for him in the least.

"And Rose, make sure you consider this, as well."

She stopped and faced him. "What?"

"I visited my solicitor this morning. He seems to think that given our circumstances, I won't have much trouble laying claim to Andrew and bringing him up to London without you, if necessary."

Her lips pinched and her face turned ashen. "I thought I'd misjudged you, but you're ruthless and selfish—"

"I'm fair and honest, unlike you've been in most of our recent dealings."

The door opened at the front of the house and the murmur of indistinct voices filtered down the hall. She frowned. "Why would you want a wife you have to force to wed you?"

The question cut deep. Before she'd fallen in love with Harry Keen, she'd planned to marry him without hesitation. "This has nothing to do with wanting a wife at all. It's about making certain I have a proper claim on my son. You've already proven willing to keep him from me when it suited you. If not for finding that note by chance, I may never have known he existed."

She opened her mouth to reply, but a footman tapped on the half-open door. "Sir?"

"What is it?" Sam snapped.

"Miss Ratner is here," the footman said with a hint of apology. "I told her you were occupied, but she insists you wish to see her."

Without another word, Rose quit the room. He watched her go, attuned to her footsteps fleeing up the stairs.

"Send her in," he told the footman. He might as well tend to Ameila and finish the business before she set up camp in the front garden. He stood and rounded the desk.

The footman didn't have a chance to carry out his instructions. Amelia pushed her way into the study.

Dressed in cream satin and emeralds she seemed the epitome of a well-bred young lady until she opened her mouth. "Why did I see that tart of a maid ascending the stairs? What is she still doing here and why is she dressed like a queen?"

Chapter Eleven

"Miss Ratner." A cool smile turned his lips as he watched her sail across the carpet toward him. "To what do I owe this unexpected visit?"

She stopped before his desk. Her fisted hands on her hips, she looked at him with disdain as though he were some errant lackey. "Don't play games with me, Sam Blackstone. After the way that hussy threw herself at my father and Mr. Winters, she was supposed to be discarded with the rubbish."

He ground his teeth together as anger flared in him like a bonfire. Until this moment, he'd had no more than suspicions to prove Amelia's part in seeing Rose sacked. But hearing her voice the same exaggerated complaints as the Malbury servants confirmed she'd put them up to the deed. What had he ever seen in this heartless virago? "She was, you'll be happy to know. Malbury's housekeeper received your missive and cast her out in a storm."

"Then how did she come to be here?"

"After the way you used my name to slander her,

I felt it was my duty to find her and offer a measure of protection."

Amelia's eyebrow arched and her shoulders stiffened. She crossed her arms over her chest. "And now she's your bit of stuff, I presume? How could you? I know dogs like to lie with dogs, but this is too much even for a mongrel like you."

He laughed without humor. "I agree. It is too much. Miss Smith is no dog and of the two of you, kindly recall, you're the one with the pedigree."

Incensed, color flooded her pale face and seeped down her throat. "Why you filthy guttersnipe! How dare you insult me in such a manner?"

"I thought you'd like a taste of your own medicine. Thanks to your lies, Miss Smith has been denied her livelihood. She was booted into the streets of a dangerous city she's unfamiliar with, beaten and robbed."

She waved her hand as though Rose's plight meant nothing. "I doubt she had much to steal, anyway."

He glanced at the clock on the mantel to divert his attention. He'd never been tempted to strike a woman until this moment. "She'll have plenty once I convince her to marry me."

"*Marry* you?" Her mouth dropped open and her dark eyes blinked in outrage. "You can't be fool enough to choose a baseborn Jezebel over a viscount's daughter."

"I'm no fool and she is no Jezebel. As far as choices go, I'd pick her over anyone."

"Do you believe yourself in love with her?" Her shrill laughter rang through his study. "How quaint. Have you considered you can have us both? I'm not naive. I know men play away. You can have her once you and I marry as you've led me to believe—"

"I did no such thing," he said, disgusted by her and her filthy offer. "I confess I considered a proposal once you broached the subject, but I never intimated as much. You and your father took it upon yourselves to prattle on to half of London." He returned to his satchel containing his books and other important papers. "Now, if you'll excuse me, I'm to depart in a few minutes' time and I still have much to prepare."

She grabbed his arm. "Ah, yes, you're headed to Devonshire. You declined to go there with me on holiday, but you're making time now. When will you be back?"

Irritated that she must have questioned his servants, he shook her off. "My business is none of your concern."

"Indeed it is. I've been hither and yon in search of you this morning. The Ellistons have written to inform me our party was a great success. We've been invited to dine with them Tuesday next at eight o'clock sharp."

He marveled at her thickheadedness and inability to comprehend that he meant to disassociate with her and her schemes. "You'll have to give them your regrets or take another in my stead. As you seem to need bluntness, let me be clear. You and I are as finished as if we'd never met."

"You can't be serious."

"I'm serious as death."

She opened and closed her mouth as though her words were choking her. "I'll make you sorry for thinking a lowborn piece of rubbish like you can treat me in this shabby fashion."

He smirked, quite confident he had nothing to fear. "I doubt it."

Without saying more, she raced for the exit. She careened to a stop at the threshold, before pivoting to face him and declared overloud, "It matters not what hold she has on you. You and I are both aware you'll always be mine. In your heart of hearts you know I speak true, even if you deny it to the ends of the earth."

She fled down the hall, her heels clicking in the corridor. "Get out of my way, you dolt," he heard her shout, forcing the commotion of the footmen moving trunks in the entryway to stall.

The front door opened and slammed, shaking the windows. Relieved to have met with the end of Amelia's dramatics, he was embarrassed that he'd ever displayed the slightest interest in the self-important shrew. Had it been but a matter of days ago that his life had been empty enough to consider marriage to a woman he neither liked nor respected in exchange for a place amongst a bunch of snobs?

He pulled on his coat, mulling over the oddness of her last little speech. She couldn't be that half-baked, could she? There had never been love between them, only business. She'd sounded as though she'd spoken for someone else's benefit. Like a two-bit actress addressing an audience....

His stomach sank and he raced into the hallway. Relieved to find the space empty except for a footman, he gripped the banister of the grand staircase. Thankfully, he'd been wrong to suspect Rose had been there to overhear Amelia's ludicrous tirade.

In the entryway, the clock chimed noon. Hodges gave clipped directions to a variety of servants con-

cerning the remaining articles that needed to be stowed
for the journey. Sam appreciated the butler's efficiency.
They could not leave London soon enough. Not only
did he have a driving need to meet his son, he longed
for a change of pace and the chance to convince Rose
that life with him needn't be so bad.

At precisely twelve o'clock, Rose, Prudence and
Mrs. Frye descended the stairs for the second time in
the past ten minutes and gathered on the portico outside the townhouse's front door. The storm the previous night and the following onslaught of wind had
made for a clear but chilly day.

Three coaches awaited their party. Gibson and a
handful of under footmen busied themselves with
strapping the last trunks to the top of the second coach
while several housemaids finished packing the boot
of the third.

Trying to be discreet, Rose searched the surrounding block covertly to be certain Miss Ratner was well
and truly gone. Unnerved by the other woman's emo-
tional display, she'd been on the staircase when the
shrew left Sam's office. Having backtracked immediately to her chamber, Rose had given the matter to
the Lord. There was nothing else she could do. Sam's
connection to Miss Ratner was a continual source of
disquiet—as was the knowledge that she would be denying him the woman he truly wanted if she agreed to
his decree that they should marry for Andrew's sake.

She hated being Sam's second choice. It made her
sick inside, knowing she would always wonder if he
was disappointed he'd been saddled with a kitchen
maid instead of a viscount's daughter.

"Don't worry." Mrs. Frye patted Rose's shoulder. "That haughty little minx is well on her way by now."

"Perhaps we shouldn't be uncharitable toward Miss Ratner," she said. "She and Mr. Blackstone may be fathoms deep in love just as she claims."

Prudence snickered. "Right-O. And I'm Queen Victoria."

The door swept open behind them, drawing startled exclamations from each of the trio.

"My apologies, ladies," said Sam. He offered his arm to Rose in a gentlemanlike fashion that drew pleased smiles from Prudence and Mrs. Frye.

Rose accepted his arm, her fingers finding hard muscle beneath the soft wool of his gray coat. After Miss Ratner's stormy departure, she hadn't known what to expect of his mood, but he seemed at ease, a far cry from the upheaval of her own unsettled emotions.

He escorted her down the steps and saw her comfortably placed in the well-sprung coach before consulting with Gibson, the other two drivers and Mr. Hodges. Prudence and an additional maid, Mary, rode in the second vehicle, whilst Sam's valet, William Hern, and the other male staff traveled in the third.

The coach swayed as Sam climbed aboard and took the seat across from her. Although a large man in height and the breadth of his shoulders, it was the energy and vibrancy of his presence that filled the coach to bursting.

A footman closed the door behind him as Sam tugged off his gloves. He hung his hat from a hook beneath the window and combed his hands through his hair, mussing the thick, dark strands.

The carriage lurched forward. She waved goodbye

to Mrs. Frye and Hodges, who stood on the top step waving back.

They'd traveled a block by the time Rose dared to look at Sam. He'd loosened his cravat, and the snowy-white neck cloth provided a strong contrast to the bronzed hue of his skin.

The tension between them built with each turn of the coach's wheels. Sam's close proximity and the delicious scent of his cologne sent her thoughts spinning. Her reaction to his nearness was intense, uncontrollable and beyond the bounds of ridiculous when she was so furious with him. She was a grown woman who should be able to manage her reactions and feelings, but Sam had always possessed the powerful ability to turn her reason on end.

Disappointed by her lack of good judgment, she glanced out the window, staring blindly as they passed rows of brick townhouses, carriages and brightly dressed pedestrians out for a stroll in the fine autumn weather.

Sam shifted on his seat. "We have a long journey ahead of us."

"Said the spider to the fly?" She frowned at him.

He laughed. His dark eyes caressed her face until her skin grew hot beneath his perusal. "Are you suggesting you're not safe with me?"

"Of course not." She wished she had a fan. "I have every faith in your self-control considering your heart belongs to Miss Ratner."

His humor died. "You overhead her, didn't you?"

"How could I not? Her caterwauling was loud enough to rattle half of London."

His lips twitched. "Where were you?"

"On the stairs."

"I didn't see you there. How much of our conversation were you privy to?"

She decided to goad him a bit. "I heard it all. Every word. From your declarations of undying love to her—"

"You little liar. I made no such declaration."

"No? Hmm…then I suppose I should confess I heard her from the time she stopped at your study's threshold on her way out. I didn't want to be caught in the middle of a lover's spat, so I went back to my room once she decreed you would always be hers."

She weighed his reaction. He watched her with intense interest but offered no response other than silent encouragement for her to continue.

"I have no inclination to come between the pair of you. I realize you have a full and busy life, Sam. My return out of the blue, and certainly Andrew's existence, must be the cause of more than one difficulty for you. I've accepted that you want to know Andrew, that you can give him more than I can and I expect you to. I love and am grateful that you want to be a father to him, but…"

"Yes?" he urged, his expression as readable as rock.

"I don't see how marriage is the best course of action for us. We're clearly not suited to each other anymore. We believe different things. You believe my religious beliefs are claptrap and even if I dressed in beautiful clothes and tried to act the part of a rich man's wife, I don't feel I could ever be comfortable in your world. On the other hand, I truly doubt you want to leave London for tiny Torquay."

"Decent parents make sacrifices for their children's sake and I'm willing to do whatever is necessary. You say we believe different things, but I believe children ought to be born within the bounds of matrimony. Clearly, we failed on that score, but I wish to correct the matter. Of course, if living in the lap of luxury with me is so abhorrent to you, then give Andrew into my care and you can be as free as a bird."

"I don't want to be free from my son."

"No, you just want to be free of me."

"I don't want to be browbeaten into marriage!"

"I suppose you ran down the aisle to that Henry fellow." His lips firmed into a thin line. "How did he propose? With a bouquet of roses in one hand and a sack of sweets in the other?"

"Leave *Harry* out of this. He was a better man than you'll ever be," she said, her anger running away with her. "He cared about my happiness and wasn't selfish or cruel."

"I'm far from cruel."

"You've threatened to take my son from me if I don't fall in line with your wishes. What is that if not cruelty?"

"I'm sure I could allow him to visit on the odd holiday or for a few days between school terms."

Fear gripped her. She'd seen his ruthless streak that first night in London and she wasn't willing to test him when her place in Andrew's life was at risk. "You're intolerable. You say you're willing to make sacrifices for Andrew, but you don't care how much he'd be hurt if his mother suddenly disappeared. I'm the only parent he's ever known, and you may not like it, but you can't just ignore that I love him and he loves me."

"I'm not ignoring your feelings, I'm simply giving you a choice."

"No, you aren't. If you think I'd give my innocent son into the hands of a hateful blighter like you then you're very much mistaken."

"Shall I consider that a yes, then?" he asked coldly.

She ignored him and looked out the window, too livid to speak. The coach slowed at the crossroads to accommodate the hectic state of the traffic. Sam shifted his feet, his long, booted legs stretched across the space between the two seats, bringing their knees within touching distance.

They traveled for some time in strained silence. Close-set buildings, stained by coal smoke and filth, began to thin until green fields dotted with sheep and apple orchards stretched out along both sides of the road.

Sam reached for the window. "Do you mind?"

"If I did, I doubt you'd care."

He adjusted the pane. Fresh, cool air swept through the vehicle along with the sweet scent of late-blooming wildflowers and the sound of a rushing stream.

The rock and sway of the vehicle tempted Rose to sleep. Deciding slumber was the best way to avoid him, she closed her eyes and leaned her head against the tufted side wall, but the bumps in the road caused her head to bounce and the stiffness of her bonnet plagued her with sharp pains in her swollen left cheek. Aiming to brace herself, she adjusted her spot on the seat several times before she found a bit of comfort.

Darkness was descending when she awakened and the coach was slowing to a stop.

"We've arrived at the inn where we'll spend the night," Sam said.

It took her a moment to realize he'd crossed to her

seat and provided his shoulder as a pillow. Dismayed to realize she was drooling on his coat sleeve, she came fully awake and jerked upright. Mortified, she turned away and wiped her mouth. "How long have I slept?"

"About an hour." He opened the door and climbed out. "Of course you were snoring like a locomotive for most of it."

"I was not!"

"That is when you weren't railing against that Pickles woman at Malbury's."

"Mock me all you like, but I know better. Andrew has assured me I'm quiet as a grave when I sleep."

"Either he's a liar or he's just being nice." Snickering, he planted his hands on her waist and lifted her down to the ground as though she weighed no more than a basket of feathers.

The sun had set and full darkness was upon them. Lanterns illuminated the small country inn's stone walkway and yellow front door.

Thanks to Sam's forethought and the rider he'd sent ahead of them, their entire party had rooms for the night and consequently, no one would have to sleep in the stables.

While Prudence and the footman saw to the trunks, Rose waited for Sam near the front desk while he discussed arrangements with the innkeeper.

"It seems we've missed dinner and the few surrounding shops are closed," he said when he returned to her side. "The innkeeper's wife agreed to bring some tea and sandwiches to your room, but it may take a little time."

He sounded apologetic, but she saw no cause for him to be. "I'll be content with whatever they provide."

"I knew I could count on you to be reasonable." He lifted her hand to his lips and pressed a warm kiss to the back of her knuckles. "You always are with everyone but me."

She searched for a saucy retort, but her brain was empty of everything except Sam's handsome face and the delightful shiver his kiss had sent racing up her arm.

Keys jangled behind her and the innkeeper's wife called, "I'll see you to your room if you're ready, madam."

Though she tried to gain her freedom, Sam didn't release her with alacrity. Their joined hands lingered until the last possible moment, then slipped apart from necessity as Rose moved to follow the proprietress. She glanced over her shoulder, discombobulated by the unexpected tenderness of the moment they'd shared.

He took a step forward. "Sleep well, Rosie. I'll see you in the morning."

"You, too," she whispered back.

In her room, Prudence joined her and helped her prepare for bed before seeking out her own chamber for the night. Once she was alone, she convinced herself she'd imagined the warmth in Sam's eyes and her reaction to his kiss. Not wanting to be a ninny so easily swept off her feet, she tried to push him from her mind by listing all the ways he'd been deplorable, but once she was abed reason abandoned her. For a few unguarded moments, she allowed herself to revisit the long-forgotten dream of Sam, Andrew and she living together as a family. The dream was so wished for, yet long denied, she was tempted to throw logic to the four winds, give in to her weakness and accept Sam's demand that she marry him.

"And then what will you have?" she whispered into the darkness. "A husband who wishes you were someone else and a position in life you'd fit into as well as a draft horse at a tea party."

She cringed at the idea of being an embarrassment to either Sam or Andrew. From what she could tell, Sam was well connected, and Andrew was a lively little boy bound to make friends wherever he went. She'd be a joke once their friends learned she was little more than an illiterate servant.

She rolled onto her side and pulled the bedcovers up to wipe away the sudden well of tears in her eyes.

"Dear Heavenly Father," she prayed into the dark. "I'm walking blind more than usual. I want to do Your will. Please lead me, light my way, give me wisdom and protect me from the longings of my heart. Please reveal Yourself to Sam and make Yourself real in his life. Keep us both from making a mistake. Thank You for bringing me this far, and most of all, for being trustworthy even when I'm unable to trust myself."

Chapter Twelve

The next morning arrived in a blink. Washed and dressed, Sam helped Rose back into the coach and made certain the rest of their party was assembled to leave. The rising red-gold orb of the sun glowed in the still purple sky while the smell of smoke and the earthiness of livestock carried on the cold, crisp air.

Sam set a hamper of food on the far side of his seat and climbed in to take his place across from Rose. Today was their one full day of travel. Tomorrow they should reach Torquay by midafternoon if his plans came to fruition—not that much had gone as he'd planned since Rose had returned to his life three days ago.

The carriage lurched forward and the wheels crunched over the gravel drive. "Are you well?" he asked. "Your bruises look better and your lip appears healed."

"I'm much improved, thank you." The dark smudges under her eyes hinted at a different story. He suspected she'd slept as much as he had, which was next to nil. He'd spent most of the night worrying Andrew would reject him, and mentally making a list of questions about him to pose to Rose. On the rare occasions when he'd closed his eyes, he'd recalled the feel of her resting in his arms, trusting him as she used to do. The floral scent of her hair and the softness of her skin teased his memories, reminding him of sweeter days when she still loved him.

Unlike now.

Yesterday had been quite an education with regards to her feelings about him. Apparently, she considered him heartless and bone-deep cruel. She believed him monstrous enough to take their child from her and she considered marriage to him akin to torture.

Pain edged with bitterness cut into his soul. How could she think so low of him? He didn't care if he was being unreasonable, but it infuriated him that she hadn't seen through his empty threat to take Andrew to London without her. All their lives, he'd tried every day to see her safe and make her happy. Despite his apology, had a few hours of bad temper three nights ago really been enough to convince her he'd become a villainous cur?

The light pink blooms of sowbread enlivened the hedgerows growing along the low, stone walls on both sides of the road. Beyond the hedgerows, green pastures dotted with white sheep spread out as far as the eye could see.

"What's the matter?" He indicated the wicker hamper. "Are you hungry? Or perhaps tired? I know I wouldn't mind a nap after the terrible night I've just passed."

She eyed him dispassionately. "What kept you from your rest?"

"This and that." He opened the basket and withdrew a warm bundle wrapped in brown paper. The scent of baked apples and cinnamon sweetened the air. "Would you like an apple tart? They're your favorite. Or at least they used to be."

Something similar to grief flitted across her countenance. "They still are. I'm surprised you remember."

He handed the package to her and extracted two small bottles of milk from amongst the other items of food within the hamper. "I remember everything about you. You like hedgehogs and swallows, but you don't care for butterflies."

She grimaced. "They're flying worms."

He chuckled. "You enjoy roast chicken but dislike eggs. Your favorite color is yellow, your preferred scent is rosewater. You love winter because the cold affords you more opportunities to cuddle. You've always wanted to live in a cottage by the sea and have a dozen children—the first boy to be named Andrew. You're beautiful and a fine artist. You have the kindest heart I've ever known, but once your trust is lost it's gone for good. You discount your worth because you're ashamed you can't read. You—"

"That's enough." Her hand trembled as she set aside the unopened pastries. "You have an excellent memory, always have had. What does that prove?"

That I wish I'd never left you. That if I could turn back time I would. "Nothing, I suppose."

"Shall I tell you what I remember about you?"

"Is any of it good?"

A whisper of a smile turned her lips. "You're the cleverest man I know. Too clever for your own good sometimes. You're brave and courageous enough to go after what you want in life. You're determined and stubborn to the point of vice. I remember how happy we were and how that wasn't enough to keep you with me."

"Rose—"

"No." She lifted her gloved hand to stop him. "I don't want to discuss this anymore. It does no good to revisit the past over and over again. Today and tomorrow are what matter."

He wished he had the ability to sweep away their past as easily as she did. She sat across from him, tense and wary. Her anxiety confirmed his suspicions and her bad opinion *hurt.*

"Will you promise me something, Sam?"

"I don't know. What is it?"

"Please promise you won't take Andrew from me."

"And give up my leverage? I think not."

"Andrew isn't a deal to be struck. He's a precious little boy with feelings and a heart."

"And you think I don't have one?"

"You used to. Since coming to London, I haven't seen much proof of it."

"Is that so? Has it occurred to you that I might say the same of you?"

She frowned.

"When have I ever given you a reason to believe it's my wish to torment you or cause you pain?"

"You're hurting me now. Without your promise, every mile that we travel closer to Andrew is a torment of uncertainty."

"That's not my intention. I told you before, you might try trusting me."

"I trust your word. That's why I asked for it."

He slowly unwrapped the tarts while he considered that revealing bit of information. At least not all of her trust in him was gone. "You're worried I'll take Andrew, but how do I know you won't keep him from me?"

"I wouldn't. I promise. He needs you and I want him to know you."

Her love for their son touched him deeply. Neither of them had known a parent's love or concern for their welfare. That his son had a protective mother who adored him was a priceless blessing he respected and appreciated. "All right, if you agree to consider my proposal, I'll vow not to take Andrew from you. But there's one caveat."

"One what?"

"A stipulation. A requirement."

"I should have known." Her lips thinned into a reproachful line. "What is it?"

"You have to eat at least two of these pastries and tell me what you've been doing for the last nine years."

She relaxed. The edges of her mouth softened and the stiff line of her shoulders eased. "I can't promise to eat two of them. Perhaps one and half of another."

"You always were a natural negotiator." He handed her the tarts. "Stark should have taken you to London. You could have taught him a thing or two, I'm sure."

She bit into the pastry and closed her eyes to savor the sweet confection. Bits of flaky crust settled on her velvet cloak and a spot of stewed apples perched at the corner of her mouth. Tempted to lean over and kiss the sweetened spot, he looked out the window to catch himself. The hills had flattened into emerald-green grassland with the occasional tree to offer variety. A sky as clear and blue as Rose's eyes reached out to the horizon.

"Aren't you going to try one?" she asked.

He reached for a pastry and took a bite. "Delicious."

"I agree, although not quite as good as mine."

His eyebrow arched dubiously. "Hodges told me you're a kitchen maid, but I still can't believe you can cook. As I recall it was always my job to make the beans and yours to burn the toast."

She wrinkled her nose at him. "I've learned quite a few things since we parted."

"I don't doubt it. I regret not giving you a better listen the other night. I realize times can't have been a laugh for you after I left."

She leaned back against the seat, clearly uncomfortable, but at least somewhat pacified. "You know I've been working at the Malbury family estate a mile outside Torquay."

He nodded. "Were they good to you?"

"Yes." She smiled fondly. "I'll always be grateful to them. They agreed to hire me because they respected Harry and his mother, but given my deficiency no one would have thought less of them if they hadn't."

"What deficiency?"

"You know I can't read. I'll never be a cook or upper servant because I can't make head nor tails of the receipt books or household accounts. The most women like me can hope for is to be a kitchen or housemaid, but they gave me the chance to improve myself and I made cook's assistant even though I have to memorize the receipts and be twice as careful when I assemble the ingredients."

"I'm not surprised. You may not be able to read, but

you've always been quick. You're talented and hard-working. And despite your rough life, you still have a good heart that makes people want to be near you."

She shook her head. "That's kind of you, but—"

"You've never been able to take a compliment."

She began to deny the charge, but grinned, instead. "I'll take the compliment if for no other reason than to prove you wrong."

He laughed. "There's the Rose I know."

"Mrs. Keen says the same thing." She smiled fondly. "I lived with her for several years after Harry died. She cared for Andrew while I worked to help with expenses. It was a comfort to know he was in loving and capable hands. Because of that time she's like a grandmother to Andrew and a mother to me."

"When did you move to Hopewell Manor?"

"When Andrew started school. Baron Malbury was kind enough to pay his tuition, but the school was too far from the Keen farm. The family offered us a room at Hopewell because it was close enough for him to walk."

"I see I have much to thank the Malburys for."

"Yes, the whole family is dear to me. They gave me my first glimpse of a true and happy family. They seized life and always gave thanks to God for their blessings. Guests and laughter were the means of the day. By watching them, I saw how life could be and I wanted that for myself and Andrew. I accepted the Lord as my own thanks to their and the Keens' witness. For the first time, I met Christians who treated me with love and friendship instead of judgment.

"It was a sad day, indeed, when the baron and his wife drowned last August. Their daughter, Miss Holly, is…was my employer, but she and her parents always treated the staff with dignity."

"As well they should."

"You know some employers don't." She smiled at him. "I have to say, I'm impressed by how highly your servants think of you."

"Yes, well, I'm not quite as heartless as you imagine."

She rolled her eyes and continued. "I consider Miss Holly a friend. She's especially fond of Andrew, and he fancies himself in love with her. He doesn't think anyone knows, so please don't mention it, but to see him with her is quite adorable."

The coach rolled on. With all their talk of the past, the subject of how she'd met her husband lingered in the air. His curiosity chafed him, but he could not bring himself to listen to the story of how she'd fallen in love with another man.

The carriage began to slow. He consulted his pocket watch. Where had the past three hours gone?

They came to a stop in front of a small coaching inn comprised of whitewashed walls and a thatched roof. Trees with the first flush of autumn color surrounded a gravel park crammed with a rainbow of coaches and carriages. Stables awaited the horses at the back of the main building.

"I suppose everyone could do with a break and a chance to stretch their legs." He took hold of the latch but waited to open the door.

"What is it, Sam?"

He hesitated, soaking her in. She was so pretty in her cream-colored bonnet with its edge of lace and satin ribbons.

"I appreciate your honesty. For what it's worth, I'm proud of you for making the most of your opportunities. With all my heart, I thank you for the sacrifices you made to keep our son. I want to make it up to you. I owe you that. Marry me and give me the chance to see that neither of you wants for anything ever again."

She studied him with the frankness of a seasoned investor who couldn't decide if he was worth the risk.

"Is taking a chance on me really so distasteful?"

She glanced away. "You don't owe us anything, Sam, and we don't need your charity."

"I'm not offering charity."

"Then what is it?"

"I want my son. I want him to have everything I never did."

"And I'm his mother so you have to put up with me."

"I wouldn't offer marriage just to put up with you."

"But you don't love me, either."

How dare she put him on the spot and ask for a confession when her own heart belonged to a dead man. "Love has nothing to do with this. We have a child to think of. We were good together once. If I make the necessary sacrifices, I believe we could be so again, especially for the sake of our son."

Chapter Thirteen

The rain began to fall in earnest a few miles outside of Torquay. Since their sojourn at the coaching inn yesterday, they'd enjoyed few stops save an uneventful night at a small, countryside inn.

Weary of travel and bone-rattled by the incessant sway of the coach and every bump in the road, Rose watched the passing scenery while Sam read to her from a local newspaper.

His blunt honesty yesterday had stung, but she was determined to use it to her advantage. By accepting that he did not love her, she hoped to overcome the incessant heartache that plagued her. If she could win that particular battle, perhaps she could be satisfied with friendship between her and Sam. Many couples survived on less.

The paper crinkled, drawing her attention. Sam peered at her over the upper corner he'd folded down. "Do you think he'll accept me?"

Sam's nervousness had increased tenfold since they started out this morning. He hid the wounds of his childhood so well, she sometimes forgot he suffered from the same fears of loss and rejection that she did.

"Andrew? Of course he will." She offered him a reassuring smile. Since their reunion, he'd struck her as equal parts arrogant and exhilarating, so his uncertainty now seemed all the more sweet. "He's wanted to meet you for ages."

His lips quirked. "What have you told him about me?"

"Let's see. What *have* I told him?" She pretended to give significant contemplation to the matter. "Oh, yes, now I remember. I've told him you're an ogre with green skin, one goggly eye and no teeth—"

"You're wicked." He folded the paper and tossed it aside. "Be serious."

"You slobber when you eat and growl in your sleep."

His dark eyes narrowed with a hint of humor and promised reprisal.

"And, of course, you never bathe. You stink to the moon and back."

"That's it!" He grabbed her and dragged her over to the seat beside him, tickling her without mercy. "Be warned, this is what happens to brats."

"Stop, stop!" She squirmed and kicked, laughing until her ribs ached. She gasped for air, proving herself a liar when she took in his delicious, spicy scent. "You win, you rotter."

She slapped his hands away and managed to escape back to her side of the coach. Settling into the corner, she straightened her gown and bonnet, glad he'd gotten some of his assurance returned.

"Truth to tell, I haven't told him much," she said. "I've answered his questions the best I could whenever he inquired. He knows your name and that you're employed in London, that you might return for him someday if you're able."

"If I'm able? It distresses me greatly to think a chance sighting of you on the street a few days ago is all that is between me knowing my son and missing him altogether."

"Perhaps it wasn't chance. Maybe it was Providence and you should be thanking the Lord for this opportunity."

"Why would God bother with me when he's ignored me until now?"

"Are you crazed? I've never seen a life so blessed by God as yours."

"Nonsense." His brown eyes gleamed with anger. "Was it my privileged upbringing you're referring to or the fact that I've worked sixteen to twenty hours a day for almost a decade to achieve a measure of success in the world?"

"Sam—"

"I'm not complaining, mind you. At least I've succeeded where so many others have fallen flat. But don't pretend I moved to London and coin rained down from the clouds."

"I never imagined it had." The coach turned onto the road she recognized as the way to the Keens' farm. "I think you're blessed for a number of reasons. I see the hand of God on you."

"How so?"

That he didn't scoff as she expected encouraged her on. "I see Him at every bend in the road your life has taken. It's true we both had miserable beginnings, but He was with us even then. We could have been baby farmed as infants and who would have noticed if we'd been killed? Our asylum was harsh, but at least we didn't starve or perish from fever. We went to the workhouse, but we were provided with an education unlike so many others. Or what of your meeting Mr. Stark? Just when you were about to settle for a life you didn't want in service he made an unlikely visit to our backwater town and happened to see your potential during a single hand of cards. Without your education would meeting him have mattered, anyway? And in London, such success you've achieved. You dine with lords and ladies and enjoy every material comfort.

"Someone might claim one of those instances is a product of chance or plain hard work, but taken as a whole, I'd say you have to be willfully blind not to consider God's been guiding your life and keeping you in His hand."

Watching him, she worried she'd said too much too soon. He stared out the window, silent and contemplative. *At least he's not arguing.*

The coach took another turn. Despite the sheets of rain pouring down, she recognized the stone bridge and wooden fences that belonged to the tenants of Mrs. Keen. The other two coaches in their party were continuing on to the village proper and their lodgings farther down the road.

"We'll be there soon," he said. "I remember this lane all too well."

"You do?" He possessed the memory of an elephant, but when had he ever been here? "How?"

"I followed you here from Ashby Croft when I came to take you back with me to London."

"I didn't know." The thought of their needless years

apart filled her with agony. "How did you learn of my marriage in the first place? You wouldn't tell me that first night in London."

The carriage began to slow and turn as it followed along the curved drive.

"Your friend, Molly, told me you'd come here, and the clerk in the records office sent me to the Keens', but Alistair, that weasel you worked for, blathered on about the marriage first. I didn't believe him and I left him with a black eye for lying to me."

"I'm sorry you found out that way. You and Alistair were never friends."

He gave a noncommittal grunt. "What caused me to believe you were truly wed was the Keens' housekeeper. She didn't know me and had no reason to fabricate. She said you were as 'happy as a clam' on your honeymoon in Paris."

"You're certain?" she asked through a veil of disbelief and pain. She could not imagine anyone wishing to hurt her so badly. "I've never been on a honeymoon, and Mrs. Keen's never employed a housekeeper in all the years I've known her."

"Why not? The place looks moderately prosperous."

"It is. Mind you, Mrs. Keen's not wealthy, but she enjoys a small income from a handful of tenants that keeps her comfortable."

"I only know what the woman claimed."

"What of her looks? Was she old or young?"

Sensing her rising pique, Sam didn't press the point. "She had graying brown hair and a plump figure. She was short, as I recall."

"A short, plump, brown-haired woman. She could

have been one of a dozen women I know, including the previous cook, Bessie."

"I wasn't in the best frame of mind to remember particulars that day. Perhaps that's who I spoke to and thought she was the housekeeper." He shrugged. "How long did you live here with Harry?"

"With Harry?"

She turned her attention to her lap. She didn't like talking about her husband. Was it too painful?

"Not long," she said. "He passed on within weeks of my knowing him."

"Weeks?" He couldn't hide his surprise. What kind of marriage had she had exactly? She'd already admitted it hadn't been a proper one. But she had loved and wed the bloke within a short time of meeting him. Curiosity gnawed at him. "What happened between the two of you?"

She squirmed uncomfortably. "Why do you wish to know now? I offered to tell you days ago, but you weren't interested."

"I was jealous, Rose. I couldn't bear to hear the tale of how you fell in love with another man."

Her eyes dimmed with sadness. "I'd rather not tell you the whole story. You won't like it and there are things you're better off not knowing, believe me."

"Perhaps, but I'd like you to tell me, anyway."

The tip of her tongue moistened her full upper lip. "All right. If you must know, I'll start shortly after you'd gone."

He waited anxiously while she gathered her thoughts.

"At first, everything went as we planned," she relayed in a voice without emotion. "I missed you terribly, but I knew you'd had to go and I wanted you to have your chance. But when you didn't come back within the time you said you would, the doubters were emboldened to cause me trouble."

"The doubters?"

"Yes, everyone who doubted you'd come back for me."

Everyone in Ashby Croft had known how much he loved her. "There couldn't have been many?"

Her lips turned in a cheerless smile. "Nearly everyone, Sam. Some of them even made bets."

"Well, everyone was wrong," he sneered. "What did they do?"

"I was robbed. They stole the money you left to help me meet expenses."

"Who was the vermin responsible?"

"I can't prove it, but I'm certain it was Farley Bobbins or one of his other louts. Around the same time, I fell ill and soon realized I was expecting Andrew."

Guilt piled on him like a mountain slide. "So you really didn't know about your condition before I left."

"No."

"I hate that I wasn't there for you—that I've missed out on Andrew."

Her eyes glittered with unshed tears. She looked toward the window and the pastures rolling by. "I'm sorry, too."

He waited while she collected herself. "What happened after you realized you were expecting?"

She took a deep breath before going on. "My old friend Molly let it slip that I wasn't up to snuff. Alistair appointed himself my minder as though I was some helpless child. I told him to take a flying leap, but he ignored me. He started to dock my pay because, according to him, if I wasn't going to pay for his trouble with my body, I'd have to compensate him in the usual way."

Rage coursed through Sam. His hands clenched into fists. "I'm going to murder that worthless piece of—!"

"You won't have the chance. I heard he died in a tavern brawl some three years ago."

"Good riddance."

"If you're going to fly off the handle at every turn, I'm not going to tell you any more."

He ground his teeth together.

"*You* wanted to hear this story," she reminded him. "I told you, you wouldn't like it."

The coach bounced over a rut in the road. "I'm fine now. Please continue."

Her mouth tightened as though she wasn't inclined to, but eventually she relented. "By the time you'd been gone six months, I was at the end of my tether. My job had become unbearable and I was unable to find another because Alistair had blackened my name, calling me bone idle and lippy. Molly and I had tried to room together in order to economize, but her mum took to her bed and Molly moved home to care for her.

"I didn't know what I was going to do. I'd already moved into a hole in the wall and I didn't dare not work. The dribs and drabs Alistair felt inclined to pass on to me were fewer and farther between, but up to then they'd been just enough to keep a roof over my head. And sometimes I was fortunate to find food left behind in the rooms I cleaned."

He tugged his fingers through his hair. Worse and worse. "Rose, I promise I sent money in the letters I posted. I never meant for you to suffer a single moment."

"I believe you." She studied her hands. "Perhaps Alistair got them. I don't know. At the time, I just wished you'd come back."

More guilt crushed him. No wonder she didn't believe in him after the way she'd suffered. He deserved her scorn, nothing less. "I see why you married Harry after I failed you at every turn."

She sighed. "It wasn't like that, Sam. I still hadn't abandoned hope you'd return for me. I knew you'd done what you could to see me safe and provide for me before you left. It wasn't your fault I was robbed or that Alistair took advantage of the situation. But the morning I met Harry, I'd been dislodged from my room. Alistair had refused to pay my wages for over a week and Molly said she saw him speaking to my landlord. I literally had nowhere to go unless I wanted to give in to Alistair's plans to keep me."

He saw a shudder ripple through her. He wanted to take her in his arms, to assure her he'd never let her suffer again, but he'd already offered to take care of her and she'd turned him down every time.

"I was cleaning the last room at the inn when a man by the name of John Bowden arrived. He was a reverend from Exeter and a genuine Good Samaritan. He'd found Harry shot and left for dead by the side of the road. The Reverend Bowden was certain nothing could be done to save him, but he asked me if I'd like the task of caring for him until he passed on.

"As you might expect, I could hardly believe him at first. But the Reverend Bowden was true to his word. He brought in a physician and gave me a tenner to pay for a room and anything else Harry or I might need. I'd never seen ten pounds all at once in my life, and I was shocked he promised to bring more when he came back through town in a fortnight."

"So you came to love Harry while you nursed him back to health?"

She nodded. "The physician extracted the bullet and I did my best to make Harry comfortable. After a few days, his fever broke and he began to regain his strength. We talked and talked about so many things. I told him about you and how I knew you'd be back soon. He told me about the Lord and his farm and how thankful he was for both.

"A week went by. I started to believe he'd recover, but then, without warning, he began a steady decline. He knew he was going to die and the physician agreed with him—something to do with his blood being poisoned. Knowing my circumstances, Harry asked me to marry him. I said no. I was waiting for you and I didn't want to lie to him. He told me it didn't matter since he'd be gone soon. The marriage was to please his mum. She'd be happy to take in his wife, and I could start fresh in Torquay where there were possible jobs to be found for respectable widows. I agreed because I knew once he passed on, I'd be alone again and out on the street."

"And you must have been heavy with child."

"Yes." She lowered her gaze to her lap where her hands were clasped tight. "I'd have done anything to keep from giving our baby away, Sam. I would have even gone with Alistair if I could have counted on him to keep the child safe. I used to lie awake nights wondering about our mothers and how they felt when they left us on the orphanage steps. I came to believe it must have broken their hearts."

Sam switched seats and pulled her tight against him. Instead of fighting to get away, she settled closer. He'd never considered the idea that his mother may have wanted him or that abandoning him might have been a sacrifice.

While growing up, he and the other orphans had often heard they were unwanted. They were products of bad blood, a burden to the women who'd borne them and a blight on society. Had his mother thought perchance that she was doing her best to see to his welfare or at least trying to give him a better start in life? He'd never know, but the new perspective intrigued him and the pain of abandonment he'd carried all his life eased a smidgen.

"The Reverend Bowden came back through town just as he said he would," Rose continued. "Harry told him our plan and he married us that same afternoon."

"It couldn't have been legal," he pointed out. "There was no time to post the banns or get a special license."

"True. The Reverend Bowden explained that if Harry lived, we'd have to see things done right and proper."

"Is that why you never took the Keen name?"

"I did for a short while, but I never felt it was honest once Harry died. Harry's mum understood and thought so, too, although I think she would have preferred otherwise."

He dug in his pocket for a clean handkerchief and handed it to her. She wiped her eyes and dabbed at her nose. "We took the stage to Torquay the morning after the marriage, but not without leaving word with

Molly to tell you where I'd gone. Harry wanted nothing more than to be at home when his time came. He introduced me to his mum and she took me under her wing. She never once batted an eye at my condition or made me feel unwelcome.

"Harry survived another few days." Her voice weighed heavy with sadness. "In the end, he got his wish to die in his own bed, in his own room with sunlight streaming through the window. He was well loved and most of the town came to pay their respects."

Rain beat against the coach and the wheels splashed through the puddles along the dirt lane. "I'm sorry I wasn't kinder when I spoke of Harry," Sam said through a haze of shame. "It seems he *was* a paragon."

"Yes, he was. Perhaps now you can understand why I loved him. Few men would have taken someone like me on as he did with no benefit to himself. But he had an open heart and a true love for the Lord. Never once did I hear him condemn the men who jumped him and left him for dead. He was convinced everything, good or bad, was a step on the path God designed for his life. I'm certain he had no wish to die, but he believed that if and when he did, it was simply the Lord calling him home."

Without a word, he held her tight until the coach came to a stop in front of a smallish stone house with emerald-green shutters and a matching door. Boxes hanging beneath each of the four front windows displayed a colorful mix of anemone, cornflower and zinnias.

Rose pulled away. "I believe I should speak with Andrew first."

"Whatever you think best. What do you plan to say?"

She reached for an umbrella hanging on a hook by his hat. "I'll tell him the truth. We met in London and you hoped to visit with him."

He scowled. "That sounds too temporary for my liking."

"I think it's best if we go slowly with him." Without waiting for a footman, she opened the door and unfurled the umbrella against the downpour. Quietly, she added, "Things can happen and circumstances can change. I don't want him to be disappointed if… if you're called away."

"You mean if I leave."

"I didn't mean to imply you'll leave us on a whim. I meant if something happens that you can't stay as long as you intend to." She sighed. "Let's not argue. Andrew will sense our bad temper. I want the first time he meets you to be a cheerful occasion."

He nodded, knowing she was right. He already feared having his son reject him, and the odds of that were bound to increase if the boy believed he'd made his mother unhappy. "I do, too."

Chapter Fourteen

Rose dashed the short distance to the front door, lifting her skirts to keep the hem from being muddied. While Sam sent Gibson and the others around to the stables, she knocked on the front door and jiggled the knob. To her surprise it wasn't locked. Sam joined her. They stepped inside and Sam shut the door against the crash of rain behind them.

"Hello," she called from the small entryway. "Where is everyone?"

She hung her cloak and bonnet on a rack by the door. Sam placed his coat beside hers, then noticed the small boy's jacket made of gray wool.

"He's very small?"

"No, he's just right for his age. A bit tall, actually. Lanky like you were as I recall."

"You were five years old when I was his age."

"Just so, but you'd be surprised at what I remember." She led Sam down the hall toward the parlor. "Andrew? Mrs. Keen?"

The old wood floors creaked but shone from a recent scrubbing. Warmth and comfort reigned in the rest of the snug, homey cottage. Simple, overstuffed furniture and worn, soft rugs filled the tiny, vanilla-scented parlor. Mrs. Keen's prized orchids enjoyed the area's temperate climate and were in full bloom across the mantel above the fireplace. Embroidered samplers, pretty plates and framed charcoal sketches she'd drawn of Andrew through the years decked the walls.

"You can wait in here," she told Sam. "Make yourself comfortable."

He noted the sketches right off. "Are these—?"

"Yes. I'll be back in a moment."

Behind them, footsteps thumped down the stairs. "Mummy!" Andrew's happy voice rang through the house. Her gaze flicked to Sam, who had gone stock-still and paled beneath the natural warm shade of his skin.

She sprinted into to the corridor, her own nerves running rampant all of a sudden. Andrew launched off the next-to-bottom step and raced toward her. His joyful face brought happy tears to her eyes. She'd missed him until her chest ached. She'd been gone a week, but so much had changed it seemed like a year or more.

"Mummy, you're home!" He threw himself into her arms and she caught him up against her. They hugged each other tight, his beloved giggles shrill in her ears, his dangling feet banging her knees.

"I take it you missed me, darling?" She soaked up his love like a sponge. "I missed you like mad. I think you've grown a foot."

He pulled back, his bony arms looped in a loose circle around her neck. "I thought you weren't coming back for two weeks. Granny and I have been marking the days off. Did you get my letter? We sent it in the evening post the day you left."

"I did. A friend read it to me." His excitement was contagious. His sweetness squeezed her heart. She smiled as she brushed the wisps of coal-black hair off his brow. His resemblance to his father was undeniable, but the years apart had diffused her memories of Sam. With his image vivid in her mind again, she marveled at the likeness between the two of them. She saw no part of her in Andrew except the shared blue of their eyes. "Where is Granny?"

"Asleep in her room. I'm supposed to be taking a nap."

She clucked him under the chin. "After the racket you just made, I'm quite sure you've woken her up."

A lightning strike flashed outside the window. The clouds had turned black as the storm progressed.

"Did you bring me a pressie?" Andrew asked. "Max Somerton's papa went to London and brought him back a box of toy soldiers."

"I didn't bring you soldiers," she said. "But I do have a surprise."

"A surprise?" His face lit up. "Where is it?"

Hearing his son's voice for the first time, Sam froze. Over the past few days, he'd imagined this moment more times than he could count, but nothing had prepared him for the wave of raw emotion and protectiveness that threatened to undo him.

He took a seat on the settee, hoping to calm himself before his son arrived. He recognized Rosie's handiwork in the sketches on the walls. Gifted with natural talent, she'd captured Andrew at a variety of ages.

From babyhood, with his chubby cheeks and tooth-less grin, to boyhood, climbing a tree with a bit of the imp in his eyes.

The loss of all those years tormented him. Fortunes could be earned or lost, but there was only one chance for a man to hold his newborn son, to watch him take his first step or hear him utter his first word. Worse, he knew what it meant to be fatherless, to wonder if he was truly safe in the world. It galled him that his son had suffered the same experience when he'd promised himself his own children never would.

"Max Somerton's papa went to London and brought him back a box of toy soldiers," he heard Andrew say from the hall. Rosie murmured something indiscern-ible, then, "A surprise?" Andrew exclaimed. "Where is it?"

Equal parts excitement and dread plagued Sam. As much as he wanted to meet his son, he feared the boy's rejection.

"He's in the parlor," said Rose.

"He? Is it a puppy?" The hope in Andrew's voice made Sam cringe. The boy was bound to be disap-pointed he wasn't one of the canine variety. First thing tomorrow they were headed to town. If his son wanted soldiers and a dog, he'd see that he had them.

"No, I didn't bring you a puppy," he heard Rose clarify.

He hadn't prayed since childhood, but he was tempted. Rose's talk in the coach had challenged his conviction that God wanted nothing to do with him. Before today, he hadn't thought a single conversa-tion could alter his whole outlook, but something had changed in him. Though he couldn't place his finger on precisely what, he felt as though he'd spent his whole life in darkness and the sun was starting to rise.

"I met your father in London."

Hearing Rose's hesitation, he struggled to remember the Sunday lessons from his boyhood. Nothing special came to mind, just a pleading from his heart, *Please, God, let him like me.*

"He's very eager to meet you," she said.

Silence followed. The whole house seemed to join Sam in holding his breath.

"Andrew, wait!" Rose called. "Just a moment, luv."

Sam hung his head. His worst fear had come true. The boy had run off, wanting nothing to do with him. He stood and turned, desperate to find something— anything—to lessen the expanding ache in his chest.

"Papa?"

He spun toward the small, solemn voice. Andrew stood in the doorway, his bright, hope-filled eyes exact replicas of his mother's. He looked like Rose with the same generous mouth and slim nose. He saw himself in his son's black hair and square jaw, the golden hue of his skin. Rose had been right. He was long limbed and taller than he'd expect for a boy his age. His clothes were a simple white, cotton shirt and blue breeches that had been mended more than once, especially at the knees.

"Are you really my papa?"

He swallowed hard and blinked the mist from his eyes.

"Yes, I am," he rasped, not altogether in control of his voice.

The pouring rain beat against the windows as Andrew studied him, taking his measure with a wide, sky-blue gaze. "Where have you been?"

He struggled to remember the explanation Rose had given him, but his brain wasn't functioning as well as he was used to. "I was lost, but I'm grateful now I've found you."

"I got lost the first time I had to walk here from Hopewell Manor by myself. I was frightened so I climbed a tree and waited for someone to come for me." Andrew stepped closer, hesitant, yet curious. "Mummy told me you work in London."

Sam stood firm, giving the child a chance to get used to him. "Yes, I do."

"What do you do there?"

"I buy and sell things."

Andrew sidled up to one of the overstuffed chairs. "Do you have a dog?"

Recognizing an opportunity when he saw one, he tried not to smile. "No, but I've been thinking I should get one."

"Really?" Andrew inched closer. "What kind?"

His mind went blank until he recalled his conversation with Lady Elliston. "A pug?"

Andrew's mouth twisted in silent disappointment as he crawled up on the settee. His legs hung over the edge, but his feet missed the floor by several inches. "They're nice, I suppose."

Careful not to send him running, Sam slid onto the cushioned seat next to him. "What sort do you like best?"

"I want a bulldog." He pushed his lower jaw out and curved his arms to emulate one of the odd-looking beasts. "Did you know they used them to bait bulls? I think they must be very brave animals."

"I had no idea," Sam said. "Where did you learn such a thing?"

Andrew pulled his legs up and circled his shins with his arms. "From a book Baron Malbury loaned me. He drowned in the fishing pond. I miss him. I like to read, do you? Mum can't, but I read to her."

"Yes, I like to read. What does your mum enjoy best?"

Without warning, Andrew crawled onto his lap. Startled, but overjoyed, he placed a gentle arm around his boy's narrow shoulders.

"Stories. The Bible the most," he said. "Mum likes Ester, but I like how Jesus rose from the dead and how God made Balaam's donkey talk to him. Don't you think it would be a lark to hear what a donkey has to say to you?"

"I've never considered it." Sam smiled, delighted by his son's clever and inquisitive mind. Andrew leaned against him and laid his head on his chest. Perhaps it was wishful thinking, he possessed no real experience to know for certain, but he felt the uniqueness of a father-son bond already forming between them. Sam tightened his hold, grateful for his first answered prayer. *Thank You, God. I'm in Your debt.*

"When are you leaving?" Andrew asked in the quiet moment that followed. "You don't have to go, you know. I could ask Mum if you can stay—if you want."

Hearing the undercurrent of longing in Andrew's voice, he closed his eyes and pressed a light kiss to the top of his head. Both delighted and humbled that Andrew wanted to be his son as much as he wanted to be his father, he vowed, "Now that I've found you, I'd have to be dead to ever leave you again."

From the corner of his eye, he saw Rose leaning against the door frame. She looked pained, with her full mouth tight and her eyes bloodshot. Judging by her appearance, he could not decipher whether she was pleased or saddened by his and Andrew's first meeting. He wished he possessed the ability to read her mind. He held his free arm out in an invitation for her to join them.

She stepped forward, but a creak on the stairs caught her attention and lured her back to the hall.

"My word, Rose, when did you come home?" An unfamiliar female voice carried in from out of sight. "How did you get that bruise on your face? And where in creation did you come by that magnificent dress?"

"That's my granny," Andrew whispered. "She's nice."

Sam nodded and whispered back, "Let me listen for a moment. I want to hear what your mum tells her."

Andrew quieted and strained to eavesdrop with him. Sam forced himself to be at ease lest Andrew sense his growing hostility. Ever since his talk with Rose, he'd wondered if Harry's mother might be the "housekeeper" who'd lied to him. He understood that Rose wanted to believe the best of her, but if he was right, the old lady deserved his eternal antipathy.

"I'm quite well," Rose assured her. "I came in a little while ago. Andrew said you were resting. I didn't want to disturb you."

"So you've seen the scamp?" Sam heard the fondness in Mrs. Keen's voice and more creaks as she descended the stairs. "I'm surprised it's so quiet. He must be as wild as a hare now that you're home."

Sam and Andrew shared a speaking glance. Sam smiled and Andrew stifled a giggle.

"Yes," Rose said. "He came down from his nap straightaway. He's in the parlor with a visitor I brought back with me."

"A visitor? Who is it? Shall I fetch some tea and biscuits?"

"No, there's no need. His name is Sam Blackstone." Another lightning strike, this time accompanied by the rumble of thunder. "He's Andrew's father. We met again my first day in London."

"Granny, come meet him!" Andrew shrieked.

The feminine voices in the hall died away.

Sam sighed. "You were supposed to be quiet."

Andrew looked up at him with remorse in his gaze. "I'm sorry. I just couldn't help it."

He squeezed him. "Likely story."

"Yes, do come and meet him," Rose said.

The two ladies entered the parlor together. He recognized Mrs. Keen the moment she appeared in the doorway. She was older, of course, a little rounder, her once brown hair all gray. But there was no denying she was the liar who'd dashed his hopes of finding Rose.

Were he to guess, he'd say Harry's mother was close to sixty years of age. More striking than handsome, she was short and stout. She wore a plaid gown with a black velvet collar and matching fingerless gloves. She'd pinned her white-gray hair in a tight bun on the crown of her head. If he saw her on the street, he'd count her as a perfect granny, not the confidence trickster he knew her to be.

She recognized him, too. The moment she saw him, she turned ashen and refused to look him in the eye. Red-hot anger infused him. If not for his son's presence, he might be tempted to strangle her.

"Sam." Rose stepped into the silent fray. "This is my mother-in-law, Mrs. Keen. Mother Keen, this is Mr. Samuel Blackstone—"

"My papa!" Andrew shrieked, throwing up his hands and feet in a happy explosion that narrowly missed Sam's chin.

"Hello." Mrs. Keen wrung her hands.

Sam prodded Andrew off his lap and stood. His hand on his son's shoulder to keep him close, he offered a polite bow that belied his lack of respect for her. "Hello, Mrs. Keen. I would say it's a pleasure to meet you, but then we've met once before, haven't we?"

Her gaze snapped up to meet his. Guilt scored her face, proving to him she remembered what she'd done. Tears filled her eyes. Whether crocodile or genuine, he didn't know or care. He was far from inclined to forgive her. Perhaps, if he were a gentleman, he'd possess the ability to smile, nod and pretend all was well, but as it was he enjoyed seeing her squirm.

"Sam." Rose sent a pointed glance toward Andrew, warning him to hold his peace while the child was present. She ushered Mrs. Keen to a chair near the orchid-lined hearth and helped her be seated.

"What's wrong with Granny?" Andrew said, confused by the sudden pall in the house.

"She's surprised I'm here." He looked to Rose. She'd gone quiet. This couldn't be easy for her. His vindication meant her heartbreak.

"I'm sorry, Rose," he said.

She turned to him. Her chin quivered. "What have you to be sorry for? You're the one who deserves an apology—especially from me."

Sam felt Andrew grasp his hand. "What did you do, Mummy? Were you naughty?"

Her gaze flicked to Andrew. "Go to your room, luv. Your father and I have a few questions to discuss with Granny."

"But why? What did you do?"

"She didn't do anything wrong." Sam crouched in front of him. "You need to do as she says and go to your room. We'll fetch you in a few minutes."

The boy didn't argue, but he made no pretense of being happy about his banishment, either. Sam followed him out into the hall and watched him drag his feet up the stairs as though he were climbing the gallows. Once he was certain Andrew was in his room with the door closed, he set his jaw and headed back to the parlor.

Grateful Sam had taken Andrew to his room, Rose contemplated the woman who'd been as much a mother as a mentor. As late as an hour ago she'd been convinced Mrs. Keen was incapable of deceiving her. It came as a crushing blow to learn she'd been wrong.

Lord, please show me the truth. Help me to know what to do.

"Sam said he came here to find me eight years ago. Tell me you weren't the one who sent him away."

Mrs. Keen closed her eyes and slumped in her chair. Her shoulders bowed, she shuddered and covered her eyes with her age-spotted hands. "I wish I could."

Rose's lungs seized. Was there no one in the world

who wouldn't leave or betray her? "How could you when you knew how much I loved him?"

"I'm so sorry, my dear!" Lifting her head, Mrs. Keen reached for her hand, but Rose pulled away. "Please, you must forgive me. I was trying to protect you."

Anger turned her cold. "From what? A man I've known and loved all my life? My son's own father? The choice wasn't yours to make." Her heart was as heavy and hard as a stone behind her ribs. "You claimed to love me, yet you've lied to me for years on end. And poor Sam! What did he ever do to deserve your cruelty?"

Tears rolled down Mrs. Keen's ashen face. "The day he came here I was in a haze of grief. We'd buried Harry less than a month earlier. Andrew was no more than a week to the day and you had yet to recover from the hard labor you'd suffered. Caring for the two of you gave me a purpose. I couldn't bear to lose you so soon after Harry. I felt God had given you to him and then entrusted you both to me. I was selfish, I see that now. I should have given the matter to God, but at the time, I'd convinced myself Blackstone didn't deserve you. When you came here you were without shelter, starving, barely a bag of bones. To Harry and me, it seemed he'd abandoned you. And when he did bother to return it wasn't until it suited him to do so."

"That isn't what happened," Rose said, her throat scratchy and tight. "Where was I when he came here?"

"You were upstairs sleeping." She wiped the moisture from her wrinkled cheeks. "Andrew had kept you up all night."

Mrs. Keen stood and tried to embrace her, but Rose

brushed her hands away. "No, don't come near me. You have no idea what damage you've done. You knew the agony of losing a son but saw no wrong in forcing that same pain on Sam. You denied Andrew a chance to know his father and the life of comfort he could give him. And me, you convinced me you were trustworthy, that you loved me like a parent, knowing how much I wanted to believe in you. Yet you let me suffer all these years thinking I'd been forsaken when you knew Sam had come for me." She swallowed hard, trying to maintain her composure when she longed to rant and rave at the unfairness of it all.

"Rose, listen to me," Mrs. Keen pleaded. "Ever since Harry brought you here I've loved you like a daughter. All that I've done was for your sake and Andrew's. I knew the moment I saw that man in his fancy suit and with his city ways—"

"City ways? We grew up in the same country orphanage, attended the same charity school." She laughed without humor. "Is there nowhere to go? In London they judge a body for not having money, but here, you're judged if you do."

"I don't know about London, Rose, but I wasn't born this morning. A young man with that much flash? I'm certain he meant to drag you to London with no intention of doing right by you."

"No," Rose said, her conviction unwavering. "You don't know him or how we were together. He's always done right by me. He went up to town because he would have been foolish to squander the chance when people like us had so few opportunities."

"And what of now? Has he mentioned marriage?"

"Yes, he has," she said, happy to refute Mrs. Keen's apparent belief that he hadn't—or wouldn't. "But—"

"But what?" Mrs. Keen prompted.

"I've held him off."

"Why, when you have Andrew to consider?"

"I'm afraid he only wants me now because of Andrew. That should be enough I know, but he cares for another woman now and would prefer to have her for his wife."

Sam chose that moment to reenter the room. From across the parlor, Rose felt his fury crashing off him in waves. He ignored Mrs. Keen altogether. "Rosie, the storm has let up. I'm leaving. I hope you and Andrew will come with me."

She turned, expecting to find an iceberg where he stood, but his eyes were warm and pleading. "Of course we'll come with you, Sam. Will you fetch Andrew and his belongings? Mrs. Keen and I need a few more moments."

Sam's stiff posture eased. "I suppose I can spare you another five minutes."

As soon as Sam disappeared, Mrs. Keen railed, "How can you take my boy from me when I've done so much to help raise him?"

Rose faced her, dreading what had to be said. The woman she'd loved had destroyed her best chance for happiness and denied Sam his son. "I'm not taking him from you. I'm returning him to his father. A father who will love and cherish him, I'm certain. Had you told the truth eight years ago, you would have been welcomed with open arms into our family. Sam is like me in so many ways, so in need of a mother's care. I know he could never have replaced Harry in your heart, but he would have loved you like a son."

Mrs. Keen hung her head and picked at a line in the plaid of her skirt. "I didn't know."

"Nor did you try to learn." As she turned to leave, she took in the small parlor. Memories of her time there flashed through her mind: Andrew taking his first step, the two of them playing hide-and-seek. Mrs. Keen teaching her how to knit and the many hours she'd spent sketching before the fire. In so many ways the Keens' house had been her first real home and she was saddened to leave it behind.

"I made a mistake, Rose. I let fear cloud my judgment. I've asked the Lord for His forgiveness. What can I do to earn yours?"

Rose stopped at the door. She was angry, hurt and beyond disappointed by Mrs. Keen's unthinkable behavior, but that did not mean she despised her. "You have it. I understand how treacherous fear can be, believe me. I know we've all done wrong at some time or another and I have no wish to condemn you. But neither can I pretend the trust I had in you remains or that Sam hasn't been *deeply* mistreated."

Mrs. Keen wandered to the fireplace. She clutched at the mantel for support. "Will I ever see you again?"

She heard Sam and Andrew outside the parlor. "I can't say for certain." She hated that they'd come to this when the situation might have easily been much different. "I'll pray for you and I hope you'll pray for us. Beyond that, we'll have to do what you've always taught me and see what the Lord has in store."

Chapter Fifteen

Rose joined Andrew in the hall. He held a small basket stuffed with toys and jumbled clothes neither he nor Sam had bothered to fold. "Where did your papa go?"

"He went to the stable to fetch the coach. Where are we going?"

She knelt down on one knee and helped him pull on his only pair of shoes, which she'd cut the toes out of to give him extra room to grow. She smiled to encourage him as well as herself. "We're going on an adventure. Tonight we're staying at a hotel in town. Tomorrow, we'll have to see what awaits us."

His face brightened, then shadowed. "Are you sure papa's coming, too?"

"Yes, you needn't worry." Her chest tightened at his need for reassurance. Convinced only time and Sam's steadfast presence would heal his insecurity, she stood and bent to kiss him on the forehead. "Go and tell Granny goodbye. We may not see her for some time."

He ran into the parlor and did as she bid. Mrs. Keen followed him out into the hall, stopping a short distance away. Her clenched hands and uncharacteristic hesitancy softened Rose's heart. As angry and pained as she was, she did not possess the ability to disregard the past eight years of camaraderie and memories.

The coach pulled up outside. She took Andrew by the hand and turned to go, but the image of Mrs. Keen's stricken face tugged her back. She gave the older woman a lingering hug and whispered, "Goodbye," before making a hasty exit onto the portico.

The sun had decided to make an appearance and the warmth that followed was a welcome respite from the earlier storm. Just as she pulled the door of the house closed, Sam opened the coach and helped them climb inside the comfortable interior.

To his credit, Sam made no mention of Andrew's ragged clothes or altered shoes, though she was certain he had noticed both. As the vehicle rolled down the gravel drive, Andrew pointed out the window. "Look at the rainbow, Mummy."

She glanced at the sky, not from interest, but to keep Andrew from noticing her melancholy. "It is beautiful," she said, heartened by the prism of bright colors more than she thought she would be.

Rose looked back to her family in the seat across from her. Andrew had commandeered Sam's top hat from the hook beneath the window. Several sizes too big, it looked to be swallowing his head. He sat tucked under Sam's arm, peering up at him from under the hat's rim as the two of them chatted as though they'd been best friends for years.

Her spirits lifted. Although she felt the loss of Mrs. Keen acutely, she could hardly fathom the wonder in front of her. Other than the Lord, who could have foreseen the three of them together as little as a week ago?

"Isn't the rainbow a sign of something?" Sam asked.

"That God won't ever flood the world again," Andrew informed him.

"Ah, yes, I remember. But I think this particular rainbow is a sign that God is here with us now."

"He's always with us. He never leaves us," Andrew said cheerfully. "It's promised in the Bible. Didn't you know that?"

Rose tried not to laugh at Sam's chagrin. Encouraged by his changing attitude toward the Lord, she agreed, "Yes, and you can always depend on God's word."

The coach turned off the lane and onto the main road that led to Torquay. Although Hopewell Manor was located fewer than two miles away, she'd had neither the time nor the inclination to visit town in recent memory.

This close to the water, the air took on a salty tang. Along their journey, Andrew looked out the window, pointing at various birds, a cloud in the shape of a dragon, a rabbit near the hedgerow and, finally, as they reached the center of town, the unique planting of palm trees that had become a symbol of the seaside resort's warm, Mediterranean clime.

As Andrew exclaimed over boats in the harbor, Sam nudged her foot with his. "How are you?"

She smiled, appreciating his concern after her confrontation with Mrs. Keen. "I'm bruised, but I'll rally."

"I'm sorry you were hurt." He glanced at Andrew, who was leaning out the window. Taking him by the waistband, Sam pulled him back inside and plunked him on the seat. "Have a care, my boy. You're a human not a monkey."

"Eeee, Eeee, Aaah, Aaah." Andrew took the proclamation as a challenge. Curving his arms—one to scratch his head, one to scratch his ribs—he mimicked the monkey Sam claimed he wasn't.

Sam rolled his eyes and ruffled Andrew's hair. "That will teach me."

"It's your fault he's in such high spirits." Rose was still laughing when they stopped before a Georgian terrace that had been refashioned into a luxurious harborside hotel. Although not as fashionable as Bath or Brighton, Torquay had been rising in the estimation of wealthy, winter tourists for the past decade. The mild, healthful temperatures, lovely seaside walks and favorable sailing conditions made an ideal respite from London's cold winters.

A uniformed doorman welcomed them into the rich, but understated reception area. The melodious song of a piano greeted them from a connecting parlor. Gilded beams crisscrossed the plastered ceiling and acres of thick, red carpet covered the floor.

Taking Andrew firmly by the hand, she instructed him to be calm and well behaved before escorting him to an antique settee tucked away in a corner where they might go unnoticed.

While Sam saw to their arrangements, Andrew rested against her as they listened to the music, a popular tune by Chopin that she'd often heard Miss Holly play at Hopewell Manor.

The hotel was renowned throughout the county and never once had she dared to imagine she'd be a guest here one day. Cream wallpaper with a complex vine and red pomegranate design provided a perfect backdrop for the red-silk drapes framing the windows that overlooked the sparkling sea. A forest of ship masts bobbed in the water beyond the sickle-shaped wharf.

Fashionable ladies and gentlemen milled about the parlor or strolled arm in arm on the shop-lined street.

"Doesn't she know one is supposed to leave the urchins on the street outside?" A young, well-dressed woman smirked in an aside to her companion as they passed her and Andrew.

Rose's protective instincts rushed to the fore. She drew Andrew closer and arranged her skirt to cover his ragged shoes and bare shins.

"Who is that man, Mummy?"

"What man?" She dismissed the rude woman from her mind and looked down into Andrew's troubled face before searching the parlor for any suspicious characters.

"He's gone now. He was looking in the window, frowning at you."

She gave him a reassuring squeeze. "I shouldn't worry, darling. I don't know anyone here. The man, whoever he was, was probably trying to locate someone or perhaps had the sun's glare in his eyes."

Sam found them. Tall, strong and radiating energy, he claimed the interest of everyone in the parlor, especially the ladies if the sudden outbreak of fan fluttering and curious whispers was any indication. With a room full of eyes on him, Sam offered a polite nod of his head before dismissing them all to focus on her. She could not help smirking at the woman who'd insulted her and Andrew earlier, before smiling up at Sam.

"All is set," he said. "The servants arrived an hour ago. They're seeing to the room and unpacking at present. We've engaged the whole second floor. You and

Andrew have a suite and I'm across the hall. Prudence and Mary are next to you while the male servants are split up amongst the balance of rooms."

"How generous of you to keep them all here."

He shrugged. "It's easier."

She didn't comment, but he was the first employer she'd come across that didn't house his people over the stables or in the cheaper attic rooms that were always too cold or too hot.

His kindness pleased her, but then he'd always been kind. In anger she'd accused him of the opposite while they were in London, but his thoughtfulness toward her and his servants had proven her wrong time and again.

Andrew wiggled in his seat. "Mummy, are we going to tea soon? I'm hungry."

"Yes, Mum, when are we going to eat? I'm famished." Sam grinned at her. "The concierge mentioned there's a tearoom a few doors down. Does that suit?"

"It suits me," Andrew opined.

Rose laughed. "It suits me fine, as well, but shouldn't we visit our rooms first?"

"Whatever for?" Sam looked her over from head to toe. "You look lovely as always. Even travel-worn you put these other ladies to shame."

Her face heated. He had to be joking, but his compliment gave her confidence. "Andrew needs to change his shirt."

"He's fine—"

"Yes, I'm fine," Andrew agreed. "Besides, if I spill something on this one it won't matter."

Sam's smile widened and his dark eyes sparkled with mirth. "Try and defy such logic. I dare you."

"I wouldn't know where to begin," she said as Sam

mimicked Andrew's exaggerated pout and hopeful, puppy-dog eyes. "The two of you are pitiful."

Seeing the two males exchange triumphant grins, she stood in a mock huff. "Now I see how it's going to be with the two of you rascals always banding together against me."

Outside the hotel, they walked along the cobblestoned high street, the three of them holding hands with Andrew in the middle. Although the light was still bright and warm, the sun had begun its initial decline toward evening. A slight chill invaded the salt-tinged air. Water lapped at the sea wall while gulls screeched and swooped overhead. A symphony of other sounds—the clack of horse hooves, the melody of a street musician's flute, the bark of a dog and the conversation of other pedestrians—made for a pleasant and lively promenade.

"There's the shoemaker's shop," Sam said. "Let's stop there to order a new pair for Andrew."

Andrew started to protest, but a silencing glance from Sam cut the objections short.

"He never quiets for me with such ease." Rose laughed at her son's downcast face. "How is that?"

"He's trying to impress me." Sam opened the door to the shoemaker's. The ring of a bell announced their arrival as Andrew skipped across the threshold. "When he's accepted that I'm truly a part of his life, no doubt he'll try to defy me, as well."

The tang of leather and tobacco pervaded the shop. A menagerie of shoe forms and patterns hung on the back wall. Shoes, boots and a selection of materials formed a colorful display on a long table in the middle of the narrow room.

A balding man with a swooping mustache joined them from the workshop behind a blue curtain. Smoke rose from the pipe at the corner of his mouth. Dressed in trousers and his shirtsleeves, his braces dangling from his waist, he looked ready to retire for the night. "What can I get you?"

Sam stepped forward. "We'd like to order shoes for my boy here."

Rose moved back, watching the process unfold. It was a novel experience not to have to worry about the expense of a necessity. Andrew sat like a statue as the man bent down to make an outline of his foot. He'd never had shoes made to fit since Rose acquired his from the church's charity box or bought them second- and third-hand.

Within a quarter of an hour, they were back on the street. Andrew's old shoes had been replaced with a pair of soft, leather slippers and Sam had ordered two more pairs of sturdy shoes, an additional pair of walking boots and another pair for riding. To Rose's disbelief he'd paid triple their price to have the lot ready by the day after the next.

As they made their way to the tearoom, Rose's head was spinning. Since Andrew's birth, she'd borne the heavy responsibility of fulfilling all of his needs on her own. God had been good and provided her with help in the shape of Mrs. Keen and the Malburys, but she'd never been able to escape the underlying sense of guilt and indebtedness that accompanied the constant need to rely on the favor of others to survive.

"I sat very still while the man drew the pattern of my foot," Andrew told her as though she hadn't been there. "Are you proud of me?"

"I'm always proud of you," she assured him. Seeing his excitement was bittersweet. Although the Lord and careful money management had stretched her meager wages to provide for their needs, there had been few if any extras. Like any proud mother, she wanted her child to shine and be happy. Always having to deny Andrew's simplest request for a toy or to dress him in ill-fitting clothes because she could afford no better had been a burden that chipped away at her own self-worth.

"What are you thinking?"

"That you were right. Money does make the world go round. In a quarter of an hour you were able to swoop in and buy him more happiness than I've been able to manage in the last eight years."

"What are you talking about? He's tremendous."

"Thank you. I think he is, too. Don't misunderstand me, Sam. I'm grateful, truly. What mother doesn't want her child to have the best of everything? I've done my best to provide for him, but as you can see, I haven't succeeded very well."

"The children I know have everything in terms of material possessions but aren't half as well cared for or cheerful. You are an excellent mother and I'm grateful my children will have you for theirs."

"Children?" She stumbled on a cobblestone, but Sam steadied her before she fell.

"We will be having more, won't we?" he asked straight-faced. "You always said you wanted a dozen."

"And I want a brother," Andrew piped in, his attention divided between the conversation and a ship sailing by.

Her gaze caught Sam's to warn him they should be more mindful of what they said in front of the child.

He nodded in understanding. "Ah, here we are." He opened the door of the tearoom and waited for them to precede him.

Inside, the aromas of coffee, chocolate and sugar mingled with the citrus scent of lemon, smoked meats and fresh-baked breads.

Sam moved through the crush of waiting patrons with ease to speak to the host taking names.

"The wait won't be long, I shouldn't think," he said upon his return. Rose found that hard to believe considering the number of people ahead of them, but she was pleasantly surprised when he turned out to be correct and the host called, "Blackstone."

She began to expect foul play when they were led to a coveted table in front of the window overlooking the street. Dressed in embroidered linen and graced with a small vase of wildflowers, the table employed a cushioned window bench along with two chairs for seating. The window was bedecked with lace that had been stained with tea for a soft, antiqued effect.

"How did we come by this excellent table so fast?" she whispered to Sam. "Did you bribe someone?"

"What's a bri—?"

She covered Andrew's mouth with her palm. "I'll tell you later, darling."

Sam frowned. "Why should you think I'd do such a thing?"

She arched her eyebrow. "I remember how impatient you can be."

"Fine," he grouched. "Although I wouldn't call it a bribe. I merely mentioned to the gentleman we would like the first available table by the window and he happened to prove open to the suggestion when a fiver dropped from my wallet in front of him."

"Five pounds…?" She shook her head, feeling squeamish at how easily he discarded money. The amount was more than she earned in months, and his deep pockets underscored how different their lives were. "That's ghastly. You'd best be careful or you'll beggar yourself. You were already robbed by the shoemaker."

A serving girl delivered menus. Rose managed to make out a few of the dishes on offer before the letters began to rearrange themselves. She handed the crisp sheet of paper to Andrew. "What does it say, darling?"

As he perused the list, she told Sam, "Next time you decide to purchase something let me bargain for you. Clearly, you're out of the habit, or have you simply lost the knack?"

"I saw no need to quibble. In London, I'd pay thrice the price I paid, so I managed quite well if you ask me."

"If you say so."

"I do." He served her a meaningful glance. "Sometimes getting what you want is worth any price."

Including marrying her for Andrew's sake and sacrificing his happiness with Miss Ratner. "What if what you want can't be bought?"

"Then one employs a great deal of patience and waits for the right moment to take it."

Was he reneging on his promise not to take Andrew if it suited him?

"Well, I want chocolate," Andrew said, oblivious to the underpinnings of their conversation.

Sam turned to him with a smile. "Anything you want, son—"

"A bulldog?" he asked sweetly.

"Anything you want to eat," Sam amended. "Just don't make yourself ill. Your mum will be cross with me if you do and that will make me cross with you."

The serving girl returned with a china cup and saucer for each of them before asking for their order. Sam sat back, allowing Andrew to pick and choose from the menu, an unusual event given the prevailing wisdom that children should to be seen and not heard.

Andrew hesitated at first but soon warmed to the task. Along with tea for her and coffee for Sam, he requested a pot of chocolate for himself. He chose a variety of savory sandwiches, crumpets with Devonshire cream, jam, raisin cake, berries and sweet biscuits.

"Is that all?" Sam asked drily. "Don't you think you should order something for your mother?"

"I ordered her tea," Andrew said without skipping a beat.

Rose pulled a face at him. "Just remember, sweetling, in most families the parents eat first."

Chuckling at Andrew's aghast expression, the waitress departed, but soon returned with their hot beverages and a small stack of plates. As they waited, they sipped their drinks and commented on the activities outside the window. Andrew found several hats worthy of his amusement. "That one looks like she's wearing a skunk." They noted the gulls diving for their supper and the setting sun's vibrant display of red, gold and purple.

Their food began to arrive. Displayed on a tower of three plates, the dainty sandwiches were made of cheese, smoked salmon with dill sauce, cucumbers with butter, and ham with rich, brown mustard. The raisin cake came next, then a basket of crumpets. Crocks of Devonshire cream, butter and jam were squeezed into the center of the table, followed by another round of drinks.

Andrew's eyes widened a bit more with each new offering. Rose understood his reaction. Many times, she'd crafted similar fare for her employers and their guests, but it was a rare treat for her and Andrew to partake of such a luxurious bounty.

Andrew took each of them by the hand. Sam looked at him askance. "Papa, pray for us and hurry, please. Those sandwiches look lonely."

Looking to Rose for encouragement, Sam cleared his throat. She doubted he'd prayed since his youth, but he didn't decline the duty, either. "Dear God, thank You for this food and for bringing my family back to me. Amen."

Rose prepared Andrew a plate of sandwiches and raisin bread, which he slathered with butter and tucked into with verve. By the time she and Sam had filled their own plates he was reaching for a second helping.

Andrew ate and ate, while she and Sam enjoyed the repast at a more leisurely pace.

"Have you ever been to Torquay?" Rose asked Sam. "We talked quite a lot about coming here to enjoy the seaside, but we never could afford the trip before you left."

"No, but I'm starting to suspect my mistake. The town's charming enough and has a fine reputation to build upon. With a relatively minor infusion of capital, I'd say there's great profit to be found here."

"Are you always focused on turning a profit?"

He took a drink of his coffee. "It's habit. I haven't done much else in the last nine years."

"Are you very rich, Papa?"

He winked at Andrew. "Very."

"Then can I go to school? I heard Mummy tell Granny I might not be able to since Baron Malbury died."

Mortified, Rose stiffened as understanding dawned in Sam's eyes. "We'll see you go school, son. You'll have the best education money affords."

More food came. A side table was unfolded, covered in a pretty floral cloth and laden with bowls of berries and sweet, crisp biscuits.

"Can I have the last salmon sandwich?" Andrew asked.

Sam looked at him, amazed. "Where did you put the last one?"

"Mum says I have a hollow leg." He grinned. "Today I seem to have two."

The tally arrived. Sam read the piece of paper and released a low whistle under his breath as he reached for his wallet. "Your mother's right, my boy, you're bound to beggar me at this rate, but I suppose you're worth it."

"Too bad I can't bargain for you here," she said, taking a sip of warm tea.

"No matter. We'll save your powers of negotiation for something important."

"Such as?"

"When we buy a new carriage or house." He chuckled. "Oh, what fun *that* shall be. Winters won't know what hit him."

"Winters? Wasn't he the fine-looking fellow at your dinner party? As I recall, he flirted with me like mad."

"Is that so?" His jaw tightened and he sounded almost...jealous. "I suppose I can't blame him. You've always been beautiful. He'd have to be blind not to want you."

"Well, he can't have her." Andrew popped a berry in his mouth. "She's ours."

"Quite right," Sam agreed. "She definitely is."

Warmed by the sudden regard in his gaze, she endeavored to change the subject before she did or said something foolish. "You were saying?"

He didn't laugh outright, but she could tell he enjoyed her discomfort. "Jake Winters is my friend and business associate. He manages the bulk of the firm's real estate. He's a genius and ruthless, but you're sure to make mincemeat of him."

"I assure you, I don't know what you're talking about."

"Precisely." He extracted several coins from his pocket and placed them with the bill on the table. "That, sweetheart, is what makes you dangerous."

Chapter Sixteen

"Papa, I've been thinking about what we should do today."

As he finished tying his cravat, Sam met Andrew's gaze in the mirror. A week of getting to know his son had gone by since he and Rose had first arrived in Torquay. Every day the three of them were together made him long to make their family official, and he was at his wits' end trying to convince Rose to marry him.

He'd given up resisting her at the teahouse their first night in town. He had tried to make himself believe he didn't want to love her again, but the fact was he'd never stopped. For all his efforts to set her from his mind over the years, he'd been unable to forget her or to ply her from his heart.

Seeing her with Andrew had shown him what it meant to have a worthwhile life. For so long he'd been limping along, certain he knew what was important when his existence was as empty as the massive mausoleum he called a house.

"Shall I guess?" He smiled fondly at his son, still not quite used to the joy of having him in his life. So far, they'd explored the local highlight of underground caverns, watched seals sunning on the rocks, collected shells from the various beaches and gone fishing with one of the town's many old salts. "Why don't we start with a hearty breakfast, followed by a trek through the forest above the cliffs and then—"

"Did you forget today is Sunday? We need to go to church."

He faced Andrew, who was sitting with his knees pulled up to his chest and tucked under his billowy sleep shirt.

"You *want* to go to church?" He hadn't been to service since he'd left the orphanage at sixteen, but he couldn't deny there had been a change in his attitude toward God of late. Ever since Rose had pointed out the blessings in his life.

Andrew nodded. "Don't you?"

"To be honest, I haven't considered it. I haven't been to church in a long time." He pulled on his boots. "You've been doing a fine job reading the scriptures to us each evening. Indeed, I've rather enjoyed discussing them with you. Wouldn't you prefer to continue in that vein?"

"Reading the Bible isn't the same as going to church."

"Church is a building, son, nothing more. I've heard some people believe God can be worshipped anywhere."

"I suppose He can, but that's not church. We have to go."

Seeing the boy's obvious distress disturbed him. He remembered the fire-and-brimstone sermons of his youth and wondered what sort of guilt-laden nonsense they were teaching him. He began to wonder if it wouldn't do Andrew good to skip a few services just in case he'd developed some sort of unnatural dependence or unhealthy religious beliefs. "Perhaps next week."

"I want to go today," Andrew insisted.

For the first time since they'd met, he began to get annoyed with the boy. Rose had warned him a clash was bound to happen, but he'd thought the disagreement would arise from declining to buy a trinket of some kind or not allowing him to eat as many sweets as he wanted, not from refusing to take him to church of all places.

He started to put his foot down, but something inside him warned him to ask, "Why do we *have* to go?"

Andrew picked at the bedcover. "I like the music and I always learn something from the vicar…and… do you promise you won't tell Mummy?"

Big, blue eyes peered up at him, pleading for him to understand. He began to worry. Had someone threatened him? Hurt him in some way that he felt forced to go to church as some sort of penance? He shifted uncomfortably in his seat, completely out of his depth and starting to doubt he had the stuff to make a good father. Where was Rose when he needed her? "Andrew, I can't promise to keep a secret from your mother when I don't know what the matter is about. If you're in some sort of trouble—"

"Oh, no, I haven't been naughty. You can't tell Mum because she's…she's a girl."

Sudden understanding, followed by massive relief swept over him. His son was in need of a man-to-man chat. Tenderness engulfed him. How long had the child been suffering with this secret and wishing he had another male to confide in? He patted his lap. "Why don't you come over here and tell me the whole story."

Andrew jumped off the bed and scrambled into his lap. "We have to go to church because Miss Holly is going to be there." His expression turned wistful. "She's the prettiest, nicest, most perfect girl there is besides Mummy. She has red hair and green eyes... I want to marry her when I'm grown up."

He smiled fondly. "Maybe you will. I was about your age when I decided to marry your mum— although I knew I loved her long before then."

"You did? Then why didn't you marry her? Mummy thinks you don't want to anymore."

"Impossible." He'd asked her, threatened and reasoned with her ever since he'd learned about Andrew. "What makes you think so?"

"I heard her talk in her sleep. Usually, she's quiet, but sometimes she's not. One time she had a whole row with Granny."

He forced a laugh, but his mind had wandered to Rose in the suite across the hall. He'd been quite clear with his intentions of marriage. She was the one who perpetually denied him.

He shook his head in disbelief. "Andrew, I do intend to marry your mother. It's my fondest wish and sincerest hope that the three of us are never parted again."

Andrew's face lit up. He threw his arms around Sam's neck and squeezed until Sam couldn't breathe. "We're going to be a real family! The lads at school won't be able to call me bad names anymore."

Stung by that inadvertent admission, he tightened his arms around the boy. A ball of emotion thickened in his throat. He'd been called those foul names, as well.

As a child he'd felt the insults like a lash. He hated that his son had known that kind of pain because of him. Not that he needed one, but here was another reason he should have married Rose and done things in the proper order all those years ago. He pressed a kiss to Andrew's forehead, wishing once again he could turn back time.

Another knock on the door. "Come in," Andrew called.

Rose poked her head into the room.

"We're going to church," Andrew announced with a happy grin before she managed to speak a word.

A ripple of surprise crossed her face, and her eyes met Sam's in a fleeting glance. She smiled at Andrew. "That's wonderful, darling. We'd better see you dressed."

Andrew wiggled off his lap. He stopped at the door. "Thank you, Papa."

Rose watched him go. The door clicked shut across the hall before she said, "I didn't think you'd care to join us."

His eyebrow arched. "You mean you planned to go without me?"

"We never miss Sunday service if we can help it. Andrew loves to see Miss Holly. What changed your mind?"

He shrugged. "He asked me to come. How could I deny him?"

"I'm glad you didn't."

"Aren't you concerned the gossips' tongues will wag when they see us together?"

"I'm more concerned for you. If I'd known a simple invitation would stir you, I would have offered one myself."

"Rose?" He called when she turned to leave.

She turned back. "Yes?"

"Andrew said those twits at school tease him because he's illegitimate. Did you know?"

She glanced away. "Yes. I've done my best to ease his mind and for the most part he gets on well at school, but there's only so much I can say or do to address that particular point."

He nodded. She knew the boy's trials as well as he did. Her own childhood had been fraught with ridicule, not only because of the circumstances of her birth, but because of her learning difficulties.

He stood and went to her at the door. Dressed in a cream-colored gown edged with yellow satin, she looked young and wholly feminine. He took her hand and brushed his thumb across the tiny, white scars where her teachers had rapped her knuckles to motivate her to read. "You know he suffers and you still won't marry me?"

She flinched. "That's so unfair."

"But what you're doing is right and proper? Tell me the truth, not excuses. Why do you insist on rejecting my proposal?"

Her arms banded about her waist as though she wished there was a wall between them. "Because I'm certain we'd be making a mistake. No one is sorrier than I am that Andrew suffers because of our past sins, but we're bound to cause more problems for us all if we continue to do what we know is wrong."

"And spending the rest of your life with me is wrong?"

She swallowed deeply and refused to look at him. "Yes, yes, it would be."

She disappeared into her room. He slammed his own door behind him, mentally kicking himself for the folly of broaching the sensitive subject in the first place.

He sat on the edge of the bed, his elbows on his knees, his face in his hands. "Dear God, are You there? Can You hear me? What should I do?" The questions startled him. Discomfited to be talking to the air, he reclined against the soft pillows and crossed his booted ankles at the foot of the long mattress.

Why was Rose so determined to believe that being together would be a mistake? Surely, she wasn't so in love with Harry Keen that she'd sacrifice her son's best interests on an altar of loyalty to a dead man, would she?

"Papa?" Andrew rapped on the door. "Have you called for the carriage?"

He swung his legs over the side of the bed and joined Andrew in the hall. "You look dapper, son." The boy beamed in obvious pleasure of his new, blue sailor suit with white piping on the collar.

Rose ventured from her room. "I hope I didn't keep you long." She'd added a yellow hat, embroidered purse and yellow gloves to the cream gown she'd been wearing earlier. With her blond hair and smooth complexion, she reminded him of a daisy.

How she believed she'd never fit into his world was beyond him.

A half hour later, they arrived at an ancient parish church a mile outside of Torquay. Situated on a cliff overlooking the sea, the church was surrounded by moss-covered grave markers and gnarled oak trees dressed in a display of vibrant autumn color. The distant crash of waves against the beach below mingled with the song of bells emanating from the square-shaped tower.

The moment all three of them left the carriage, Andrew tugged on his hand. "We have to hurry. I want you to meet Miss Holly. I wish we could sit by her, but Mummy's one of her kitchen maids and Mrs. Michaels says we have to sit with the servants."

Frowning at that bit of news, he allowed Andrew to lead them into the cool interior of the dimly lit church. Mrs. Michaels must be the cook or housekeeper in charge of the Malburys' female servants. He wondered if word of Rose's dismissal had reached the household from London and how surprised they'd be when she turned up this morning.

As the three of them progressed up the center aisle, Sam removed his hat and nodded politely to the onlookers casting interested, though not unkind, glances his way. Candles flickered on the altar and the aged pews shone from a recent cleaning with pine oil, judging by the scent in the air. Sunlight pierced a stained-glass window, spreading a prism of color across the chancel and altar.

He hadn't been in a church in years, but against all his expectations, he didn't feel out of sorts. Indeed, he felt strangely welcome.

"Where are we going?" asked Rose. "These pews are for the local gentry. We usually sit farther back."

He decided then they'd sit up front. "I'm following Andrew."

"He's probably looking for Miss Holly," she said,

waving to someone behind him. "I'll return in a moment. I see a friend I wish to give my regards."

Rose wasn't more than a few steps away when Andrew came to a sudden stop. "There she is," he said, his whisper excited, but hushed so as not to disturb the reverent quiet of their surroundings. "The girl with the red hair in the black dress. Isn't she wonderful?"

Amused by his son's dreamy expression, he perused the general area and small clutch of parishioners waiting for the service to begin. Based on the description he'd been given, he found Andrew's beloved standing beside the second pew, surrounded by a circle of people trying to speak with her at once. Although she smiled and nodded appropriately, she appeared to be looking for someone. Her auburn hair and pale, flawless skin contrasted vividly with the mournful black of her gown and short, cage veil.

"She's a stunner, my boy, but don't you think she's a mite too old for you?"

Crestfallen, Andrew looked as though he'd shot him. "I don't think so."

Sam groaned inwardly. Again, he should have handled the situation better. When would he get the hang of this father business? Besides, who was he to question the ways and means of love when his own romantic life was such a muddle?

"And she's only nineteen," Andrew grumbled.

"Nineteen, eh? Well, what's eleven years when it comes to matters of the heart?" he said, trying to patch up his previous blunder.

Andrew scowled. "I thought you'd understand, but you think I'm too little to know what love is like."

"No, I don—"

The powerful notes of an organ drowned him out, signaling the start of service. Rose came up behind him and tugged on his sleeve. "I have seats for us in the back."

"I'd prefer to sit near the front. I want to be certain I can hear." He didn't give her a choice except to follow unless she preferred to sit by herself. She came with them, but he sensed her unease with the attention they drew and the curious glances directed at him.

He steered Andrew into the second row across the aisle from Miss Malbury. Rose followed suit before he sat beside her. "It's a church," he whispered in Rose's ear once they were settled. "You have as much freedom to sit where you like as everyone else."

The congregation stood and began to sing "Awake, My Soul, And With The Sun." As she sang the words, she seemed to consider his statement with a furrowed brow and a thoughtful frown. Before his eyes, her expression slowly transformed until she smiled up at him.

"You're right," she said for him alone. "In God's house I'm first-rate, not second."

Bravo, he thought in silent approval. It was a small improvement, but her realization that she was as good as anyone present was a step in the right direction. She claimed they were worlds apart, but if he succeeded in convincing her of her worth, perhaps she'd accept her place as his wife.

He tipped his head down to her level. "You're always first with me, sweetheart." He turned his attention to the service before she could brush him off. From the corner of his eye he saw Miss Malbury cast Andrew a kind smile and mouth, "Hello." She must know the boy's fondness for her and aimed to treat him gently.

Several more hymns were sung before the congregation sat down in unison. The candles on the altar flickered. Despite the well-attended service all was quiet, reverent.

The vicar approached the pulpit. A middle-aged man with thinning, brown hair, he slipped on a pair of spectacles before he opened his notes. "Our scripture for today is from the book of Revelation, chapter three, verses nineteen through twenty-one. 'Behold, I stand at the door, and knock: if any man hear My voice, and open the door, I will come in to him, and will sup with him, and he with Me.'"

As the vicar continued to speak, the scriptures spoke to Sam as none others ever had. The words flowed through his veins like a living, breathing force, pinning him to the pew. Unwilling to move lest he lose this marvelous sense of clarity, he didn't precisely understand what was happening.

Although he'd heard of Christ's love and that He'd died for the sins of the world, he'd been taught about God's wrath and judgment more times than not. He'd been led to believe God wanted perfect people, not flawed wretches like he was, so the image of Jesus knocking on a man's heart spoke to him. Far from being distant, disinterested or wrathful, Christ desired to be his friend.

What a fool I've been, Lord. We haven't spoken for years, but I ask you to forgive me and hear me now. Knock on my heart no longer, but come in and take up residence, instead.

From the corner of his eye, he noticed Rose watching him with concern. He smiled and reached for her hand. Their fingers intertwined.

He listened to the service. Rose had been right that day in the carriage. Looking over his life, he saw the hand of God at work as far back as his first memory.

Forgive me for my blindness and stupidity, Lord. All these years I thought You'd forgotten me, but now I see You've been beside me all the while. Thank You for protecting my family and restoring them to me when I don't deserve them. Be the Father I never had and help me be the father my son needs.

"Are you all right?" Rose asked quietly.

His heart was full and overflowing with a newfound love for God. His whole life seemed brighter and filled with hope. He lifted her hand and kissed the back of her knuckles. "Better than I've ever been."

The last note of the organ was still reverberating through the church when Holly Malbury crossed the aisle to greet Andrew and Rose. She reached into her black, jet-beaded reticule and removed a sweet wrapped in paraffin paper for Andrew. "This is for after your tea unless your mother permits it before then."

Andrew looked up at her lovingly and offered a polite, "Thank you," before tucking the sweet in his pocket. "Would you like to meet my papa?"

"I'd love to, sweetness." Holly turned spring-green eyes on Sam. "I did wonder at your visitor."

Rose stepped in and finished the introductions. To Sam's way of thinking, the friendliness between her and her former employer spoke well of Miss Malbury.

Once they exchanged pleasantries, Holly held Andrew's hand as the four of them meandered outside.

Many of the coaches and carriages had already departed, but other parishioners mingled in the churchyard, enjoying the cool, autumn breeze.

Sensing Rose wished to speak with her friend in private, he put on his hat and motioned for Andrew to come to him. "We'll be in the coach. Take as long as you like."

Disgusted to be shuffled off, Andrew dragged his feet. "Why did we have to leave?" he complained as he climbed into the vehicle.

"Because the ladies want to be alone. You don't want Miss Malbury to think you're a nuisance, do you?"

"I guess not," he said glumly.

Rose and Holly moved to stand by one of the ancient oaks. "Here." He lifted Andrew onto his knee. "You have a perfect view of your ladylove, but keep in mind it's bad form to let her catch you staring and even worse to drool."

Andrew leaned back against his chest as the two of them watched the objects of their affection.

Andrew chuckled.

"What's so amusing?"

"With Miss Holly in black and Mummy in white, they look like salt and pepper, don't they?"

Laughing, Sam agreed.

Wind rustled the trees, sending a flurry of colorful leaves across the churchyard. One man's top hat went flying and more than a few women had their hair curls ruffled.

"Andrew, when did you become a Christian?"

"Last year," he said, his attention remaining on Miss

Malbury. "I asked Mummy to pray with me and Jesus moved into my heart. When did you?"

"This morning."

Andrew twisted around to look up at him. "This morning? But you're old. What took you so long?"

Sam choked on his laughter. "Foolish things and misunderstandings. I wish I'd been wise like you and come to my senses at your age."

A few moments later, the women hugged and parted ways. Andrew moved to the other seat in order to watch Holly Malbury climb into her own coach, a gleaming green-and-gold pair in hand with matched bay geldings.

The footman opened the door for Rose, and Sam gave her a hand up.

"I'm sorry to keep you waiting," she said as the coach sprang into motion. "Miss Malbury received word of my dismissal yesterday. She wanted to know what happened and assured me I still have my place at Hopewell Manor if I want it."

Sam tensed. "I hope you told her you didn't."

She glanced out the window without answering him.

"I'm hungry," Andrew announced. "Can I have my sweet from Miss Holly?"

Rose turned to him. "Wait until after we eat. You'll spoil your meal if you don't."

Andrew pulled the small treat from his pocket and held it up in front of her. "I promise you, Mummy, my stomach is bigger than this."

"If you're going to be cheeky, I'll toss it out the window."

He buried the treat back in his pocket. "Why are

you cross? You should be happy. Papa became a Christian today."

She gasped and swiveled back to Sam. Her brilliant smile lit up her whole countenance and made him warm inside. "Is that true? When?"

He nodded. "During the service. I realized you were right. I could cry coincidence for the good turns in my life, but I know that's a lie. Far from being distant, God has been right in front of me, leading my way. When I heard the verse about Christ knocking on the door of a man's heart, I knew He was knocking on mine and I had to answer."

The coach rounded a bend. "I could tell something special had happened. I can't begin to express how thrilled I am. I…" Happy tears rained down her face. "This is marvelous…just brilliant…wonderful."

Joyful himself, he couldn't help laughing at her reaction. He reached into his coat pocket and handed her a clean handkerchief. "It is rather wonderful. I see now that I was an imbecile to wait so long."

"Yes, but—"

"You needn't agree so readily on that point."

She smiled. "As a Christian, I strive to be honest."

Andrew giggled. "Oh, Papa, Mummy got you there."

He ruffled Andrew's hair. "She certainly did. Now I'll have to see if I can get her."

Chapter Seventeen

Sam strode through the hotel's reception area. Piano music wafted in from the parlor along with a cool breeze through the open windows.

In the three days since he'd opened his heart to the Lord, the trappings of his life had changed little, but his true self had altered in ways he was just beginning to understand. For years he'd believed he was alone and unwanted except for his wealth. Left to his own devices he'd built walls to protect him from returning to the degradation of his youth and, ultimately, an existence as joyless as a one-note tune.

To his amazement, in the space of a fortnight, the Lord had changed him and his life beyond recognition. Faith had replaced his fear and he'd been given a priceless blessing in Andrew. As yet, Rose still had to be convinced to stay with him, but her mere presence in his life was a marvel given that he'd thought he'd lost her irrevocably. For a man used to having more money than he could ever spend, he suddenly found himself in deeper debt than he could ever repay.

Sam glanced at the clock above the reception desk.

Quarter past eleven. A few minutes remained until Rose and Andrew were due to return from their outing to fetch the boy's clothing they'd ordered the previous week. In their absence he made some purchases of his own. For Andrew, he'd found a kite and for Rose, a proper set of art supplies. He hoped they'd be up to a picnic on a secluded beach they'd found earlier in the week.

He stopped at the concierge's desk. An earnest, young fellow with fashionably long sideburns and an overabundance of pomade in his combed-over hair hastened to greet him. "How may I help you, sir?"

"I'd like to have a hamper prepared within the hour." He named several foods he knew Rose and Andrew enjoyed. "And any other delectable items on offer."

"Very good, sir. I'll see to it immediately."

Sam made his way to the second floor as quickly as the crowded stairs allowed him. He set his purchases on the table and tossed his bowler hat on the bed before taking up a stack of correspondence from his office that his valet had delivered to the room in his absence.

He'd just opened the third envelope when he heard footsteps in the hall. Thinking Rose and Andrew had returned, he left his desk and opened the door. Startled, he pulled back at the sight of an upraised fist.

"My apologies, Mr. Blackstone." The concierge dropped his hand to his side. "This is Officer Cross. He's from the local constable's office."

"May I come in?" said the officer, a serious-looking gent with fierce, dark eyes. "I think it would be best if you sit dow—"

Instant dread snaked through Sam. "I don't need to sit down. Are my fiancée and son well?"

"Your fiancée, sir?"

"Yes, Rose Smith is my intended. Where is she? Has she or my son been harmed? Out with it, man, explain."

Officer Cross looked grim. "Leave us," he said to the concierge. "This is a personal matter I can see through from here."

"What's going on?" Sam demanded. "I insist you inform me at once."

The inspector waited until the younger man had disappeared down the stairs. "Sir, Miss Smith is in fine health, you needn't worry about her. It's the boy…it appears he's been abducted."

Sam's heart stopped. His blood turned to ice and his entire body went numb. "No…there must be some sort of mistake."

"No mistake, sir. We have a ransom note. If you'll come with me, I'd be much obliged. Miss Smith is asking for you. As you might suppose, she's quite upset."

"She's not harmed? You're certain?" He forced himself to rally for Rose and Andrew's sake. Laying hold of his room key, he locked the door behind him and made for the stairs, the police officer beside him.

"Miss Smith wasn't with the boy at the time of the abduction. From what we've gathered, she stayed behind to complete a purchase of clothes for the child while he and two servants, a Miss Prudence Lively and a Mr. Archie Rivers, visited a sweetshop on the Strand."

"What of the servants? Where are they?"

"Mr. Rivers was shot in the shoulder when he attempted to foil the brigands. At present, he's at the mercy of a physician."

"And Miss Lively?"

"At the time of the abduction, she was rendered unconscious and left in an alleyway."

Fueled by equal parts rage and fear for Andrew's safety, Sam climbed into the constable's coach. "What happened precisely? Where is the ransom note?"

As the vehicle joined the flow of traffic, the inspector took a small notebook from his breast pocket and consulted several pages. "According to Miss Lively's account, Andrew was pulled into an alley by a masked assailant. When she and Mr. Rivers gave chase, they met with two additional assailants who prevented them from following the child and his captor. During the altercation, Mr. Rivers was shot in the shoulder and Miss Lively was rendered senseless due to a blow to the head. According to Mr. Rivers, he called for help and informed his rescuers of Miss Smith's whereabouts before the pain of his wound caused him to lose consciousness."

Aware that if he succumbed to his fear he'd be useless, Sam fed his anger. Part of him wanted to pray, but the other half rejected the notion. An hour before he'd been at ease and overflowing with gratitude for the Lord's presence in his life. He'd gone against years of ingrained distrust and stepped out in faith. He'd dared to believe in God's goodness and that He cared for him.

Had he been duped, manipulated or betrayed? It had to be one of the three. Otherwise, how was he to reconcile the notion of a good God allowing his precious son to be stolen?

"What of the ransom note? Have you any clue who sent it?"

"No, sir, not as yet. Miss Lively's rescuers found it left on her person. The demand for the child's safe return is…" The constable glanced at his notebook, and then read it again as though there must have been a mistake. His eyebrows climbed up his forehead.

"How much?" Sam pressed, his voice dark with impatience.

Cross looked at him over the top of his spectacles with blatant curiosity. "A fortune of fifty thousand pounds. It's a ridiculous sum. I'm inclined to believe it's a mistake."

"No matter. I'll arrange the demanded amount with the bank. How much time do I have?"

The previously unflappable constable blinked several times in rapid succession. "Five days at most, sir, but fulfilling a ransom is not recommended. The ruffians will be encouraged—"

"What good is having money if I don't have my son?"

Cross didn't answer, leaving Sam to stew in dread, fury and the uncertain hope that the Lord had not truly forsaken him.

"Do you have any idea who may have done this?" Cross questioned several minutes later.

"No. I have few acquaintances here in Torquay, and although I have rivals in London, none of them are aware of Andrew's existence."

The coach stopped in front of the constable's office. Unable to reunite with Rose fast enough, he left Cross to trail after him.

Inside the brick building, the smell of human filth and coffee mingled to create a sour stench. Inside the holding pen, several coarse-looking blokes sat on the bare floor forlorn or egging on another pathetic pair engaged in a drunken display of fisticuffs.

Various officers sat behind desks, filling out forms or contending with resistant criminals. Abandoned coffee cups and half-eaten sandwiches littered more than one empty desktop while foul-mouthed outbursts, cries of innocence and weeping in general punctuated the incessant rumble of conversation.

His breathing labored, Officer Cross caught up with Sam. "Mr. Blackstone, follow me, if you please. Miss Smith is in a holding room. It would be unseemly for such a fine lady to wait here with these dregs of humanity."

Sam followed him to a small room down a quiet corridor. "Your people are with her," said the constable. "All except Mr. Rivers, whom I expect is still with the physician."

Cross opened the door, and Sam saw Rose immediately. She sat behind a long table. Her forehead resting on her palm displayed the smooth silken crown of her plumed, blue hat. Prudence sat next to her, the right side of her cherubic face a swollen mass of purple bruises. A footman paced the floor at the opposite end of the room.

"Rose?"

Rose raised her head. She looked despondent, beaten. "Sam! I'm so glad you're here." She stood and raced to him. He gathered her in his arms and held her tight against his chest. Wishing he could assure her that she had no need to worry, he held his tongue, fearful of telling a lie when so much remained uncertain.

"Sam, have they told you what's happened? Andrew's gone missing. The men who stole him are demanding a fortune for his safe return."

"Yes. Once I deliver you safely to the hotel, I'll make arrangements with the bank."

"They're demanding fifty thousand pounds. Surely, even you don't have a sum so large."

"I do, and you're not to worry. We'll get Andrew back if it costs me the whole of my fortune."

She looked up at him, her eyes disbelieving, her cheeks chafed red and stained by tears. "Who could have done this evil? He's just a young boy. I can't imagine how frightened he must be."

"I'm so sorry the both of ya," Prudence interjected in a forlorn voice. "You trusted me with that dear, little scamp and I failed you."

Sam frowned. "No, this whole debacle lies at my door. I should have had you better protected. In London, I would have, but here I believed there was no cause for alarm."

An argument erupted in the corridor. "Please, just take us out of here," Rose said. "I… We need to pray and—" She choked, overcome by emotion. "I'm so frightened. What if they hurt him? What if—"

"We're going to see him returned. You mustn't give up hope. Whoever did this did it for greed's sake. They won't harm him if there's a chance their demands will be met."

"Do you promise?"

How could he promise when there was no guarantee? "I'll do everything in my power, Rosie. The rest we'll have to leave to God's mercy."

Devastated and frantic with fear, Rose entered her hotel suite an hour later. Sam had gone to the bank. Signs of Andrew were everywhere. The army of toy soldiers he and Sam had bought together was lined up on the writing desk beneath the window. His toothbrush was lying beside the pitcher and basin on the dresser. Last night's sleep shirt was strewn across his pillow.

She sank down onto the side of the bed and buried her face in her hands. "Dear heavenly Father, I know You hear me. I don't know why You've allowed my baby to be taken, but please, I *beg* You, bring him back to me." She continued to pray for what felt like hours. Until her body was numb with grief and parched from an endless flow of tears.

Her fear that Andrew was hungry and cold or being hurt somehow plagued her without ceasing. Still, she refused to give up hope. How could she without facing the prospect of losing everyone important to her? She loved Andrew more than life itself. He was her baby, her blessing, her heart.

He was also her best and last link to Sam.

A knock on the door jolted her.

"Rose?"

Sam's voice drew her into the adjoining parlor and across the room at speed. She yanked open the portal and froze. Blinded by her own fears, she hadn't been attuned to his grief earlier, but now she saw the devastation in his eyes. He looked older somehow, utterly heartbroken and ravaged by worry.

"It's done," he said. "My firm has accounts with the bank here. It took less time than I expected. How are you holding up?"

"I'm trusting in the Lord." She took him by the hand and drew him inside the parlor. She closed the door and removed his hat before leading him to the settee. She'd had so much practice trusting the Lord, but Sam's faith was brand-new. "How are *you?*"

His dark eyes roamed over her face. He raked his fingers through his hair. "I'm struggling, if you must know." His deep voice was dark and tinged with anger. "I want to have faith, but the more I think of what's happened the more I question God's goodness. Tell me how to do this. Tell me how you can believe God cares after what's happened today. How can you still believe in prayer?"

She understood his doubts; she struggled with them herself. "After what happened today, Sam, how can I not? Where would I go if not to the Lord?" Tears welled in her eyes as more fear stabbed her. She wasn't willing to speak of losing Andrew for good, but she wasn't ignorant of the possibility. "Sam, no matter what happens, please promise me you'll stay strong and trust in the Lord. I've never been so frightened in all my life. Before all is said and done, you may have to have faith for the both of us."

His jaw tightened. His warm palm cupped her face, and his thumb stroked her cheek. His eyes turned solemn. "I won't disappoint you. I admit I started to sink today, but you've brought me back to solid ground."

"Rose?" A voice called from the corridor. "Rose?"

"Who is that?" he asked darkly.

"I don't know." She tore herself away from him and stood. "It sounds like Mrs. Keen."

"What is she doing here? Did you send for her?"

"No. I wouldn't do that after what happened, but please, let's hear what she has to say." She opened the door before he could object and found Mrs. Keen about to knock on the door across the hall. "Mrs. Keen?"

The older woman spun around to face her. "Rose! There you are. I didn't know which room was yours. I'm so pleased I've found you before I embarrassed myself."

"How did you find me?" she asked. A part of her was still angry with the other woman for the lies she'd told and the years she and Sam had lost because of them, but another part of her had missed the only mother she'd ever known, and she was truly glad she'd come.

"I learned you were staying here from Edwina Mason. She reports for the *Telegraph* at present and she came to the farm to learn my full account concerning Andrew."

Rose stepped back to admit her into the parlor. "What does she know?"

"Very little from what I surmise." She untied the ribbons holding her bonnet and handed the lacy article to Rose. "I told her… Oh…hello, Mr. Blackstone, I didn't realize you were here."

Sam had already stood. The two of them exchanged a polite bow and curtsy, but Rose feared she might get frostbite from Sam's cold demeanor. "Won't you have a seat?"

The older woman glanced nervously to Rose. "Yes, please have seat, Mrs. Keen. Tell us, what have you heard?"

Once they were seated, Mrs. Keen continued, noticeably unnerved by Sam's dubious attitude toward her. She cleared her throat. "Where was I?"

"Edwina Mason's visit," Rose supplied. "She inquired after Andrew."

"Oh, yes. I told her I hadn't heard a word, but she

said half the county is abuzz with the terrible news. It seems the initial witnesses have spread the word he was snatched off the street like a stray kitten. I hastened here straightaway, hoping you'd let me pray with you, at least. Once Andrew's found, I'll leave you be, but you must know how much I love that darling boy. I would do anything to help bring him back to you."

"I know." She glanced at Sam, pleading with him silently to let her friend stay, but her loyalty belonged to him.

To her relief, his stony expression softened. "In times like this we need all the friends and prayer we can muster."

"Thank you." Mrs. Keen wrung her hands. She looked first to Rose, then to Sam. "I know what I did to you was wrong, that I must seem the worst sort of villain," she said quietly. "But I ask your forgiveness with my whole heart, fully aware I deserve nothing but your contempt."

Rose waited on pins for Sam's response. "I'll endeavor to try, Mrs. Keen. God has forgiven me of enough sins this week."

He stood and aimed for the door.

"Where are you going?" Rose asked.

"Mrs. Keen's given me an idea involving the newspaper. I'm going to offer a reward for Andrew's safe return. I should have thought of it already. The two of you continue to pray. I'll return within the hour."

Chapter Eighteen

Two days of unbearable torture passed. At the constable's direction, they'd remained at the hotel instead of moving to the Keens' farm or to Hopewell Manor as Holly Malbury suggested in case the abductors attempted to contact them.

Prudence and many of Rose's friends from Hopewell had come by at various times to join the constant prayer vigil being held in the parlor of Rose's suite. Holly had been the one who'd come and set up camp, not only lending her voice to the prayers, but quietly organizing food and blankets whenever the need arose.

To Sam and Rose's amazement, finding Andrew became a community endeavor. Concerned citizens joined search parties throughout the surrounding area, freeing police to investigate the variety of leads that seemed to pour in on an hourly basis.

Sam took note of it all. He'd never seen so many people ban together in such single-minded communion, and their concern for his son touched him beyond measure.

"Mr. Blackstone." Miss Malbury approached him

the moment he walked into the parlor. "I take it the search party found nothing?"

He shook his head. "Not yet. How is Rose?"

"She's taking nourishment—finally. She's been a rock, but I fear she's exhausted and has yet to sleep. I convinced Mrs. Keen to go home for a bit. She'll be back tomorrow morning. When did you last eat?"

"In all honesty, I can't remember."

"Go and sit with Rose. I'll bring you a plate."

Too tired to argue, he did as she suggested. "Rose, do you mind if I sit with you a bit?"

She seemed not to recognize him as she looked up, but then he realized she looked dazed because of the unshed tears in her eyes. She handed him her untouched plate. "I can't eat. I keep imagining Andrew hungry and cold and I can't bear it."

He crouched in front of her, nodding to the others to continue whatever they were doing. "You have to eat for Andrew's sake. We're going to get him back and he's going to be his normal, rambunctious self. How will you keep up with him if you make yourself weak and sick? Please, take just a few bites, if nothing else."

"Do you really believe we'll get him back?"

He curled a stray strand of hair behind her ear. "Yes, I do. I feel it in my gut. It's the same feeling I get when I know I've found a new investment or stock that's about to earn me a fortune."

A wan smile curved her lips. "That's faith."

"I suppose so. I've never considered it that way."

He coaxed her into eating a few bites of cheese and a nibble of bread before fetching her a cup of tea with milk. "Here, I want you to drink this. All of it," he warned. "Or I'll pour it down you myself."

"Mr. Blackstone?" Prudence approached them. "The constable's at the door."

Sam turned to see Officer Cross in the doorway. His grim face sent an arrow of dread through Sam. Rose set down her cup, sloshing tea into the saucer. She sprang to her feet and rushed to the policeman. "Have you news?"

As a hush fell over the room, Sam ushered Rose and the officer into the corridor. If Cross had come to tell them the worst, he refused to hear it in front of an audience.

Another man with a thick beard and bushy brows stood there. Dressed in dark green from head to toe, he clutched a brown leather cap in his beefy hands.

"Who are you, sir, and why are you here?" Sam demanded.

"This is Mr. Ansel Morton," Cross said. "He's come with me."

"Fine." Sam shuffled the lot of them into his own room. His hands were shaking. "What have the two of you to tell us?"

Officer Cross pulled out his notebook. "Mr. Morton is a gamekeeper at Winter's End, Lord Digby's estate about three miles from here. He's offered a sound lead we're investigating."

"The Digby estate?" Sam's brow pleated.

"Yes, are you familiar with the place?"

Sam considered the name. Something about it niggled in his exhausted brain, but he couldn't place why. "Not that I recall."

Rose stepped forward. "Thank you for coming today, Mr. Morton. What have you seen?"

Morton smiled down at her anxious face. "I noticed

something amiss a few days ago when one of the abandoned hunting cottages on the outskirts of the estate was boarded up for no good reason, m'lady. Given that a shooting party arrived three days ago from London it would have been more prudent to shut up the cottage once they left since the weather this time of year can be tricky and shelter is sometimes necessary. When I learned of your boy's disappearance last night over supper, I went back to the cottage to have a look and nearly got shot for my trouble."

Rose gasped.

"Shot?" Sam said. "Did you approach your master? What has he to say on the matter?"

"I didn't go to him. I heard of the reward you're offering and I took my chances. If his lordship's guilty of somethin', I didn't want to give him an opportunity to move the boy and cheat myself out of a ten-thousand-pound fortune."

"I don't blame you," Rose said.

"No, m'lady, I won't ever have to work again."

"Why are we still standing here and not on our way to investigate?" Sam demanded.

"There's the rub," Cross said, scratching his chin. "The cottage is within the perimeter of the Digby estate. If his lordship is somehow involved in this crime, he's not likely to leave the boy there once he's notified of our interest."

"Then we don't notify him," Sam said through clenched teeth.

"We must. He's gentry. We can't tramp through his estate without a warrant."

"Bother that." Sam frowned. "I appreciate your services, Cross, but they're no longer required."

"Sir, this is a criminal investigation—"

"And yet, you're not investigating. Do you think I give a farthing about anything except my son's welfare and safe return to me and his mother?"

"Don't you want to see his abductors punished according to the law?"

"I want him home."

Rose intervened. "Forgive me, Constable Cross, but do you really think a peer will be arrested in such a matter as this? And even if he was, what proof would there be to convict him in court? Do you suppose he's written his intentions down? Or do you hope his servants will testify against him? I bow to your greater expertise in these matters, but I think we're both aware that although a man of his station might order such a deed, he would never carry it out himself or leave a trail to his own guilt, don't you agree?"

The constable nodded. "I'm sure you're right, but the law—"

"Is not in dispute." Sam glared at him before he looked to the gamekeeper. "Mr. Morton and I are going for a walk. We'll return shortly. Cross, you're free to come with us, but there's food in the other room and you look famished."

Cross appeared undecided. "I've already eaten, but I could use some fresh country air."

An hour later, the three men crossed onto the Digby estate by way of a gamekeeper's trail which, according to Mr. Morton, few knew about, let alone used.

The setting sun cast an orange-gray pall over the trees. The chirp of insects and the hoot of an owl interrupted the silence.

A breeze rustled the trees. A short distance ahead of

them, the boarded cottage appeared dark and gloomy amid the coppery glow of twilight.

The click of a gun being cocked drew Sam's attention behind him. Mr. Morton grinned. Given his earlier brush with a bullet, the gamekeeper had insisted they fetch rifles from his own stock of weapons.

The three men inched closer. Cross snapped a twig beneath his boot. Crisp leaves crunched beneath their every step, but there was no turning back. Goaded on by the stillness of the cottage, they moved to within a few feet away and took cover behind a copse of trees.

"There's no one here," Sam whispered as they studied the hovel in the waning light. "Notice the front door. It's half-open."

Agreeing with the assessment, the three men sent Cross to the back of the cottage to avoid any surprises while Sam and Morton took the front. Sam took the steps first. Oddly, there was a frying pan lying upside down on the sagging porch.

Inside, the musty damp of the forest pervaded the tiny structure. Dim light from the doorway exposed a narrow, unmade cot pushed against the back wall. Foodstuffs lined a shelf above a small stove. Someone had been here, but no more.

A low groan alerted them they were not alone. Sam raised his rifle. Squinting into the direction the moan had risen from, he saw the outline of a body on the floor. He moved quickly, turning the man from his side onto his back with his booted foot.

"Light a lamp, would you?"

Fumbling noises came from Morton's direction, followed by the flare of a match and the golden glow of a lamp.

Noting the trail of dried blood flowing from his temple down his cheek, Sam aimed the rifle between the prone man's glaring eyes. "I'm going to count back from ten. I suggest you tell me who you are, who you work for and where you've taken my son. Ten—"

"I don't know what you're talking about."

"Nine."

"Who do you think you are, barging—"

"Eight."

"Get out of my house."

Cross joined them. "What's happening?"

As Morton explained, Sam continued, "Seven, six."

"The name's Harley Simmons."

"Five."

"I work for Lord Sanbourne."

Sam froze. Rage exploded through him. The name Digby made sudden sense. Amelia had invited him to accompany her to the Digbys' the night of the dinner party. "Four."

"I don't know where the sniveling brat is!"

"Three."

"Honest! He blindsided me. Knocked me out cold." He reached for his temple. "Don't you see all this blood?"

"Two."

Simmons squeezed his eyes shut. "I promise on me mother's grave!"

Officer Cross intervened. "Put the rifle down, Mr. Blackstone," he said in a calm voice. "I think we all understand emotions are high. Wouldn't you rather leave this good-for-naught to me while you search for the boy? Take Mr. Morton. He knows the area."

The thought of Andrew lost in the woods penetrated

the depths of Sam's rage. Breathing heavily, he wrestled his temper under control.

"Mr. Blackstone. Night will have fallen completely in a short time. I have Mr. Simmons. I've heard his confession. He isn't going anywhere. Now go, find the child before some other danger befalls him."

Sam lowered the rifle. With a swift kick to Simmons's midsection, he turned to Morton. "Bring the lantern."

With the sun fully set and the moon on the wane, the two of them stayed together due to the lack of light.

"Andrew," Sam called, fearing to draw unfriendly attention, but lost for another way to find him.

Hours ticked by. They covered acres of forest and farmland but to no avail.

Rose was never going to forgive him. When she learned the Ratners were responsible for Andrew's abduction and the torment she'd been forced to endure, she'd want nothing to do with him, and who could blame her?

The situation had been bad enough when they'd believed his wealth had been the object of a stranger's random greed, but this attack had been personal and directly related to his own faulty judgment.

If not for his false pride and need to prove to the world that he was something he wasn't, he never would have overlooked Amelia's vicious character or her father's penchant for lies.

He deserved to be punished for his stupidity, but Rose did not. She'd already suffered enough because of him. She didn't deserve to lose her son.

"He's not here," Morton said as the first ray of light

broke the horizon. "We have to get some rest and enlist more people to help look for the boy."

Even Sam had to agree. Worry for Andrew's safety and the cold of night had worn him down. He had to stop for a few hours or he'd be no good to anyone.

They returned to the hunting cottage. Cross was asleep in the chair. Simmons remained on the floor, his hands and feet bound with thick rope. Sam let the door slam.

Cross jumped to his feet even before he was fully awake. "Yes, sir!" he exclaimed with a salute.

Sam might have been amused if the situation weren't so dire. Aiming the pistol at Simmons, he kicked the bottom of the cretin's boot. "Wake up."

Simmons grunted. Cross untied his feet for him to stand. Sam escorted him out of the cottage at gunpoint and into the carriage awaiting them out front. While Morton drove, Sam held the pistol on Simmons, who wisely kept his mouth shut.

"According to him," Cross motioned to Simmons, "he's been following you and Miss Smith since the day you left London. Do you know a woman by the name of Amelia Ratner?"

Sam nodded. "Unfortunately."

"She seems to think of you more fondly. Simmons says she was quite upset when you broke off your engagement."

"There was no engagement outside of Amelia's own mind."

Cross looked surprised. "She and her father thought otherwise. Again, according to Simmons here, Lord Sanbourne was—is—heavily in debt."

"Yes, the information is hardly a secret. My firm

carries the notes on all three of his properties and I've heard he's exceeded his credit with half the shops in London."

"Then it's understandable as to why they might seek a marriage between you and Miss Ratner, considering your wealth could then be called upon to solve those concerns."

"Miss Ratner intimated as much. For my own reasons I considered the match, but ultimately declined."

"Because of Miss Smith?" asked Cross.

"What does she have to do with this?"

"Miss Smith was their intended target, but when Simmons alerted the Ratners to the child, they changed their focus to him. I don't think it's a stretch to believe that when you broke off with Miss Ratner, they felt you owed them and intended to collect a piece of your fortune by fair means or foul."

Sam shook his head, once again disgusted by the Ratners and his foolishness at becoming involved with them. "And how do you intend to prove all of this? I doubt a jury of Sanbourne's peers will take the word of a kidnapper over one of their own."

"I doubt we can," Cross admitted. "But I thought you might care to know the reason behind this misfortune. At least Simmons won't go free."

"And the toffs escape yet again." Bitterness burned inside him and a plan began to take shape in his head. "Not this time. Mark my words, Amelia and her father will be punished for what they've done. I'll call in Sanbourne's debts and land him in prison one way or another."

"Debtor's prison?" Cross considered the idea. A slow grin curved his mouth as he nodded. "Brilliant idea. Their sort values pride above all else. Debtor's prison will cure them of their airs and graces and ruin them in the bargain."

After leaving Cross and Simmons at the constable's station, Morton drove Sam back to the hotel before returning to his own home.

As Sam walked through the hotel's reception, he tried to pray, but exhaustion turned his thoughts to gibberish. He dreaded facing Rose and seeing her heart break again when he appeared without Andrew in tow.

All of his life, he'd relied on himself, bending things, people and situations to his will. This time he was helpless. His precious son was lost. The thought of Andrew suffering afraid and alone twisted his gut in a knot. He'd never been such a failure or felt more useless. The mountain of money he'd amassed to protect himself from the deprivation of his childhood had proved worthless.

He had no other option except to trust the Lord.

He stopped at Rose's door. Muffled voices sounded behind the portal. Grateful and humbled that so many people were still praying for Andrew's safe return, he took a deep breath, turned the knob and pressed open the door.

"Hello, Papa!"

Chapter Nineteen

Andrew jumped down from the settee where he sat between Rose and Holly Malbury. He raced across the room.

Shocked, Sam sank to his knees in time to catch him. Love, pure and fine, coursed through him as Andrew's arms circled his neck and he kissed his cheek. "I didn't think you'd ever come back. Where have you been?"

Sam buried his face against Andrew's throat and breathed in the clean scent of lemon soap. He closed his eyes to stem the flow of tears. *Thank You, thank You, Lord, for bringing him home.* "Me?" he rasped, his throat sore from the painful emotion lodged there. "I've been looking for you. Where have you been?"

Andrew frowned. "I was in a cottage in the woods."

Sam's gaze flicked to Rose's happy face before his eyes met Andrew's. "You weren't hurt?"

"No. I was so frightened when that man took me, but I knew the Lord was with me since He never leaves us and that you would want me to be brave."

Sam swallowed hard. The boy knew more about

faith and trust in God than he ever would, but from this moment on, he'd make a more concerted effort to learn. "How did you get away?"

Andrew looked back to Rose. She smiled and nodded in encouragement. "I wanted to come home, but that man wouldn't let me. I hit him with a fry pan when he wasn't looking and ran as fast as I could."

"Bravo, my boy. I'm so proud of you."

"You're not cross that I hurt someone?"

He stood and settled Andrew on his hip. "I would never be angry at you for defending yourself—not that you ever need to look for a fight."

Andrew grinned at Rose. "You were right, Mummy."

"She usually is, son. The faster you learn that fact, the better off you'll be. Where did you go after you left the cottage? I've been scouring the countryside."

"I got lost." He picked at Sam's shirtfront. "I thought about climbing a tree like I did last time, but then I remembered Mummy telling me how she prays when she gets lost and can't read the road signs. She said God always helps her find her way."

"Really?"

"Mmm. It wasn't very long after that, that I saw the lane to Granny's. She got home a little after I did and brought me right back here to Mummy."

Rose joined them. "You weren't gone more than an hour when they came in, Sam. I wasn't certain where to find you or I would have sent word. I know how worried you've been. As it was, we've been praying for your safe return."

"I'm grateful…to all of you," he said to everyone in the room.

It wasn't long before their friends began to leave,

and within an hour the three of them had been left alone. Andrew struggled to keep his eyes open and Rose insisted he go to bed.

"Don't go anywhere, Sam. I'll be back in a minute."

He watched the two of them disappear into the bedchamber while he waited in the adjoining parlor. His hour of reckoning had come.

"He was asleep before his head touched the pillow," she said on her return. A smile curving her lips, she shut the door behind her. "I can't tell you how grateful I am to you. For all that you did to bring him back safe and sound."

Guilt gnawed at him. Andrew would never have been in danger if not for him. "I didn't do anything. In the end, he saved himself and the Lord guided him home."

"Don't belittle your part in this."

"I'm not, believe me."

"I don't know how I would have gotten through this ordeal without you."

"If not for me there would have been no ordeal."

"Don't blame yourself—"

"Who else can I blame?"

"The wicked people who perpetrated their scheme. Just because you have money doesn't give anyone the right to steal your child."

He sat heavily on the settee. "You're right, of course you are, but you haven't heard the whole truth. I'd prefer not to tell you, but you're bound to learn of it somehow."

"What truth, Sam?"

He rubbed his forehead, wishing he was anywhere but there. "Won't you sit down?"

"Tell me what you have to say first."

"All right." On the verge of losing his nerve, he stood and began to pace. "Constable Cross informed me a short time ago that the Ratners were responsible for Andrew's abduction."

Rose sank into the chair across from the settee. Her sudden calm and loss of color alarmed him. He crouched before her. "Rose, I'm sorry. The miscreant they hired to perform the deed let it be known they felt entitled to the portion of my wealth they believed they'd receive if and when I wed Amelia."

"I'm sorry," she said through ashen lips. "You must have been devastated. I know you care for her. She's not my cup of tea, but I realize you gave her up for Andrew's sake and if not for us you would have chosen to marry her."

He shook his head. He must be more exhausted than he realized because he was hearing the most preposterous things. He sat back on his heels. "I *was* devastated. Not because I'd learned of Amelia's treachery, but because it was my foolishness in becoming involved with those miscreants that got Andrew abducted. How could you believe I would choose her over you when you're the only woman I've ever loved?"

She bit her bottom lip. "When we met in London you were on the verge of an agreement with her. She was acting as your hostess—"

"Just the once."

"—and her father made it clear he approved of a match between the two of you. Even your servants believed an engagement was imminent. How could I *not* think you were in love with her, that you preferred her over me when you yourself told me how suitable she was and what a perfect wife she'd be for a man like you? And then you spoke of the sacrifices we'd have to make for Andrew's sake. I thought you meant you were being forced to give her up."

He groaned. "I only told you that because I'm rabidly jealous of your perfect Mr. Keen. I'll be forever grateful to the man for helping you in my absence, but do you have any idea how frustrating it is to long to break every bone in the body of a man who is already dead?"

Her lips twitched. "Sam—"

"I hate that you ever loved any man but me, Rosie. I know that's unreasonable, but I can't seem to help it."

"I did love him," she said. "Like a brother or dear friend. Like I told you, he was a gift from God and I'll always be thankful that he introduced me to the Lord." She leaned forward and wrapped her arms around his neck. The unexpected move startled him, but he began to hope. "But I never loved him like I love you, Sam. I gave you my heart years ago and I've never been able to take it back."

He leaned forward and pressed his lips against hers in a kiss filled with a lifetime of love. "Please marry me, sweetheart. I don't want to spend another day in fear of losing you again. Just the thought fills me with terror. When I saw you in London that first day, I was desperate to have you back in my life. I didn't want to love you. I convinced myself I had a choice because I couldn't face the prospect of losing you again. I told myself I wanted you in my house to show you what you'd missed by not waiting for me all those years ago. Then, when I found out about Andrew, I saw my chance to tie you to me, to keep you close without having to admit my true feelings."

"I'm beginning to think you've been in the wrong profession all these years," Rose said. "Perhaps you should try your hand at the stage because you were very convincing when you said your proposal had nothing to do with love. Sadly, I might have accepted the offer straightaway if I hadn't believed you preferred Miss Ratner. As much as I adore my son, he'll be grown one day and I couldn't bear the thought of spending my whole life wed to a man who wished I was someone else."

"There's no chance of that." He explained about the arrangement he'd considered with Amelia. "The marriage would have been very bloodless and businesslike. As you know she and her father wanted my money, while I found it a lark to think of someone from my background taking up a place in society. Do you think you can ever forgive me for being so feckless and shallow?"

"Now that you've come to your senses, I suppose so." She turned quiet and contemplative.

"What is it, Rose?"

"Are you sure you won't regret having me for a wife? I don't want to embarrass you and I don't think I'll ever fit into your world. I've never learned all the proper forks to use at dinner. I don't know how to dance. I've never played a game of whist in my life."

"I'm a businessman, Rose, not gentry." He chuckled. "You couldn't embarrass me if you tried. I say we should make our own rules from now on. We'll use whatever fork we like and create our own dances. And if someone doesn't like us, then that's their loss as far as I'm concerned."

"Truly?"

"Truly."

"Good, because after being in contact with the Ratners, I've come to a conclusion of my own."

"Really?"

"Yes. I've decided that if they're the standard of your acquaintances, I'm not very impressed and I'd prefer not to be around them."

He laughed. "I do have other friends."

"Right, that Mr. Winters seemed quite interesting."

His left brow arched. "You may think you're amusing, but you're not."

She smiled. "And yet you insist you want to marry me."

"I've wanted to marry you since forever," he said earnestly. "Don't you remember? We're a pair. The sand and the surf, the moon and the stars—"

"A goose and 'er gander?"

They both laughed until they heard a noise in the next room. Rose jumped to her feet and made for the bedchamber door, but it opened before she reached it.

A groggy Andrew stood in the open space, rubbing his eyes with the backs of his hands. "Mummy? Where are you?"

"I'm here, darling." She wrapped her arms around him. "You're safe."

"Where's Papa?"

"I'm here," Sam said. "You needn't be frightened. We're keeping watch over you."

Andrew peered at him from around Rose's skirt. "What are you doing?"

"I'm asking your mum to marry me."

"You are?" He perked up immediately and skipped across the room to him. "Where is the ring? That's important. Girls like it when you give them a ring."

"How do you know that?" Rose asked.

"I heard two of the girls at church talking about Farmer Carl's proposal. Poor Farmer Carl. He didn't do anything right. He tried to give the girl's papa a cow instead of bringing her a ring and he didn't bend down on one knee. The girl he wanted said it would be a cold day at Land's End before she ever agreed to be his wife."

Sam tried not to laugh. "I don't have a ring, but we can correct the oversight this afternoon after tea."

"Do we have to wait that long?" Andrew looked to both of them with pleading blue eyes. "Couldn't we go now?"

"She hasn't agreed to marry me yet." He took hold of Rose's hands, and for him the whole world settled into place. "How about it, Rosie. Shall we go and find you a ring?"

"Papa, you didn't bend to one knee."

"He doesn't need to," Rose said.

"Yes, he does."

Sam laughed and bent down. He kissed the back of each of her hands and took a deep breath. "Miss Rose Smith, love of my life. I need you like a starving man needs bread. I adore you as the earth adores the sun. I want you like—"

"I want a bulldog," Andrew chirped happily.

"Even more," Sam agreed drily. "As difficult as that may be to believe."

"Now that I do find hard to believe," she said, her smile radiant and filled with love.

"Will you marry me, Rosie, finally? Please say yes. Please make me the happiest man in the world."

Her smile dulled. "I'm sorry, Sam, I'm still not certain."

He and Andrew went stock-still until she burst out laughing. "You two will never learn. Of course I'll marry you. I love you more than I can say. I want nothing more than to be your wife."

"That wasn't nice," he grumbled, standing up to kiss her. "I may have to teach you a lesson."

"You can try," she whispered against his lips. "But as you may recall, I was a very poor student. I may need a lifetime for proper instruction."

"A lifetime's a good start, but I want eternity."

She linked her arms around his neck and smiled up at him.

"I want you, Sam, just you. You were always enough and you always will be."

* * * * *

Dear Reader:

I don't know about you, but more than once in my life I've wished for a second chance. Like Sam and Rose, I've made mistakes that carried consequences I either couldn't or didn't foresee.

Thankfully, the Lord somehow manages to use our shortcomings and frailties to our advantage and for His purpose. What a blessing it is to know that when we put Him first in our lives He will guide our steps and direct our path.

Thank you for taking the time to read about Sam and Rose's journey back to each other and the love they thought they'd lost. If you are hoping for a second chance at something in your own life, I hope their story will inspire you to wait on the Lord and see what plans He has in store for you.

As always, I enjoy hearing from my readers. Please visit my website at www.carlacapshaw.com or contact me at carla@carlacapshaw.com.

Be inspired,
Carla Capshaw

Questions for Discussion

1. Rose experienced a great deal of rejection in her life. Have you experienced rejection? How did you feel and what did you learn from the experience?

2. The Bible says to pursue God above all things. Sam believed achieving wealth would fix all of his problems, but chasing after money cost him the family he always wanted. Have you pursued something other than God in your life? If so, did it cost you something important?

3. When Sam and Rose met in London, years of hurt lingered between them. Have you met someone from your past who hurt you? If so, how did you clear the pain and begin to heal? Did you give the situation to the Lord? What did He do to encourage you?

4. Rose believes she is inferior due to her upbringing and societal prejudices. Do you struggle with feeling unimportant because of the opinions and expectations of others? If so, how has God's presence in your life improved your self-esteem?

5. Sam believed in Christ as a child but allowed people and worldly influences to draw him away. Have you ever struggled to keep God first in your life? If so, what were the circumstances? What did you learn along the way that brought you back to faith?

6. For a time, Sam and the Ratners share the same outlook on life that wealth is of prime importance. However, Sam soon realizes family is more important, and his resurgence of faith gives him a fresh understanding of what really counts. However, the Ratners' continued pursuit of their own comfort leads them to ruin. Have you ever had to suffer because of wrong choices? If so, what did you learn and how did God repair the damage?

7. Because Sam experienced a great deal of rejection in his youth, he believed God wanted nothing to do with him. Have you dealt with similar feelings that made you believe God had forgotten you? Has something happened to show you He cares for you?

8. Rose is embarrassed by her inability to read and feels deficient because of it. Do you have something in your life that others seem to take for granted that makes you feel inadequate? Has your faith helped you to grow or help others who may be facing the same thing?

9. Rose feared for Andrew's safety and decided to keep his existence a secret. Was it fair of her to keep him from Sam? If you were in a similar situation what would you do to protect your child?

10. Rose and Sam had preconceived notions concerning their past and the events that broke them apart. Have you ever misjudged a situation and how did you work through it to bring about healing?

11. What was the biggest change you saw in Sam once he reconciled with the Lord?

12. Although Amelia sought to harm Sam and Rose's family, God used the opportunity to bring them closer together and solidify Sam's faith. Have you ever dealt with anyone who meant to hurt you? Did God protect you and/or use the situation for your good in the long run? Was your faith strengthened?

13. Despite her trust issues, Rose believed in Mrs. Keen and was deeply hurt when she learned she'd been lied to. Have you ever been lied to by someone you trusted most? How did you reconcile? Did you go to the Lord? How did He help you through?

14. Rose was judged unfairly by her boss. Have you ever been judged unfairly? Did the Lord protect you in the situation? How did He help you resolve it?

THE WRANGLER'S INCONVENIENT WIFE
Wyoming Legacy
by Lacy Williams

Forced into an unwanted marriage to save Fran Morris from a terrible fate, cowboy Edgar White finds that his new bride just might be exactly what he needs.

THE CATTLEMAN MEETS HIS MATCH
by Sherri Shackelford

Moira O'Mara is determined to find her long-lost brother, and John Elder is determined to leave his suffocating family behind. Brought together by a group of orphans in need of rescue, can Moira and John find hope for a future together?

PROTECTED BY THE WARRIOR
by Barbara Phinney

When new midwife Clara is accused of hiding a Norman lord's son, duty commands soldier Kenneth D'Entremont to find the child. But as his feelings for Clara grow, will he honor his duty... or his heart?

A MOTHER FOR HIS CHILDREN
by Jan Drexler

A young Amish spinster accepts a position as housekeeper for a widower and his family. She never expected he'd have ten children...or that she'd fall in love with the single father.

LIHCNM0714

REQUEST YOUR FREE BOOKS!

2 FREE INSPIRATIONAL NOVELS
PLUS 2
FREE
MYSTERY GIFTS

Love Inspired
HISTORICAL
INSPIRATIONAL HISTORICAL ROMANCE

YES! Please send me 2 FREE Love Inspired® Historical novels and my 2 FREE mystery gifts (gifts are worth about $10). After receiving them, if I don't wish to receive any more books, I can return the shipping statement marked "cancel." If I don't cancel, I will receive 4 brand-new novels every month and be billed just $4.74 per book in the U.S. or $5.24 per book in Canada. That's a saving of at least 21% off the cover price. It's quite a bargain! Shipping and handling is just 50¢ per book in the U.S. and 75¢ per book in Canada.* I understand that accepting the 2 free books and gifts places me under no obligation to buy anything. I can always return a shipment and cancel at any time. Even if I never buy another book, the two free books and gifts are mine to keep forever.

102/302 IDN F5CN

Name	(PLEASE PRINT)	
Address		Apt. #
City	State/Prov.	Zip/Postal Code

Signature (if under 18, a parent or guardian must sign)

Mail to the Harlequin® Reader Service:
IN U.S.A.: P.O. Box 1867, Buffalo, NY 14240-1867
IN CANADA: P.O. Box 609, Fort Erie, Ontario L2A 5X3

Want to try two free books from another series?
Call 1-800-873-8635 or visit www.ReaderService.com.

* Terms and prices subject to change without notice. Prices do not include applicable taxes. Sales tax applicable in N.Y. Canadian residents will be charged applicable taxes. Offer not valid in Quebec. This offer is limited to one order per household. Not valid for current subscribers to Love Inspired Historical books. All orders subject to credit approval. Credit or debit balances in a customer's account(s) may be offset by any other outstanding balance owed by or to the customer. Please allow 4 to 6 weeks for delivery. Offer available while quantities last.

Your Privacy—The Harlequin® Reader Service is committed to protecting your privacy. Our Privacy Policy is available online at www.ReaderService.com or upon request from the Harlequin Reader Service.

We make a portion of our mailing list available to reputable third parties that offer products we believe may interest you. If you prefer that we not exchange your name with third parties, or if you wish to clarify or modify your communication preferences, please visit us at www.ReaderService.com/consumerchoice or write to us at Harlequin Reader Service Preference Service, P.O. Box 9062, Buffalo, NY 14269. Include your complete name and address.

LIH13R

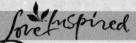
"We used to count the stars at night, Jack. Remember that?"

Oh, he remembered, all right. They'd look skyward and watch each star appear, summer, winter, spring and fall, each season offering its own array, a blend of favorites. Until they'd become distracted by other things. Sweet things.

A sigh welled from somewhere deep within him, a quiet blooming of what could have been. "I remember."

They stared upward, side by side, watching the sunset fade to streaks of lilac and gray. Town lights began to appear north of the bridge, winking on earlier now that it was August. "How long are you here?"

Olivia faltered. "I'm not sure."

He turned to face her, puzzled.

"I'm between lives right now."

He raised an eyebrow, waiting for her to continue. She did, after drawn-out seconds, but didn't look at him. She kept her gaze up and out, watching the tree shadows darken and dim.

"I was married."

He'd heard she'd gotten married several years ago, but the "was" surprised him. He dropped his gaze to her left hand. No ring. No tan line that said a ring had been there this summer. A flicker that might be hope stirred in his chest, but entertaining those notions would get him nothing but trouble, so he blamed the strange feeling on the half-finished sandwich he'd wolfed down on the drive in.

You've eaten fast plenty of times before this and been fine. Just fine.

The reminder made him take a half step forward, just close enough to inhale the scent of sweet vanilla on her hair, her skin.

He shouldn't. He knew that. He knew it even as his hand reached for her hand, the left one bearing no man's ring, and that touch, the press of his fingers on hers, made the tiny flicker inside brighten just a little.

The surroundings, the trees, the thin-lit night and the sound of rushing water made him feel as if anything was possible, and he hadn't felt that way in a very long time. But here, with her?

He did. And it felt good.

Find out what else is going on in Jasper Gulch in
HIS MONTANA SWEETHEART by Ruth Logan Herne,
available August 2014 from Love Inspired®.

LIEXP0714

*Someone doesn't want Sonya Daniels
to find out the truth about her past.
Read on for a preview of HER STOLEN PAST
by Lynette Eason from Love Inspired Suspense.*

Sonya Daniels heard the sharp crack and saw the woman jogging four feet in front of her stumble. Then fall.

Another crack.

Another woman cried out and hit the ground.

"Shooter! Get down! Get down!"

With a burst of horror, Sonya caught on. Someone was shooting at the joggers on the path. Terror froze her for a brief second. A second that saved her life as the bullet whizzed past her head and planted itself in the wooden bench next to her. If she'd been moving forward, she would be dead.

Frantic, she registered the screams of those in the park as she ran full-out, zigzagging her way to the concrete fountain just ahead.

Her only thought was shelter.

A bullet slammed into the dirt behind her and she dropped to roll next to the base of the fountain.

She looked up to find another young woman had beat her there. Terrified brown eyes stared at Sonya and she knew the woman saw her fear reflected back at her. Panting, Sonya listened for more shots.

None came.

And still they waited. Seconds turned into minutes.

"Is it over?" the woman finally whispered. "Is he gone?"

"I don't know," Sonya responded.

Screams still echoed around them. Wails and petrified cries of disbelief.

Sonya lifted her head slightly and looked back at the two women who'd fallen. They still lay on the path behind her.

Sirens sounded.

Sonya took a deep breath and scanned the area across the street. Slowly, she calmed and gained control of her pounding pulse.

Her mind clicked through the shots fired. Two hit the women running in front of her. Her stomach cramped at the thought that she should have been the third victim. She glanced at the bench. The bullet hole stared back. It had dug a groove slanted and angled.

Heart in her throat, Sonya darted to the nearest woman, who lay about ten yards away from her. Expecting a bullet to slam into her at any moment, she felt for a pulse.

When Sonya turns to Detective Brandon Hayes
for help, can he protect her without both of them
losing their hearts?
Pick up HER STOLEN PAST to find out.

Available August 2014
wherever Love Inspired books are sold.

The Wrangler's Inconvenient Wife

by

LACY WILLIAMS

With no family to watch over them, it's up to Fran Morris to take care of her younger sister, even if it means marrying a total stranger. Gruff, strong and silent, her new husband is a cowboy down to the bone. He wed Fran to protect her, not to love her, but her heart has never felt so vulnerable.

Trail boss Edgar White already has all the responsibility he needs at his family's ranch in Bear Creek, Wyoming. He had intended to remain a bachelor forever, but he can't leave Fran and her sister in danger. And as they work on the trail together, Edgar starts to soften toward his unwanted wife. He already gave Fran his name…can he trust her with his heart?

WYOMING
Legacy

United by family, destined for love

Available August 2014
wherever Love Inspired books and ebooks are sold.

Find us on Facebook at
www.Facebook.com/LoveInspiredBooks

LIH28274

Love Inspired

A reclusive Amish logger, Ethan Gingerich is more comfortable around his draft horses than the orphaned niece and nephews he's taken in. Yet he's determined to provide the children with a good, loving home. The little ones, including a defiant eight-year-old, need a proper nanny. But when Ethan hires shy Amishwoman Clara Barkman, he never expects her temporary position to have such a lasting hold on all of them. Now this man of few words must convince Clara she's found her forever home and family.

BRIDES OF *Amish Country*

Finding true love in the land of the Plain People.

The Amish Nanny

by

Patricia Davids

Available August 2014 wherever
Love Inspired books and ebooks are sold.

Find us on Facebook at
www.Facebook.com/LoveInspiredBooks

LI87902